3-25-17   .50

DI046786

WITHDRAWN

Swift Justice

Swift Justice

LAURA DiSILVERIO

Minotaur Books

A THOMAS DUNNE BOOK

New York

This is a work of fiction. All of the characters, organizations, and events portrayed in this novel are either products of the author's imagination or are used fictitiously.

A THOMAS DUNNE BOOK FOR MINOTAUR BOOKS.
An imprint of St. Martin's Publishing Group.

SWIFT JUSTICE. Copyright © 2010 by Laura DiSilverio. All rights reserved. Printed in the United States of America. For information, address St. Martin's Press, 175 Fifth Avenue, New York, N.Y. 10010.

www.thomasdunnebooks.com
www.minotaurbooks.com

Design by Kathryn Parise

LIBRARY OF CONGRESS CATALOGING-IN-PUBLICATION DATA

DiSilverio, Laura A. H.
    Swift justice : a mystery / Laura DiSilverio.—1st hardcover ed.
        p. cm.
    "A Thomas Dunne book."
    ISBN 978-0-312-64150-4
    1. Women private investigators—Fiction.   I. Title.
PS3604.I85S95   2010
813'.6—dc22

                                    2010028039

First Edition: October 2010

10 9 8 7 6 5 4 3 2 1

To my mother and best friend, Joan Hankins,
with oodles of love and gratitude

Acknowledgments

Many thanks to the wonderfully talented and generous people who shared their expertise, encouragement and/or criticisms with me: Patrick Butler (for letting me use the name of his wine store, Purple Feet); Ellory Gillis-McGinnis; Don Jordahl; Commander Bob Kean (Retired), Colorado Springs Police Department; Mariko Layton; Chris Myers; Lin Poyer; Paulla Schreiner; Heather Robinson; Paige Wheeler (agent extraordinaire); and all the folks at Thomas Dunne/Minotaur Books, including my fabulous editor, Toni Plummer, and copy editor, India Cooper, whose suggestions greatly improved *Swift Justice*. Thanks to my daughters and my dog for getting me out from behind the computer for school stuff and walks and shopping and the really important things in life. Most of all, thanks to my husband, Tom, for his continuing love and support, and for being the best husband *ever*. Being with him for seventeen years has made me a better person.

Swift
Justice

1

(Monday)

The bear had toppled my bird feeder again, the two aspirin I'd gulped with a swig of Pepsi weren't making a dent in my headache (note to self: don't try to match Father Dan drink for drink ever again), and I was late for my first appointment of the week. As the owner and currently sole employee of a private investigation business teetering on the edge of solvency, I couldn't afford to piss off potential clients by being tardy. Unfortunately, the woman tapping her foot outside the door of Swift Investigations did not look like a happy camper when I screeched to a stop in my Subaru Outback.

I assessed the waiting woman through the windshield as I gathered my purse and laptop. She was taller than my five foot three and rangy, dressed in a spiffy red suit and low-heeled pumps. Midthirties, at a guess. Everything about her said "wound too tight," from the French-braided hair pulling the skin of her face taut to the way her eyes skittered to her watch, to me, and to the infant car seat at her feet. Shit. Who brings a baby to a business meeting?

I got out of the car and offered her my hand. "I got tied up with a burglary," I said in lieu of an apology. I'd bet the burglar had snarfed down at least fifteen dollars' worth of the primo seed blend I put out to attract songbirds. "You must be Melissa Lloyd. C'mon in."

She bent to pick up the baby carrier as I unlocked the door and flicked the light switch. The illuminated space was simple, clean, and organized, just the way I liked it. Off-white walls made the office look larger than it was. My desk filled the back right corner by a window with wooden blinds. A matching desk, currently unoccupied since my last assistant left to become an aromatherapist, sat with the long side making an L with the door. A closed door led to the small bathroom in the back left corner.

"You *are* Charlotte Swift, the investigator?" Ms. Lloyd paused just inside the door.

"Last I looked." I crossed the nubby, green-flecked carpet and sat behind my desk, stowing my stuff beneath it. Swiveling my chair, I pulled a Pepsi from the mini fridge against the wall and popped the flip-top. I offered one to Ms. Lloyd with a gesture, but she shook her head, looking repulsed. I could see the word "coffee" hovering in her mind, but she didn't speak it. Just as well, because I don't even have a coffeemaker; I don't want to encourage people to linger. There's a café two doors down if they're that desperate to feed their addiction.

She wasn't. She settled the baby on top of the empty desk, tucked a yellow blanket around it, and seated herself in one of the uncomfortable chairs.

"Cute kid," I said perfunctorily, barely able to make out a wisp of dark hair poking from beneath the blanket. "How old?"

"A little over a week."

Melissa Lloyd looked damned trim for someone who'd just popped out a baby. Maybe she was into Pilates. I drew a legal pad toward me. "You said on the phone you need to find someone?"

"Yes. Your Yellow Pages ad said missing persons is your specialty, right?"

Since her furrowed brow seemed to indicate she needed reassurance, I said, "I've been in business here for almost six years. For the past four, I've specialized in finding missing persons. Before becoming a PI, I was in the Air Force Office of Special Investigations, the OSI. You've seen *NCIS*, about the Navy investigators? Like that, only without Mark Harmon. Overall, I have more than thirteen years' experience as an investigator. You can check with these people if you want." I slid a piece of paper containing the names of clients who'd agreed to provide references across the desk.

She took it, creased it in half, and tucked it into the envelope purse on her lap. "That's okay," she said, sounding as if references were no big deal.

She'd be dialing one of those numbers before her car was out of the parking lot.

"What can I do for you?"

She leaned forward, her uncertainty replaced by a businesslike air. I knew she owned an interior design business in Monument—I'd checked her out after she called—and I could suddenly see her bossing wallpaper hangers around, coaxing homeowners into replacing their mauve shag carpet, and trolling furniture stores until she found just the right lamp or ottoman. I figured this air of command was more natural to her than the earlier indecisiveness. It matched the suit, too.

She took a deep breath and said, "The baby's not mine."

"You're babysitting?"

"No. Well, sort of." She bit down on her lower lip.

Oookay. Not her baby. Not babysitting. If she was going to confess to kidnapping, I needed to get it on tape—and I'd have to hope there was a reward for the child's safe return, because clearly Ms. Lloyd wouldn't be handing over a retainer check. I surreptitiously pushed the button on the underside of my desk that started a voice-activated recorder.

"So, if the baby's not yours, whose is it?"

She laughed, an unmirthful sound. "God, I'm screwing this up. Someone left the baby on my porch a week ago."

The stork, maybe. That sounded about as likely as Father Dan converting to Buddhism. I know my clients don't always tell me the truth; in fact, most of them probably pitch me lies like Nolan Ryan throwing heat, but I like them to have some glancing acquaintance with reality.

"Why would someone do that?" I tried to keep my skepticism out of my voice.

She half rose, glaring. "Look, if you're not going to take me seriously—"

I threw up my hands in a surrender gesture. If she'd kidnapped the baby, I needed to keep her calm, convince her to tell me where the baby belonged. "I'm listening. Really. Why don't you just start at the beginning?" I put on an Oprah face: nonjudgmental and encouraging.

She glanced at the sleeping baby and sank back into the chair. "This is confidential, right? I mean, discretion is very important to me."

"I'll keep what you tell me confidential unless I think there's a good reason to tell someone—something about a crime, say—or the courts compel me to tell. PI-client relationships aren't protected like lawyer-client communications." There. If she confessed to kidnapping, I could blab all to the cops with a clear conscience.

Ms. Lloyd looked marginally reassured. At any rate, she continued with her story. "Like I said, someone left the baby at my front door last Monday. I found her when I was leaving for work. She was in that car seat, screaming her head off. At first, I thought it was a mistake of some kind, or a joke, but there was a note. It was addressed to me, and when I read it I knew it wasn't a joke. My daughter had abandoned her baby on my doorstep." She stopped to take a deep breath.

I leaned forward, my forearms on the desk. "Your *daughter*? You mean the baby's your grandkid?" I mentally revised my assessment of her age up a few years. Damn, she looked a year or two younger than my thirty-seven.

"Yes, she's my granddaughter. I had her DNA tested."

"You what?" This woman looked like a normal Colorado Springs professional woman, maybe a bit more successful than most, but she was a certifiable loon.

"I thought it was necessary," she said. She reached into her purse, and I stiffened, but her hand came out with nothing more threatening than a manila envelope. "I got the lab results yesterday—money produces fast results. Olivia's definitely my granddaughter." She didn't sound happy about it.

"Okay, then, and you want me to . . . ?"

"Find my daughter."

At last, a note of sanity in this bizarre discussion. Her daughter, obviously a teenager, had a baby, panicked, dumped it on dear old Mom, and ran away. Runaways were my thing. This, I could handle. I offered her a sympathetic smile. "Right. How old's your daughter?"

"Seventeen."

I jotted a note. "Did you bring a photo?"

"No, I—"

"I'll need one. Her name?"

"I don't know. I've never met her."

Wham! Right back to la-la land. I drained my Pepsi and clunked the can onto the desk. "Ms. Lloyd—"

"I know!" She held up a hand to stop me. "I know it sounds crazy. Just hear me out."

Her eyes pled with me, and a note in her voice gave me pause. I arched my brows, inviting her to continue.

A wave of red washed up her neck and mottled her jaw. "This is hard for me. I haven't talked about it in— I had a baby. When I was sixteen, almost seventeen. I gave it—her— up for adoption. I hadn't heard of her, or from her, since the day I signed the adoption papers until a week ago."

I pushed across my handy box of tissues, but her eyes remained dry, her voice tightly controlled.

"I know what you must think of me—"

"No, you don't."

She stopped, mouth open in midword. After a second's thought, she said, "You're right. I don't. I guess I'm projecting. My husband says I do that a lot. Sometimes I feel so bad about giving up that baby, so guilty, that I worry everyone thinks I'm a horrible person. Unnatural. Like I have a scarlet *A* on my chest for 'Abandoner.' But I was only sixteen! I just didn't have what it takes to be a mother. I still don't. And my parents . . . well, let's just say my daughter's better off wherever she ended up than she'd've been with my folks."

The bitterness in her voice would give unsweetened chocolate a run for its money. Her remark about abandonment hit too close to home, and I said the first thing that came to mind. "You're married?"

"Yes. He doesn't know."

How could someone not notice a baby living in the house? "Hel*lo*?"

She almost smiled at the incredulity in my voice. "I mean he doesn't know I had a baby and gave it up. Of course he knows about Olivia, but he thinks I'm babysitting for a friend. He's not a kid person; he just about freaked when I called him to tell him last Monday. He told me not to expect him to change any diapers. He's been away, in Arizona, troubleshooting some problem for a customer . . . he does software, something to do with personnel systems. He'll probably be gone another two or three weeks, and I need to have this resolved before he comes home."

"The note says the mom is coming back. Why not just wait?"

"It could be months! I can't take care of a baby that long." She shook her head vehemently.

"Well, you could turn her over to Child Protective Services and let them find the mother."

"If she weren't my granddaughter that's exactly what I'd do. But . . . well, part of me feels like that would be giving my daughter away a second time, and I just can't do that either. Hiring someone to find Olivia's mother quickly seemed like the best solution."

Olivia's mother, I noted, not "my daughter." I studied her, the resolute line of her thin lips, the dark smudges under her eyes, the tension in her shoulders. The faintest trace of freckles dusted her nose and the tops of her cheeks, and I imagined her as a kid, playing hide-and-seek and tag in the Colorado sunshine. The baby stirred in her sleep, and we both looked over at her. One little fist now hung over the edge of the car seat.

"Okay," I told her. "I'll find your daughter. Since you don't know her name, or where she lives, or what she looks like, let's start with what you do know. When and where was she born?"

"There's just one more thing." Melissa Lloyd looked down at her fingers pleating a fold of skirt, and I could hardly hear her. "I don't want to meet her."

"What?"

She looked up at me, her blue eyes fixed unwaveringly on mine. "I don't want to see her. Olivia's mother. When you find her, I want you to meet with her, hand over Olivia. I can let you have some money to give her if she looks like she needs help. Then tell her I don't want to meet her or hear from her ever again. She's not part of my life."

When Melissa Lloyd and baby Olivia had left, I sat for a moment staring at the notes I'd taken. They were pitifully few. Melissa had delivered her daughter, "Baby Girl Hogeboom,"

on the twelfth of March, seventeen years ago, at the Community Hospital in Boulder, Colorado. She'd never so much as held the baby, signing the adoption papers before the epidural wore off. She had no idea who'd adopted the baby or whether it was even someone from in state. Not much to go on. I grabbed my third Pepsi of the morning and headed outside, hoping some sunshine and exercise would stimulate an idea.

My PI business, Swift Investigations, occupies the corner office in a strip mall on Academy Boulevard in Colorado Springs, just two miles outside the Air Force Academy's south gate. It's a classy strip mall—not a Lotto sales sign in sight—with a bridal emporium, two restaurants, an art/frame shop, and a toy store that sells educational and ecologically sound products for kids, including doll clothes made of pure Egyptian cotton and imported cashmere that cost more for one dress than my monthly utilities bill, and an Al Gore action figure. "Al Gore" and "action" struck me as a contradiction in terms; buying carbon offsets doesn't look like it burns many calories.

As I often do when I'm gnawing on a new case, I strode down the sidewalk in front of Ecolo-Toys and the frame shop—neither open yet this morning—past the Mexican restaurant doing a brisk business in breakfast burritos and coffee, the darkened bridal shop, and the bistro my friend Albertine owns at the far end of the mall, around to the alley in back where the Dumpsters hid behind discreet concrete walls and plain beige doors provided back access for deliveries. A couple of scrawny cats slinking around the Dumpster laden with Guapo Bandito's rotting enchiladas took off as I approached. Pausing to toss a couple of soft drink cans into a Dumpster, I crossed the lane behind the shopping area into a small park with a pond and two picnic tables. Hidden away out here in retail land, far from any residential areas, the park drew few visitors. I usually had it to myself. Scanning the picnic bench for bird guano, I sat and watched mosquito larvae or water striders or some other aquatic insects pock the surface of the pond, grateful for the light olive complexion of my Italian heritage—my mother's maiden name was DeBattista—so I could enjoy the sun's warmth on my face without as much skin cancer paranoia as a paleface like Melissa Lloyd must endure. I thought about finding her daughter.

Under Colorado law, parents who gave a child up for adoption can voluntarily register to have their names and addresses released if the adopted child comes looking for them. Melissa Lloyd had made it abundantly clear, however, that she had not made her data available, and adoptees couldn't sign up to release their whereabouts to birth parents who came searching for them until they were twenty-one, which Melissa's daughter wasn't. So how had Baby Girl Hogeboom found Melissa Lloyd? And why had she left Olivia with her?

The note Melissa reluctantly produced from her purse gave few clues. It was hand-printed on a page ripped from a steno pad. *Please take care of Olivia. She's your granddaughter. I can't trust her with anyone else. Her father will do the right thing, I know. Tell Olivia I love her. I'll be back. Beth.* As I pointed out to Melissa, the note told us Beth was literate and planned to come back for her daughter, and not much more than that. When I asked if there was anything else with the baby, Melissa pointed to the car seat and said there'd also been a blanket and a different set of clothes. I asked her to leave the car seat, but she had no other way of getting Olivia home safely, so she promised to drop off the seat and the other items early in the afternoon. I had scant hope of digging up a useful clue from them, but I couldn't afford to overlook the possibility. I'd also put a note on a PI bulletin board I used, asking if anyone had been hired to find the mother of a baby born at Boulder Community Hospital seventeen years ago. Melissa's daughter had found her somehow; maybe she'd hired a PI. I'd call the hospital—not much chance of finding anyone who remembered the birth after all this time—and some private adoption agencies. I knew damn well I wouldn't get anything out of the state.

With a plan of action in mind, I dusted off my slacks and headed back to my office. Getting on for ten, there were a few more cars scattered in the parking lot. A yellow Hummer sat outside my office. I figured the owner was picking up a bushel of ecologically sound toys for his grandkids, maybe the banana plantation set with its little wooden trees, cute monkeys, and authentically dressed workers. I'd suggested once to the store's owner, Lucinda Highmoor, that she sell some Agent Orange with the set to let kids replicate the experience of defoliating the jungle to plant crops, but she'd closed her eyes as if in pain and ordered me out of the store with a pointing finger. I wasn't really an eco-nazi; it just gave me joy to bust Lucinda's chops because she took it all so seriously and overlooked the irony of her customers driving gas-guzzling behemoths to pick out eco-sensitive toys for their Ritalin-pickled children.

A shadow moving in front of the window in my office distracted me from the Hummer. I didn't have another appointment scheduled until the afternoon. Hot damn, maybe I had a walk-in client. Swift Investigations' business had been slow this summer; I could use a cash infusion, above and beyond the retainer Melissa Lloyd had given me. I needed a new assistant, too, so my being away from the office for a few minutes didn't result in lost business. Wiping the sheen of sweat off my forehead with the sleeve of my aqua blouse, I floofed my bangs and pulled open the door to find a woman of a certain age staring at me, looking like Dirty Harriet with a large-caliber revolver cradled in her ample lap.

2

Gun! My training kicked in, and I leaped back onto the sidewalk, swinging the door mostly shut and standing off to the left, my back pressed against the wall. I *really* needed to start carrying the H&K 9 mm I kept locked in the safe—and locking the door even when I left for two minutes.

"Hey!" A startled voice with a southern accent that gave the word three syllables followed me out the door.

"Put the gun on the floor and your hands over your head," I called out. My hand slid into my pocket to retrieve my cell phone.

"I didn't mean . . . it's not . . . I'm Gigi Goldman, Les's wife."

I couldn't think of a reason why my silent partner's wife would be in my office with a gun. I'd never slept with the man; hell, I'd only met him twice. He'd invested some money in Swift Investigations when I was first starting out, and I sent him quarterly statements. That was the sum total of our interaction. I was hoping to be able to buy him out by next summer. I peered through the door crack. Mrs. Goldman had done as I asked. The gun lay on the floor to the side of her chair, and she was holding her hands at shoulder height. She waved at me as I cautiously poked the door wider.

"Hi. I'm sorry if I gave you a scare. I just—"

"Kick the gun over here."

She swept one plump calf to the side of the chair and nudged the gun my way with her foot. I bent to retrieve it, checking to see if it was loaded. It was. The hair on my arms prickled up.

"Jesus, don't you even know enough not to brandish a loaded weapon?"

"It's loaded?" Wrinkles creased her brow.

My God. Carrying the gun with two fingers, I walked around her to my desk and closed it in the top drawer. Then I jerked open the fridge, pulled out a Pepsi, and drank half of it, relishing the tickle of the carbonation. Leaning back in my chair, I ran the cold can across my forehead and focused on my uninvited guest. "Want one?" It seemed only polite to offer my partner's wife refreshment.

She scootched the chair around to face me and said, "Maybe an iced tea? With lemon?"

"This is a private investigation firm, Mrs. Goldman, not a restaurant. I have Pepsi, Pepsi, or Pepsi."

"I'd like a Pepsi, thank you," she said.

I handed over a can and watched her decide not to ask for a glass. Instead, she drew a handkerchief out of her purse and wiped the top of the can thoroughly before using a metal can opener, also pulled from her capacious bag, to lever open the flip-top. "Nails," she explained, wiggling her manicured fingers at me.

I studied her as she took a genteel sip. In her early fifties, she had jaw-length hair of that ashy blond color so many well-off women over fifty seem to affect, held in place by a quart of mousse and a can of Aqua Net. She carried an extra thirty pounds or so on her tall frame—I suspected she'd be at least five-eight standing—and wore a pink and cream knit suit that shrieked "expensive" and hugged her curves a shade too tightly. Her leather bag was large enough to hold supplies for a weeklong camping trip and hung from a strap over her left shoulder. I caught a whiff of floral perfume that made me want to sneeze. I could see she'd been pretty in her younger days, but time, too many fund-raising balls, and a spa-to-Saks-to-dinner-party lifestyle had stamped her with a matronly air. The closest she got to exercise was probably box seats at a Rockies game.

With my breathing returned to normal, I said, "Let's start over. I'm Charlotte Swift. Was I expecting you?"

"Oh, no. I wouldn't think so." She shook her head. "I'm Gigi Goldman. Well, it's really Georgia, but I started going by Gigi when I married Les. Georgia Goldman. G. G. Get it?"

I got it. "What can I do for you, Mrs. Goldman?" I willed her not to tell me she thought Les was having an affair and she wanted me to catch him. Talk about conflict of interest.

"This is so awkward—"

She was going to try to sic me on Les. I could feel it. I shut my eyes in anticipation of the blow.

"Well, Les ran off with his personal trainer—"

Damn, right again!

"—and I'm afraid I need money, so I'm here to learn how to be an investigator."

My eyes popped open. "Say what?"

"When Les left for Costa Rica with Heather-Anne, he closed out all our accounts and transferred all our assets. The police say he even took some money that rightfully belonged to investors." Her soft blue eyes clouded over.

"He embezzled?"

She nodded. "I'm afraid so. Anyway, my lawyer and I have been through all the papers, and the only assets he left me are the house, the Hummer, and a half interest in Swift Investigations."

She pulled some legal papers from her purse, and I recognized the partnership documents Les Goldman and I had signed. I had a matching set in my file cabinet.

"So you're saying—"

"I'm your new partner."

———————

At eight o'clock that night, I poured an inch of peaty Lagavulin single malt Scotch into a glass and handed it to Father Dan Allgood. With the morning's headache in mind, I grabbed a bottled water and leaned against the deck rail, looking out on my partially xeriscaped backyard. Father Dan, the Episcopal priest who lived next door in the rectory belonging to St. Paul's, took a sip of the Scotch and sighed his appreciation. This late in August, dusk had settled gently on the foothills, and only a thin line of light rimmed Pikes Peak to the west. I wondered idly if the bear, a three-hundred-pound cinnamon-colored creature with a taste for garbage and sunflower seeds, would wander by tonight. I hadn't had a chance to repair and refill the bird feeder, so maybe he'd skip my yard on his nocturnal rounds.

"Nectar of the gods," Dan said, setting his glass on the chair's arm with a click. "So, what's this new partner of yours like?"

I turned to face him, thinking as always that, at six foot five, he looked more like a lumberjack than a priest with his barrel chest, muscled legs stretched out and crossed at the ankles, and perpetual tan. Still, there was a quiet strength in his stillness, and the sense of a powerful intellect behind the slightly hooded brown eyes. He never talked about what he'd done before becoming a priest about ten years ago, but something about him made me think of a sniper rifle wrapped in a quilt. The outer covering seemed cozy and warm, but the man underneath might be lethal.

I propped my elbows against the deck rail. "She's a demon in human form."

He took another sip of Scotch and kept his gaze fixed on me.

I sighed heavily. "Oh, all right, she seems nice enough, but so helpless it makes me want to slap her. She's in her early fifties, I'd guess, a zaftig blonde. She probably spent more on the *ensemble* she had on today than I spent on my entire wardrobe last year. Her whole life revolved around Les and the kids and doing the charity dinner circuit until Les dumped her for a twenty-two-year-old. Now, according to her, Swift Investigations is all that stands between her and her kids and the bread line. I'm sure she's exaggerating."

"What are you going to do about her?"

"According to my lawyer, there's not much I can do." My

fingers tightened around the water bottle, and it protested with a crunching sound. "We went over all the paperwork this afternoon, and there doesn't seem to be anything I can do except take on this woman as my partner or buy her out—and you know I can't afford to do that." I gestured at the house, a "fixer-upper" I'd bought a couple of years previously and had poured all my savings and a lot of sweat equity into renovating. "Not without selling the house, at least."

"You were saying just last night that you needed a new assistant—"

"An assistant, damn it, not a partner." I ground my teeth. If my time in the Air Force had taught me anything, it's that I like autonomy, that I like making my own decisions and being responsible for the outcome. It's one of the reasons I'd set up as a PI rather than join the police when I separated from the military; cops have partners. Now, irony of ironies, it looked like I had one, too. "Where Goldman was content to let his money ride, finagle it as a tax loss somehow, she'll be drawing a salary. She'll be taking money *out* of the business, which'll make it that much longer before I can afford to buy her out."

"Maybe she'll be an asset."

"Hah! D'y'know what she did before she married Gold-man? She was a beautician!" I'd learned that much from Gigi in the hour-long discussion that had followed her bombshell of an announcement. "When I suggested she'd make more money in her old line of work, she told me she wanted to try something new and thought being a PI would be exciting. Did I tell you she brought the .357 with her because she thought PIs all ran around with guns? I think she's watched too many *Spenser: For Hire* reruns."

A half-smile stretched across Dan's face, crinkling the crow's feet that showed as white lines penciled against his tan. He watched me pace the deck. "Give her a chance, Charlie. If you're stuck with her, you might as well make the best of it. Maybe her society contacts will bring in a new class of business for you."

"You have to look on the bright side," I grumbled, secretly taken by his idea. "You're a priest."

Swallowing the last glimmer of Scotch in his glass, Dan rose, towering over me. "I'm going to turn in. I've got a parishioner having surgery first thing in the morning, and I need to be there before they put him under. You going to be okay?"

"Go." I shooed him away. "Thanks for listening."

"I live to serve."

From anyone else, it would've been a joke. He clomped down the deck stairs and I tracked his progress across the thin strip of woods that separated our houses by the sound of rustling leaves and snapping twigs. His door creaked open a hundred yards away—I really needed to go over there with my WD-40—and a faint "good night" drifted to me.

" 'Night," I called back.

The night seemed darker in the silence after his door banged shut. I collected Dan's glass and my bottle and took them inside, carefully bolting the deck door behind me. I didn't want the bear helping himself to my Oreos.

(Tuesday)

Make the best of it, make the best of it, I chanted to myself at seven the next morning as I parked my Subaru outside the office next to Gigi's Hummer. *Make the best of it.* I pushed the door open. *Make the—*

"Oh, my God!" I stared in dismay at my office. A ficus tree in a pink ceramic pot sat to the right of the door, its leaves tickling my face. The smell of coffee wafted through the room, emanating from the pot perched on a crocheted doily atop the file cabinet. Two mugs—one with Garfield the Cat and the other embossed with blue stars and the slogan REACH FOR THE STARS!—sat beside the pot. For clients, no doubt. A poster of kittens in a basket of yarn balls simpered from the wall behind the desk I'd have to get used to thinking of as Gigi's. Framed family photos, a potpourri bowl filled with stinky mulch, a dish of pink M&Ms, a foot-high plaster rooster wearing a necklace of linked paper clips, a three-tier in-box of lavender acrylic, and a small stereo spewing New Agey–sounding woodwinds obscured the desk. Gigi smiled at me from the chair she'd customized with a beaded seat and a cream-colored cardigan draped across the back.

"Good morning!" Her voice and smile were as happy as the short-sleeved yellow blouse and matching slacks she wore. She looked like a giant canary.

"What the hell is all this?" I asked, my arm sweeping out to embrace the entire office. I started toward my desk, an oasis of simplicity and bareness in this gift shop hell, and tripped over an area rug frolicking with parrots and jungle foliage.

Her smile faltered. "I just moved in a few things to make it feel more homey."

"This isn't home. It's a place of business where our clients expect professionalism, not ducklings," I said, spotting a duckling planter sprouting wheatgrass on the windowsill.

"It's my philosophy that customers feel more comfortable in an atmosphere that reminds them of home," she said, the southern accent thickening.

"Well, no one would feel at home in this unless they lived in a Hallmark store," I said. "Get rid of it."

"No."

The single word took me aback, and I stared across the room at her. Her pleasant face wore an obstinate look, and her mouth was set in a mulish line.

"It's my office."

"It's *our* office," she returned, "and since we're going to be working together, we have to learn to compromise, reach consensus."

Screw consensus. That was probably the word du jour at her charity committee meetings. I bit back the profanities that threatened to spill out and tried reason. "Look, Gigi, you might know best what works in a beauty parlor, but you've got to understand that people looking to hire a private investigator are looking for a different . . . aesthetic than women wanting acrylic nails or a perm."

She folded her own manicured nails into her palms. "I can accept that," she said after a full minute of thought. "Maybe if I put the duckling planter in the bathroom?"

Gaagh. She wasn't getting it. I felt like I was wrestling an eel. "That's a start," I choked out. "I'll help you put the rest back in your car after work."

She held my gaze for a moment, then bent her head to continue reading from the open file folder on her desk.

"What's that?" I grabbed a Pepsi from the fridge and took a swallow.

"I thought I should familiarize myself with our cases," she said without looking up. "I'm starting with the *A*'s and working my way through the alphabet."

Pepsi went down the wrong pipe and I choked. A flame of pure anger burned through me. This was *my* business, damn it, and I'd worked my butt off to get it off the ground, sacrificing a salary the first few years until I built my customer base, putting in eighty hours a week, cultivating a network of sources, honing my skills with classes and professional reading. Where did she get off redecorating the office, rifling through my client files, taking over? Resolve hardened within me. Forget making the best of it. If I couldn't dissolve the partnership, or force her out, I'd have to make her want to leave.

—*mm*—

Taking my half-drunk Pepsi with me, I left the potpourri-scented office to drag in deep breaths of mingled fresh air and exhaust from the rush hour traffic streaming by on Academy Boulevard. Grinding gears, screeching brakes, and the thud of heavy metal music from a low-rider provided welcome relief from the strains of Zamfir or Yanni tinkling in my office. I did several laps around the shopping area at a brisk pace, startling the cats in the alley and a couple of sparrows taking a dust bath on the sidewalk. Caffeinated and calmer, I returned to the office and settled myself cross-legged on the floor to inspect the infant seat and effects Melissa Lloyd had dropped off yesterday. In my haste to meet with my lawyer about keeping Gigi Goldman out of Swift Investigations—for all the good that had done—I hadn't taken time to look them over.

Nothing was embroidered with Olivia's full name, worse

luck. The car seat had nothing distinctive about it, although the loden-colored lining and molded black handle were classier than most. PEG PEREGO was stamped on the bottom, but that meant nothing to me. I pulled the Onesie with feet from the plastic grocery bag. Yellow terrycloth with a giraffe appliquéd on the chest, it also told me nothing. I examined the labels, hoping to find initials at least, but no luck. Without much hope, I pulled the blanket from the bag. It was pale pink, woven from something wondrously soft, maybe cashmere, with a two-inch-deep satin binding embroidered with white lambs. I rubbed it against my face.

"Ooh, a Delicia Furman."

Gigi's voice startled me. I looked up, self-consciously lowering the blanket from my face, to find her staring at it with delight. "A what?"

"A Delicia Furman. I ordered one for my goddaughter's baptism present, but there was a two-year waiting list." She came around her desk and asked, "May I?"

I handed her the blanket. She inspected the embroidery. "It's definitely a Delicia. She raises her own cashmere goats, shears them, and spins the yarn herself. I met her once when she donated a blanket to a charity auction I was organizing. She looks more like a goat-herder than an artist, but there's no mistaking her embroidery. Look how tiny the stitches are, and how the lambs all seem to have different expressions on their faces." Gigi stroked the blanket reverently.

"What does a Delicia Furman go for?" I asked. "A hundred, hundred fifty?"

Gigi laughed. "Oh, honey, you're not even in the ballpark. Try twelve to fifteen hundred, minimum."

Eep. For a baby blanket that was going to get drooled on and peed on? At least this told me that baby Olivia had rich relatives or friends. A thought struck me. "Do you think Delicia'd know who bought this?"

"I don't know what kind of records she keeps, but this is definitely a one-of-a-kind, so she might remember. She doesn't do duplicates or copies of anything, ever."

I tucked the giraffe outfit into the plastic bag and folded the Delicia, snorting as I realized I was thinking of it the way one would "a Goya" or "a Rodin." I placed both inside the car seat and maneuvered it behind my desk. "Thanks," I told Gigi, who had returned to her desk and was staring at her computer screen, nails clicking across the keyboard.

She wrote something on a lavender sticky note and handed it to me. "Delicia Furman's phone number and address," she said. "From her Web page. She's outside Larkspur."

"Thanks," I said again, studying the note. At least Gigi knew her way around a computer and the Internet. She even had a little initiative. "Do you want to come with me to talk to her?" The words popped out before I could stop them.

"And learn PI interrogation techniques?" Her eyes lit up.

"Think of it as an interview, or better yet, a conversation," I suggested, already regretting the invitation.

"Gotcha." She made a note on a steno pad, then tucked it into her mailbag of a purse. "Now?"

I sighed. "Might as well."

Gigi automatically headed for the Hummer after I collected the blanket, set the answering machine, and locked the office door.

"No way," I said. "We can't go visit an artist, a woman

who raises goats, for heaven's sake, in a vehicle that looks like a Sherman tank and burns more gas than small third-world nations. She'd run us off with a shotgun."

"I never thought of that," Gigi said, dropping her keys back in her purse—how did she ever find them in there?—and following me to the Subaru. "It was Les's, you know. The Hummer. He sure loved that thing when he first got it—waxed it every weekend, wouldn't let the kids eat or drink in it. I guess he couldn't figure out a way to get it to Costa Rica, so he left it. Maybe he just didn't want it anymore."

I ignored the wistful note in her voice, wondering if she saw the parallels between Les's relationship with the Hummer and with her. The bastard. My anger toward Les Goldman surprised me, and I tamped it down. If I was angry, it was only because his disappearing act had foisted Gigi on me, landing me with a partner I did not need or want.

My annoyance kept me silent throughout the twenty-five minute drive to Larkspur, a small community northwest of Colorado Springs best known for the huge Renaissance festival it hosts every summer. We drove past the festival grounds, where permanent walls, shop fronts, and castles loomed among the lodgepole pines like ghosts of medieval England. Delicia Furman's farm was ten minutes farther on, wedged into a small valley guarded by hills on three sides. The morning sun lit up a small house, a barn, several outbuildings, and fenced enclosures full of goats. A sign at the roadside announced FURMAN's in elegant gray script on white. We bumped down a rutted driveway, and I parked the car by the first paddock. As I opened the door, the scent of dung, warm animal, fresh hay, and clean water drifted in. The smell pulled me back to the farm outside Spokane where I'd spent several years off and on with Grandy and Gramps, my mom's parents, while my parents missionaried in all sorts of godforsaken crannies in South America and Africa. Grandy and Gramps had raised a small herd of Barzona cattle, big red animals with the smarts of a teaspoon, but the farm smell was the same. I breathed it in.

Gigi murmured, "Aren't they just the cutest?"

"Cute" wasn't the word I'd've chosen. The goats were as tall as my thigh in an array of colors—tan, white, brown, gray, black—but they had long horns that swooped back from their brows and twisted to nasty-looking points. The shaggy black goat in the pen closest to me eyed me suspiciously as he chewed his cud. "You're a handsome fellow," I told him. Unmoved by my flattery, he scratched the side of his head against a fence post.

Just as I was wondering where to start the search for Ms. Furman, a woman strode out of the barn fifty yards away, trundling a wheelbarrow full of what I suspected was goat poop. Thick gray hair streamed almost to her waist from beneath a blue bandanna. Stained overalls hung loosely over a white henley shirt. Knee-high galoshes enveloped her feet and calves. She stopped when she saw us and stripped work gloves from her hands as she approached.

"Help you?" Her voice and gaze were no-nonsense. Eyes that showed more gray than blue peered from beneath straight iron-gray brows. Tanned skin beginning to soften around the jawline and pouches below her eyes testified to her life outdoors. She looked like a farmer, not an artist.

I introduced myself and stumbled when it came time to present Gigi. I finally called her "Gigi Goldman, my associate." My lips wouldn't form the P-word.

Gigi looked at me reproachfully but merely said, "We've met. Remember, Miss Furman? You donated that beautiful blue afghan with the star motif to our silent auction in support of the battered women's home?"

Furman's sharp eyes focused on Gigi. "Right. I thought you looked familiar. Well, if you're here for another—"

"We need information, Ms. Furman," I broke in, "not donations."

"I'm afraid I don't deal in information," she said, "only art." She took two steps toward the pen and scratched the black goat on his knobbly head.

She'd lost me. "I thought you made blankets. We just need to know who you sold this one to." I nodded at Gigi, and she unfurled the pink blanket she'd been clutching to her chest.

"And isn't that art?" Furman asked, whipping around to pin me with narrowed eyes. From the look of satisfaction on her face, I knew I'd fallen into a trap she'd sprung many times. "You're one of the culturally stunted products of our public education system who don't consider something 'art' unless it was painted or sculpted by a DWEM, a dead white European male." She pronounced it "dweem."

I felt heat rise to my cheeks but said, "I like Georgia O'Keeffe."

"Bully for you. How about Junichi Arai or Michail Berger? Maybe Chihuly?"

I knew Chihuly did glass, but I'd never heard of the other

27

two. "Look"—I put my hands up in a surrender gesture—"I didn't come here for a seminar on alternative art—"

"Alternative?" Her brows rose haughtily to her hairline. A goat coughed behind her, sounding like it was laughing.

This was going from bad to worse. "Do you remember who bought this blanket? It was with an abandoned baby."

That brought her up short, and she stepped off her soapbox, reaching a surprisingly well formed and delicate hand to grasp a fold of the blanket.

"I think it's lovely," Gigi said.

"Thank you, dear," Furman said, tracing her thumb over one of the lambs. She nodded and looked over to me. "Aurora Newcastle. She bought it about six months ago. It was the last one I finished this spring before combing season."

"Combing?"

"You don't shear goats to get the cashmere, you comb it out of them," she said, making a motion like dragging a comb down.

I sensed another lecture coming on, this one on goat husbandry, so I asked quickly, "Was she pregnant?"

"Aurora?" Furman laughed, a rich chuckle. "She's as AARP eligible as I am. No, it was a gift for someone."

"Do you know who?" Gigi asked. She had the steno pad out, pen poised.

Furman shook her head. "No. She didn't say. And before you ask, no, I won't give you her address. You understand."

"Sure." It didn't matter. It wouldn't be hard to Google someone named Aurora Newcastle, and she apparently lived in Colorado since Furman talked like she knew her. "Thanks for your time, Ms. Furman," I said.

"I'd love to come back and hear about the goats some-time," Gigi said, real interest lighting her face.

"You do that," Furman said. "I think they'd like you." She turned away, striding back to the dung-filled wheelbarrow, rubber boots scraping a wsk-wsk sound from her overalls as she walked.

"Did you hear that?" Gigi said in an awed voice. "The goats would like me."

I rolled my eyes and climbed into the Subaru, barely waiting for Gigi to swing her door shut before reversing with unnecessary force.

mn

Back at the office, I put mental blinders on to escape the new decor and retrieved phone messages. Two potential clients. I called them back and set up appointments, well aware of Gigi following the conversations from her desk. A third call was from a client who owned a string of fast food restaurants; he kept Swift Investigations on retainer to run background checks on potential employees. This time, he needed some undercover work done at his Buff Burgers restaurant on the northeast side of town. Buff Burgers was a newish franchise that sold buffalo patties with organic produce and whole wheat buns. I groaned at the prospect of doing fast food work to figure out which employee was skimming money from the cash drawer, and my eyes lighted on Gigi. The menial nature of the job should be just the thing to convince her that investigative work was not glamorous and exciting. "I'll have an operative there in the morning," I told Brian.

I put on a serious face as I hung up the phone. "Gigi, I think I've got a case you can handle."

She all but clapped her hands and scurried over to plop down in the chair facing my desk.

"It's undercover work." That set the hook. "It might be dangerous." Yeah, grease splatters might burn her arms. "It'll be hard, nasty work." She couldn't say I hadn't warned her.

Her eyes widened. "What do I have to do?"

I wrote down the Buff Burgers address and handed it to her. "Report to this address at eight tomorrow morning. A worker quit today, and Brian Yukawa, the owner, is holding a job open for you. You'll fill out an application like anyone would, but you'll get the job. The manager'll train you for your duties. Brian thinks someone—maybe the manager—is skimming from the cash register or selling inventory out the back door or something. Your job is to figure out who and how."

"How do I do that?"

Good question. "Keep your eyes open, get to know your co-workers. See if anyone looks like they're hanging out where they shouldn't be or has more money than they ought to. This kind of undercover investigation isn't a science—you just wing it."

"Gotcha." She had the ubiquitous steno pad out, and I'd swear she wrote down "Wing it!"

"We'll get together in the afternoons when you're off shift to discuss the case. Save any questions for me till then; you don't want to make anyone suspect you're not just a run-of-the-mill Buff Burgers employee. You'll do just fine," I added with an encouraging smile.

"But what will I wear?" Gigi asked, looking down at her sunny silk ensemble.

"Not to worry," I said, waving a dismissive hand. "Brian said something about a uniform."

3

(Wednesday)

The next morning, after filling out her application and doing a pro forma interview with the Buff Burgers manager, a kid who looked barely older than her seventeen-year-old son, Dexter, Georgia Goldman stared in dismay at the "uniform" he presented.

"But that's a buffalo costume," she protested, eyeing the heavy-looking horned head with distrust.

"It's a bison, actually," the young manager, Dylan, confided. He had a nerdy air about him that convinced Georgia he'd be able to differentiate between weasels and martens or sine and cosine with the same ease he talked about bison versus buffaloes. The Daniel Boone–ish Western look of the Buff Burgers uniform merely emphasized his gawkiness. "But I guess 'Bison Burgers' didn't have the same ring as 'Buff Burgers,' so we just go with it."

"And I'm supposed to put that on?" She'd spent an hour styling her hair, and it would be crushed.

"Well, yeah. You're Bernie the Buffalo, right? Isn't that the job you applied for? When Brian called last night, he said you'd be in to apply for Trent's job, and Trent was Bernie until his folks made him quit 'cause school's started up again."

"Where do I change?" Gigi asked, resigned to her fate.

"Bathroom." Dylan jerked a thumb over his shoulder.

With the buffalo head clutched in both hands and the rest of the costume draped over her shoulder, Georgia made her way through the mercifully empty restaurant to the bathroom. No way could she maneuver the head in one of the two tiny stalls, so she balanced it on the sink and ducked into a stall to strip. Grime in the tile grout had her aching for a scrub brush and a strong bleach solution. Maybe she should say something to Dylan about it. She'd almost wiggled into the fuzzy brown costume, luckily on the baggy side, managing not to dip the tail in the toilet, when the bathroom door squeaked open and she heard a startled "Ack!" The door clunked closed.

Emerging from the stall, Georgia giggled, imagining how the sight of Bernie's head on the sink must've startled some unsuspecting girl who only needed to relieve herself. All inclination to laugh left as she fitted the shaggy head over hers and peered at her reflection through the eyeholes in Bernie's neck. Something straggled down in front of her field of vision, and she realized it was the buffalo's beard. Walking carefully to counterbalance the weight atop her shoulders, she looped her tail over her arm and trudged back into the restaurant, where Dylan was waiting.

He eyed her critically. "Hm. Well, it'll have to do. But you have to look happier. Cheery, cheery, cheery." He grinned so wide Gigi was sure it hurt his cheeks. "The kids don't want a gloomy Bernie."

Wondering how the kids would know if she were suicidal or manic beneath Bernie's shaggy head, Gigi swished her tail and shuffled off to greet a young mother with three toddlers as they came through the restaurant door shouting, "It's Bernie!"

━ᴡᴡ━

With Gigi gainfully employed asking, "Do you want fries with that buffalo patty?" I had the office to myself Wednesday morning. Ah, bliss. I'd helped her load up most of the tchotchkes last evening, graciously conceding that the ficus and the photos could stay. I plumed myself on my generosity and sneaked a peek at the photos once I had my Pepsi in hand. Most of them showed two kids, a boy and a girl, from toddlerhood to mid-teens. The boy looked older, with longish hair and a smirk as he leaned against a red Beemer in the most recent photo. The girl, about fourteen, appeared in a variety of sequined, feathered, and increasingly sophisticated skating costumes. Once she got the braces off she was going to be a knockout with blond hair, a creamy complexion, and long legs. If Gigi looked like that when Les met her, I could understand why he'd fallen for her.

Back at my desk, I reached for the phone and called a buddy of mine at the Colorado Springs Police Department. It had occurred to me last night that if Baby Girl Hogeboom was reduced to foisting her baby on Melissa Lloyd, she might be a runaway. Perhaps, just perhaps, someone had reported her missing and I could get a line on her that way.

34

Detective Connor Montgomery was willing to look through the missing persons files. "What have you got for a description, Charlie?"

"Seventeen years old, white female, recently gave birth."

A pause. I could just see his dark brows drawing together, the corners of his shapely mouth getting tight. "You're joking, right?"

"Nope, that's all I've got. I know it's not much."

"Not much? It's nothing! Jesus, Charlie, why're you wasting my time?" The sound of paper crumpling traveled over the phone line. The line went dead.

"Nice talking to you, too," I said to the dial tone. Shit. Still, it wasn't a totally wasted call. I knew Montgomery wouldn't be able to resist peeking at the missing persons files for the local area at least, and he'd give me a call if anything looked like a possible.

Aurora Newcastle was next up on my to-do list. A Google search yielded four brief items from the *Denver Post* society page about Eugene and Aurora Newcastle participating in various charity events and hosting the grand opening of the most recent in their chain of upscale wine stores, Purple Feet, in Castle Rock, a community between here and Denver. The accompanying photo was so grainy I couldn't distinguish Aurora Newcastle from Mrs. Claus or Christie Brinkley. None of my databases yielded an address or phone number for the couple—one of the perks of being rich is being able to buy privacy—so I called Purple Feet, the flagship store in the LoDo area of Denver.

"Purple Feet! We'll im*press* you with our wine prices!" answered a young female voice.

When I asked for Mrs. Newcastle, she said, "Oh, I'm sorry. Aurora won't be back till tomorrow. Or is it the next day? No, I think it's tomorrow."

"Back from where?"

"The cruise. I think they're in the Bahamas. Or is it the Caymans?"

I thanked her, hung up, and tried to convince myself that I could legitimately bill Melissa Lloyd for a trip to the Cayman Islands to track down Aurora Newcastle. I had a new bikini I'd optimistically bought at the beginning of the summer and never gotten a chance to wear . . .

The phone rang. An angry Brian Yukawa, owner of Buff Burgers, yelled on a crackly cell phone connection. Traffic noise in the background made it hard to hear. "Charlie! I just got a call from the police, something about a disturbance at my restaurant on Powers. My phone cut out before I could get it all. I'm stuck in traffic up in Denver and can't get hold of my manager. The police were saying something about an ambulance and a private eye—"

His cell phone went dead again. Not stopping to try to call him back, I grabbed my purse and bolted for the door, my mind conjuring awful images. An ambulance! Who was hurt? I'd given the gun back to Gigi Monday afternoon, telling her to take it home, lock it in a safe, and leave it there. Surely she couldn't have taken it to Buff Burgers with her this morning? Maybe someone had wrestled it away from her and she'd been shot. A twinge of guilt goosed me into the car. I fought traffic up Academy Boulevard to Hwy 83 and turned right onto Briargate Parkway. Exceeding the speed limit by a hefty margin, I headed east until I hit Powers and then swung north to the new shopping area where the Buff Burgers sat near a Target and a Petco.

Chaos met my eyes. Traffic was snarled at the intersection as drivers gawked at the two police cars, one fire truck, and an ambulance blocking the drive-through lane of the Buff Burgers. Patrons roamed the parking lot. Black smoke roiled from the rear door and drive-through window. Firefighters played a hose over the building. The stench of burning rubber mixed strangely with the smell of french fries. A uniformed cop had a buffalo by the shoulder as an EMT tended to a nearby man stretched out under the shade of the only tree in sight. Pulling onto the median, I abandoned my car and forded the unmoving lanes of traffic.

"Charlie!" the buffalo squawked.

Oh. My. God. It was Gigi in the buffalo getup, beckoning me over with one hand—hoof? My steps dragged as I approached, and my anger mounted. Now that I knew she wasn't shot or otherwise injured, I let fury rise up at the thought of lawsuits directed against Swift Investigations. I'd lose Brian's business. The entire CSPD would be laughing at me.

I showed my business card to the cop (since Colorado doesn't license investigators, I had nothing more official to present), an Officer Venetti, and he said, "The buffalo says she's working with you, ma'am?"

"Bison," Gigi said.

When the cop and I gave her uncomprehending stares, she said, "I'm really a bison, not a buffalo."

I glared at her and asked the officer, "Is she being charged with anything?"

He shrugged and passed a hand over curly black hair.

"Don't know yet, ma'am. We're still sorting it out. There's talk of arson, assault, inciting a riot . . . I don't know what all. The detectives aren't here yet."

"What the hell happened?" I asked Gigi, half thinking the cop would stop me. He didn't. "And take that goddamned buffa—bison head off so I can talk to you."

"I can't," she wailed. "It's stuck."

"Here. You push and I'll pull," I said. "Bend down."

Gigi obeyed, and I grabbed hold of her horns, tugging with all my might as she pushed at the animal's lower jaw. Officer Venetti motioned to a fellow cop, and they both watched, amused looks on their faces. Just as I was starting to think we'd need a circular saw or a hammer, the head popped off and I fell on my ass, holding one curved horn as the rest of the head rolled a few feet and stopped. Two small children standing nearby burst into tears. "She killed Bernie!"

Their mother coaxed them away with promises of ice cream, and I figured Buff Burgers had lost their business permanently to some fast food joint that didn't behead large mammals in its parking lot. The cops doubled over, roaring with laughter as I stood up, holding the plastic horn like a dagger. I wasn't sure who to plunge it in first. I fought the urge to rub my tailbone, feeling the jolt all the way up my spine and into my head.

Gigi, plump cheeks flushed red, ash blond hair flattened to her scalp on one side and standing out in a winglike formation on the other, perspiration dripping down her temples, looked at me with trepidation. I closed my eyes and took three slow breaths.

"What happened?" I forced my hand open and let the horn fall to the ground before I committed a felony.

"Well, when I got up this morning, I—"

I held up one hand in a stop signal. "This. Explain this." I gestured to the burning restaurant, the ambulance, the cops.

"Um, well, I was getting the hang of being Bernie and really kind of liking it—the children were so sweet—except it was really hot. So I went into the back to get an iced tea and get to know the kids who work here, like you said. I'm the oldest employee by a good thirty-five years, I think. Anyway, while I was chatting, I kept an eye on the business at the counter, you know, the cash registers and stuff. And after a while I realized that Jody"—she pointed to the teen now sitting beneath the aspen tree, a Band-Aid on his forehead—"wasn't ringing everything up. When a customer would place the order, he'd ring up the burger and fries or whatever, you know, the stuff that one of the kitchen workers got ready, but he didn't ring up the drinks or cookies or stuff he could get himself. He'd charge the customer the full amount, and I'm sure that at the end of the shift, he'd pocket the difference."

"She's lying!" Jody growled. In his Buff Burgers uniform, he looked like a skinny pioneer who'd gone one too many rounds with the Indians. Two buttons were torn off his shirt, and his coonskin cap hung askew, showing lank brown hair. The EMT was binding a nasty burn on his hand.

"He must be really good at math to be able to do that," Gigi added, an admiring note in her voice. "I noticed most of these kids couldn't give you change for a dollar if you bought a fifty-cent Junior Bernie Moose Froth Non-Dairy Dessert."

"I'm not. She's crazy. She attacked me!"

"I didn't!" Gigi's eyes welled up, but she firmed her mouth into a determined line. "I merely went over to *talk* to him, to tell him what I'd noticed, encourage him to do the honest thing."

I rolled my eyes at her naïveté. "What happened then?"

"He grabbed a basket of fries from the frying well and flung them at me!" Gigi's voice climbed higher. "He ruined my Bernie costume." She pointed to the large grease splotches staining the costume. "Some of the oil landed on the ranges, and it started smoking. Next thing I knew, you couldn't see anything and people were screaming and running and—"

"Bernie saved my life," put in a new voice. I turned to see a teenaged girl wearing a Buff Burgers uniform, her raven hair in braids. She looked like Pocahontas wearing pink Crocs. "I got turned around in the smoke and started to choke—I have asthma." She pulled out an inhaler to prove it. "She came after me and pulled me out of there."

I glanced over at Officer Venetti, glad to see he'd conquered his laughing fit enough to start taking notes.

"That's great . . ."

"Caitlyn. Caitlyn Carruthers," she supplied.

"I didn't *assault* him," Gigi put in. "I had to butt him to make sure he didn't run off." She lowered her head and made a motion like a charging buffalo. "I only knocked him on his keister."

A tiny seed of hope that Swift Investigations was not ruined sprouted. If Caitlyn would tell her story to the reporters I saw crowding into the parking lot in their antenna-topped vans, and no one filed charges—

"You assaulted me. My dad's going to sue your butt back to the Stone Age, Grandma," Jody said, getting shakily to his feet. "I hope those orange prison jumpsuits come in extra-large, buffalo breath."

Wow, that boy had a real mouth on him and knew how to aim for the jugular. He'd hold his own in juvie until he mouthed off to a bigger kid with a shiv.

Gigi gasped in outrage. "Bison! And I'm not a grandma. I couldn't be . . ." She paused, doing some mental math. "Well, I'm not. And a size fourteen is *not* an *extra*-large, and you're . . . you're nothing but a rude, incompetent thief!"

"I am not! I got away with more than four hundred—" He cut himself off as he realized what he was saying. Twisting out of the EMT's grasp, he hobbled away from the restaurant.

"Yea, Bernie!" someone yelled. I heard a spattering of applause as Officer Venetti trotted after Jody, handcuffs in hand. Looking around, I saw that most of the audience wore Buff Burgers uniforms. Jody clearly wasn't in the running for Mr. Congeniality.

As Venetti led Jody, arms cuffed behind his back, over to a police car, I asked Gigi, "Why'd you ever decide to confront that delinquent on your own?"

She used her tail to dab at the sweat running down her forehead and widened her eyes at me. "Well, you said to wing it."

—————

The media and police consumed most of the rest of the afternoon. A young reporter interviewed Gigi in her one-horned buffalo head after Caitlyn told everyone about "Bernie's" heroics. Exactly fourteen seconds of the interview made the local news. The anchors snickered in the studio as the reporter summed up, "What a moooving tale! Back to you, Jed." It was almost enough to make me heave, but Brian Yukawa was so pleased with the free publicity for Buff Burgers that he and I came to an agreement on our own that didn't involve our lawyers. I waived Swift Investigations' fee, and Brian agreed to take care of the restaurant damages, most of which were from smoke and water. I offered to replace the stained and ruined Bernie costume, but he laughed it off, saying they had plenty of others in storage somewhere. Gigi brought Bernie's head back to the office and propped it behind her desk, a massive trophy. It gave off an unpleasant odor of rancid grease, smoke, singed plastic, and french fries, but I didn't have the heart to banish it. Maybe if we got it dry-cleaned and mounted, glued the horn back on . . .

What was I thinking? I'd give it to Gigi as a going-away present, because surely she wouldn't want to continue working here after the day's traumas. On that hugely satisfying thought I locked up and headed for home, having persuaded Gigi to leave early. "You deserve some time off. And a long shower," I'd told her.

As for me, I deserved a long soak in my hot tub, but only after I got some gardening done. Stripping off my navy slacks and pin-striped blouse when I got home, I estimated I had two hours to work before it got dark. Weeds were poking their presumptuous heads up in one of my rock borders, and I needed to mulch some shrubs before we got the first hard frost, which could be any day now that we were on the cusp of September. Wearing faded orange running shorts and an old Hard Rock Café T-shirt, I descended the steps from my deck to the yard.

The scent of pine met me, and I breathed it in, feeling the tension drain from me.

I dragged a forty-pound bag of mulch from the small shed at the back of the property and started tamping it into place beneath my barberry bushes and lavender, taking care to avoid the barberry's inch-long spines. The musty cedar smell made me sneeze, but I liked it. The pull in the muscles of my back and shoulders felt good, and I went through three bags of mulch before straightening. With a hand at my waist, I arched back.

"Must've been a hard day," said a familiar voice from behind me.

I turned to see Father Dan, still in black shirt, clerical collar, and gray slacks, observing me from the hillock that separates my property from the church's. The last of the sun's fingers played over his rugged features and struck sparks from his blond hair. It glinted on a beer can as he raised it to drink.

"How'd you know?" I smiled, glad to see him, and bent to yank a dandelion from a river rock border.

"You always end up in the yard after you've had a particularly tough day. You missed one," he added, using the can to point at a weed. "Why don't you just let nature take its course?"

"That would be admitting defeat," I said, only half joking. "Xeriscape is a compromise between the gardener and nature in Colorado," I told him. I gestured at the area behind my house. "I get to impose a pattern, some colors, on my yard, and the weather can't ruin all my efforts by refusing to rain, because most of the plants need very little water and a lot of the texture comes from rocks and stuff."

"So you win?" Father Dan asked with a grin. He crumpled the beer can in one large hand.

"Absolutely."

"That attitude'll only make nature try harder."

"She can bring it on." I stooped to pull some more weeds from the border, stuffing them into a plastic bag. I cut a look up at him from under the bangs flopping in my eyes. "Well, don't just stand there looking priestly, lend a hand."

"Can't. Vestry meeting in fifteen minutes. I'll bring you a beer, though."

"Slacker."

He returned with a Sam Adams, and I decided to call it quits for the night. We settled cross-legged on the grass and drank our beers in companionable silence as the sun sank behind the mountain and shadows crept into the garden, coaxing the bunnies to come out and forage. I inhaled the hoppy smell of the beer and savored its cold bite as it slid down my throat. Um. The combination of the beer, peaceful silence, and hard work had lulled me half to sleep when Dan squeezed my shoulder and pushed himself to his feet.

"Meeting time." He extended a hand, and I put mine in it, conscious of its warmth and strength as he pulled me up.

"Knock 'em dead."

"Don't think the thought hasn't crossed my mind on occasion, especially when we're talking about the budget."

Showing him a shocked face, I waved as he strode back toward the church; then I headed for the deck and my hot tub. If any of Dan's vestry members wandered this way they'd get a jolt, because I wasn't going to bother with a swimsuit.

4

(Thursday)

No one, not even the bear, observed my skinny-dipping, and I set out for Denver the next morning feeling rested and rejuvenated. I was ninety-nine percent sure I'd seen the last of Gigi Goldman; I'd call her later to see if we could work out some sort of payment plan where I bought her out a little bit at a time over the next couple of years. Then I could hire the part-time assistant I really needed, someone to answer the phone, greet customers, and do some database research while I was in the field. It would all work as smoothly as my hooking up with Aurora Newcastle this morning. When I'd called Purple Feet again just after eight, a different clerk told me Mrs. Newcastle was expected by eleven. Unless traffic screwed me up, I'd be there on her heels.

Using my cell phone, I called Melissa Lloyd to update her and tell her I'd drop by her store that afternoon. With any luck, I'd have the name of her daughter by then. If she lived on the Front Range, maybe we'd be able to turn baby Olivia over to her sometime tomorrow. Melissa sounded tense—the baby wailing in the background might've had something to do with that—and agreed to remain at work until I showed up.

Most of the commuters were safely incarcerated in their soulless cubicles by now, and I traveled the fifty-odd miles to Denver in well under an hour, only slowing when I reached Park Meadows Mall on the outskirts of the city. Downtown's skyscrapers loomed on the horizon, emerging from the prairie like stalagmites. Mountains to the west, snowcapped even at this time of year, made me prickle with ski fever. In another six weeks, maybe, some of the runs would open and I could spend my weekends rocketing down the runs. If I could afford lift tickets. The thought of my rocky finances and the bite Gigi would take out of my bottom line brought my spirits down, and I finished the drive to LoDo in a gloomy mood made worse by the struggle to find a parking spot. Finally wedging my way into a spot just vacated by a Volkswagen Beetle, a good three blocks from my destination, I locked the doors and headed down Seventeenth Street to Purple Feet, the plastic bag containing the baby blanket bumping against my shin.

Purple neon outlined the store's logo of grape-stained feet and made it easy to locate my destination between a boutique and a store selling collectible maps and prints. I considered the bikini in the boutique's window for a moment, until I noticed the two scraps of fabric—not large enough to make a decent-sized dinner napkin—were priced at four hundred dollars. Eep. I pushed through the smoked-glass doors of Purple Feet and found myself in a hushed atmosphere reminiscent of a library or a cathedral, but with a heady scent far removed from dusty books and hymnals. Bottles of wine stacked in crates, arranged in sale barrels, and chilling in glass-fronted refrigerator cases took up every available inch of floor space. The price of the first bottle I looked at would've bought me half of the bikini. The Lower Downtown district was too rich for my blood.

"Are you here for the tasting?" A woman in a gray linen dress and a headscarf tied into a mini turban of pearl, lavender, and turquoise paisley that completely covered her hair approached me. "It doesn't start for another half hour, but I just opened a bottle of sauvignon blanc to train the staff"— she gestured to a man and a woman wearing lavender polo shirts with the Purple Feet logo on their chests—"and you're welcome to try it. Here."

She handed me a stemmed glass with an inch of pale yellow wine in the bottom and filled glasses for herself and the two clerks. Following their lead, I swirled my glass and peered at the liquid as if it might be the cure for AIDS.

"Strong scents of grapefruit and herbs," said the male clerk, burying his nose in the glass like a dog sniffing a new crotch. He had thick brown hair and wore a bow tie.

"And just a hint of apricot, don't you think, Roger?" the woman added. She was younger than the man and edgier, in black capri leggings, a white and black tunic top, and razor-cut black hair. She tipped the glass and rolled the wine around on her tongue. She closed her eyes. I'd had sex that didn't make me look that happy. "Mellow on the finish with a touch of licorice."

"Bright acids," put in Roger.

The three looked at me expectantly, and I took a sip. I liked it, and I surprised myself by actually tasting the grapefruit Roger had mentioned. No parsley or oregano, though, and definitely no Twizzlers. "Yum."

A hint of a smile played around the older woman's lips. "You're not here for the tasting?"

"No," I confessed, smiling back, "but I liked it. I'm looking for Aurora Newcastle."

"I'm Aurora. What can I do for you?" She took the glass I handed to her and set it and her own on a tray. Roger whisked them away, and both clerks drifted off to tasks in other parts of the store.

"My name is Charlotte Swift, and I'm a private investigator." I gave her my business card, which she studied. "I'm looking for a teenager who recently had a baby, and I believe you might know her."

"Really?" She arched penciled-in brows. "What's her name?"

"I don't know. I was hoping you could help me with that." Pulling the Delicia blanket out of the bag, I handed it to her.

Her thin fingers dug into the cashmere, and for a moment I thought she was going to faint. She nursed the blanket to her cheek; its vibrant pink made her skin look milk-pale. She was ill, I realized, finally catching the significance of the turban and the brows that were skillfully penciled on. Makeup did a good job of hiding the circles under her eyes, but it couldn't hide the weariness and pain lurking in them, or completely cover the almost blue tinge in her skin.

"Where did you get this?" she whispered, reaching out one hand to clutch my forearm.

I told her about Melissa finding a baby on her doorstep and the note that accompanied it. "My client just wants to reunite the baby with her mother," I said. "Delicia Furman said you bought this blanket, and I was hoping you could tell me who you gave it to."

Mrs. Newcastle took a deep breath. "Let's go back to my office. I get tired if I stand too long. Erica," she called. "Please conduct the wine tasting. I'll be in my office for a while."

"Yes, Mrs. Newcastle," Erica said, gliding forward to greet a gaggle of business-suited men and women coming through the door, eager to expand their knowledge of wine on their lunch hour . . . or just get snockered.

I followed Mrs. Newcastle's slim figure through a gap in a counter spread with cheeses and crackers and into a utility room with a sink and a dishwasher. The top rack was pulled out, loaded with identical wineglasses. Steam curled up from the dishwasher, filling the air with humidity and the smell of detergent.

"Lemon," I said, sniffing deeply, "with just a hint of ammonia."

Mrs. Newcastle laughed as she pushed open the door to her office, a small room with a desk and two chairs, one behind the desk, one in front of it. The walls were taupe with framed photos of vineyards providing splashes of color. A flat-screen monitor occupied most of the desk space, and wine magazines and books slumped in precarious stacks against all the walls.

"Please, sit," Mrs. Newcastle said, lowering herself carefully into the chair behind the desk. Her gaze pinned me. "You find the rituals of wine pretentious?" She still had the blanket, and now she set it atop the polished walnut of the desk.

I thought about her question. I didn't want to offend her, and not just because she could point me toward Melissa Lloyd's daughter. I liked her. She reminded me of Grandy, not so much in looks as in spirit. "Maybe not pretentious. Foreign?"

"An honest answer." She nodded her approval. "I think if you learned a little something about wine, you'd find it fascinating, just fascinating. We offer classes and tastings here, if you ever want to take one. I took my first class almost thirty years ago, and wine just grabbed hold of me. It was I who was excited about wine, you know, who wanted to open Purple Feet. Not Eugene. He had the business sense, the financial know-how. But I had the passion. When I go . . . Eugene and I don't have any children. He'll end up selling Purple Feet, I think, in the end."

She worked her fingers in the blanket, almost like a baker kneading dough. Grief hung in the room, bowing her shoulders with its weight.

"The blanket?" I asked gently.

She straightened her shoulders and fixed a businesslike expression on her face. "Right. I gave it to Elizabeth Sprouse, my best friend's daughter."

That fit with the "Beth" signature on the note. My heartbeat picked up, and I leaned forward, surging toward the finish line of this investigation. "What can you tell me about Elizabeth and her family? Where does she live?"

Aurora Newcastle drifted into reminiscence mode, crepey eyelids half shuttering her eyes. "Her mother, Patricia, and I were friends from childhood. Inseparable. She married Eugene's college roommate, and the four of us did everything together.

Strangely enough, neither Patricia nor I ever conceived, although we both wanted children. Eugene and I decided to accept our lack of children, and I channeled my energy into the wine business. In fact, Patricia's the one who encouraged me to open Purple Feet when everyone else was pooh-poohing the idea. She'd never been interested in a career herself, and eventually she and Robert decided to adopt. They were in their early forties by then. I still remember how thrilled they were when they came home with Elizabeth. They loved that baby more than life itself. I'd heard people say that before, but never understood it until I saw the way Patricia was with Elizabeth. She was a delightful child, smart and kind and loving. But everything changed when Robert died."

"What happened?"

"He was on the United flight that went down in Pennsylvania on 9/11."

The stark announcement chilled the air.

"How awful."

Aurora nodded. "Yes, indeed. It changed Patricia—and poor Elizabeth. She was only eight. She'd lost her father, and her mother just went off the deep end, immersing herself in Bible studies and prayer groups, trying to understand the God that would let 9/11 happen. She met a man, Zachary Sprouse, at some retreat. Within weeks she was married to him and moved to Colorado Springs. He adopted Elizabeth. They live in near-poverty because Sprouse is some kind of religious zealot who runs a church, 'the Church of Jesus Christ the Righteous on Earth,' that encourages people to live as Jesus did: no modern conveniences, giving most of their money to the church, carrying out biblical punishments."

I had noticed before that the longer a church's name is, the more far out its theology seems to be. "Sounds like a cult," I said.

"Oh, yes. I worried for the longest time that he would do a David Koresh, that Patricia and Elizabeth would die with him. He just seemed like the type who'd embrace martyrdom if it made him famous. I don't worry about that so much anymore because I don't think he's got the charisma to convince people to die with him." Her tone was scathing.

I'd never thought of it that way. I could just see the job advertisement for Cult Leader: "Must know Bible by memory. Must dress and smell like Old Testament prophet. Must be able to convince congregation to drink poisoned Kool-Aid." I bit back an inappropriate grin and said, "Are you still in touch with Patricia?"

"I've only seen Patricia a handful of times since she married him. She's cut herself off from everyone who cares about her."

"Or he has." Classic abuser tactic.

"Right. Elizabeth ran away the first time when she was fourteen. She came here. To me." Aurora's face brightened. "I told her she could stay, but then Sprouse showed up, accused me of kidnapping her, threatened to bring charges. I appealed to Patricia, but she would only say that the husband is the head of the household and Elizabeth must abide by his wisdom. Wisdom! The man's a lunatic."

She took a deep breath. "I kept in touch with Elizabeth as much as I could. She had an e-mail account she used to access from the library and then from school once she got to high school. Last November she wrote to tell me she had a plan to make 'big' money and escape from Sprouse. She wouldn't take money from me; she was afraid Sprouse would find out about it and take legal action of some kind."

"Did he beat her, abuse her sexually?"

Aurora scratched her scalp through the silk turban. Her eyes were troubled. "I don't know. She never said he did. But mental and emotional abuse—absolutely."

I wondered how much of this I should share with my client. I didn't think it was the kind of story that would assuage her guilt about giving up her daughter for adoption.

Aurora's gaze drifted to the doorway, and I got the feeling she was seeing something much farther away than the hall. "You know, when Elizabeth was little—maybe six or seven— Patricia left her with me sometimes, here at the store. She'd take each customer by the hand as they came in, and lead them to a wine she thought they'd like." Aurora got teary-eyed at the memory. "Every bottle she picked out had an animal of some kind on the label: a bull, a horse, a cheetah, a loon. I can't tell you how many customers bought the wine Elizabeth picked out. She was . . . winsome. That's the word. But after Patricia married Sprouse . . ." She pinched her mouth closed, whether pained by the memory or her cancer, I couldn't tell.

I gave her memory a moment of respectful silence before asking, "What was her plan? How does a sixteen- or seventeen-year-old girl make enough money to support herself?" I didn't like the only answer that occurred to me.

"She didn't say, just wrote that she'd be able to 'get away forever.' Then she e-mailed to tell me she'd left home, that she had a new place. She told me she was pregnant and sent me a post office box number."

"Do you know where she was living?"

"No." Aurora shook her head. "I tried to find out, but she wouldn't tell me. Patricia and Sprouse didn't know either, because they showed up on my doorstep, demanding that I hand Elizabeth over. Sprouse hung around the house for days, convinced I was hiding her. I would have, too, if she'd come to me! I couldn't even tell you for sure that she's still in Colorado, although the post box is in the Springs. That's where I sent the blanket when she wrote that she was going to have a little girl. I didn't even know that the baby had been born." Tears welled in her eyes. "What's her name?"

"Olivia."

"That's Patricia's middle name. I wonder if she even knows she's a grandmother."

"Do you have a photo of Elizabeth?"

"Not here," she confessed. "I can e-mail you one from home if that would help?"

"Great. Thank you." I passed her a business card with my e-mail address on it. "Can you describe her for me?"

"She's beautiful," Aurora said. "Her hair is dark, although not as dark as yours, and she has brown eyes and just a gorgeous complexion. She never had to worry about acne, lucky girl."

"How tall was she?"

"About my height, and I'm five-six. Oh, and she's very well endowed." Aurora looked slightly embarrassed. "She used to talk about getting a reduction when she was older. Her parents wouldn't hear of it, of course."

I asked for the post office box number, Elizabeth's e-mail,

and the Sprouses' address. She copied them onto the back of a business card and handed it to me. "Please ask her to come to me when you find her. I've made provision for her and the baby in my will. Even Sprouse won't be able to make trouble over that." Her eyes blazed with triumph.

I told her I'd pass along her message to Elizabeth when I caught up with her. Silently, she handed the blanket across the desk to me, and I took it. The cashmere was warm where she'd been clutching it.

"Please forgive me if I don't show you out. I need a few moments."

"Of course. Thank you for your time and information, Mrs. Newcastle." I rose.

"Find her soon."

Before I die, I read in her eyes. I shook her frail hand.

"I'll do my best."

I was halfway back to Colorado Springs, planning to stop in and see Melissa Lloyd on the way, when my cell phone rang. The caller ID showed my office number. Oh, no, don't tell me . . . I answered. "Swift."

"Charlie?"

My worst fears confirmed, I closed my eyes momentarily, then opened them to keep from rear-ending the semi that merged in front of me. "Gigi. What's up?"

"A police officer called here looking for you just a while ago."

"About you burning down the Buff Burgers?"

A moment of hurt silence traveled down the line. "It didn't burn down. There was just a bit of smoke damage. And, of course, the water made a big mess. But—"

"I was pulling your leg." Sort of. "What did the police want?"

"Oh, yes. Detective Montgomery said to have you call him about that missing person you asked about. I told him I didn't know where you were or when I could reach you, but then I remembered you had that business card holder on your desk, and I got your cell number off of your card."

She sounded like she'd accomplished a detecting feat on par with tracking down Jimmy Hoffa. "Great. I'll call him." I couldn't keep from saying, "I didn't think you'd be in today, not after what happened yesterday."

"Oh, I soaked in the tub for an hour last night and took some Motrin. After a little yoga this morning, I feel right as rain, except for a twinge in my shoulder, and I've got an appointment to get my nails redone over lunch. No need to worry about me. I'm tougher than I look."

Great.

I hung up and called Montgomery.

He sounded weary or put out when he picked up the phone. "Charlie, I think I've got a line on your missing person. She's—"

"Elizabeth Sprouse."

He paused. "How do you know that?"

"I'm a detective, remember? I talked with a family friend today who gave me her name and e-mail address. I'm planning to interview her folks later this afternoon and hope to hook up with her in a couple of days. Did her parents report her missing? Is that how you got her name?"

"No. When the coroner's report told me the Jane Doe found last night had given birth within the last couple of weeks, I put it together with the description you gave me."

Coroner's report. I slammed on the brakes and swerved onto the verge, pissing off the man in the pickup behind me, who leaned on the horn as he blew past. I returned the gesture he made. Screw him. Elizabeth Sprouse was dead. I pictured Aurora Newcastle's face when she heard the news. Wait. Maybe it wasn't the same girl. Montgomery had called his vic Jane Doe.

"Hey, Charlie, you still there?" Montgomery sounded impatient.

"I'm here. How do you know it's Elizabeth Sprouse?"

"We don't. We just have a white female, aged between fifteen and nineteen, with no identifying marks, who had a baby not long ago."

"Does she have dark hair? Was she built like— Was she well-endowed?" I used Aurora Newcastle's term.

"Yeah and yeah."

I struck the steering wheel with the heel of my hand. Damn, damn, damn. "Okay, Montgomery, thanks for letting me know."

"You got an address for the Sprouse kid's parents? I'll get in touch, see if they can make an ID."

"Let me know when you get confirmation." I gave him the Sprouses' address and Elizabeth's mailing address, the PO box. A thought occurred to me as he was about to hang up. "How did she die?" I hoped it wasn't suicide.

He didn't answer.

"C'mon, give me something. Was it an accident?"

Montgomery's voice was stern as he said, "This is a homicide investigation now, Charlie, so you keep your cute nose out of it."

The word "homicide" slammed into me as Montgomery hung up. My mind conjured lurid scenarios. Had she been mugged? Abducted and raped? Had she been collateral damage in a gang fight in the wrong part of town? Struck by a drunk driver? Or maybe it was personal, not random. Had her father caught up with her and inflicted a biblical punishment—stoning?—for the sin of fornication? Maybe she had a fight with Olivia's father, whoever he was. Of course, suicide was a subcategory of homicide, so maybe she'd killed herself after all. I shook my head to dislodge the images and carefully pulled back onto the highway. I headed for the office. I'd have to put off my meeting with Melissa Lloyd until I had more concrete information.

———

The sight of Gigi's Hummer hulking outside my office when I arrived in no way improved my mood. Nor did finding Albertine Dauphin, the owner of the bistro at the end of the shopping area, comparing nail jobs with Gigi.

"Hey, baby girl," Albertine said when I entered. "Why didn't you-all tell me you had yourself a new partner?"

A native of Haiti who had emigrated to Florida in the late seventies, then made her way to Colorado when she got tired of the hurricanes five years ago, Albertine was, as the politically correct put it, a "woman of size." She was also black, with skin and hair as shiny and sleek as obsidian. She wore her hair in complicated loops and whorls and waves piled several inches above her head and shellacked into place. Her fingernails were at least an inch long and always painted to match her outfits. Today they were orange. Large gold hoops dangled from her earlobes, and a caftan of yellow and orange and metallic gold swathed her formidable bosom and drifted to her ankles. Her wide grin and merry laugh disguised the acute businesswoman beneath the surface. Albertine's, three doors down, was only one of the three restaurants she currently owned and she was thinking of expanding to Denver. When my PI business was really slow in the early days, I'd once jokingly asked her for a job. She'd turned me down flat.

"Uh-uh, honey. No way. First time a customer complained to you, you'd dump a bowl of jambalaya on his head. You're not cut out for the customer service business. Or for working for someone else, either. Think I don't know what'd happen if I tried to boss you around?" She boomed a laugh that had early diners turning to stare.

As far as I was concerned, that response just proved her business savvy.

Seeing her now with Gigi, I felt a pang of jealousy. Albertine could've been any age between fifty and sixty-five, but any way you sliced it she was more Gigi's contemporary than mine.

"I haven't had a chance," I said, crossing to my desk. I sniffed. "What's that smell?"

"Butterscotch cake," Gigi said, pointing to a platter on the file cabinet.

"This woman can bake!" Albertine wiped crumbs off her mouth with one beringed hand and stood. "If this private eye thing don't work out for you, Georgia, you just wander down to Albertine's and I'll put you to work making desserts."

She winked at me, and I glared, knowing she was remembering her refusal to hire me in any capacity.

"Thanks, Albertine," Gigi said, clearly flattered, "but I'm just getting the hang of the PI business. Did you see me on TV last night?"

"I don't get home from the restaurant until Letterman time," Albertine said. "I'm sure you looked great."

"She looked like a buffalo."

"Charlie!" Albertine looked truly annoyed at what she took to be my mean-spirited crack.

I pointed to Bernie's head, leaning drunkenly against the wall. "She was wearing that."

Albertine's delighted laughter trailed her out of the office. "Come on down for a drink after work," she called over her shoulder. "On the house."

I was going to need a drink by the end of the day, and free ones tasted better than any other kind. "You're on," I yelled as the door swung shut.

"You got a fax a few minutes ago," Gigi said.

Her voice sounded funny, and I looked up at her. She handed me a sheaf of papers. I glanced at them and understood her reaction.

"Is . . . is that girl dead?" Gigi asked, as I spread the photos Montgomery had faxed on my desk.

Even though the photos were head shots and there was no visible trauma to the face, the girl was clearly dead. Even in smudgy black and white her skin was too pale, her lips not much darker. I read Montgomery's typically brief note: *Will let you know when ID confirmed.*

"Yes," I said sadly. "She's dead."

"Did you know her?" Gigi sank into the chair in front of my desk, stilling her trembling hands by clasping them on the plump knees revealed by a green and white striped skort.

"No. I was hired to find her."

"We've got to find out who killed her!" Gigi said, righteous indignation flaring in her eyes.

"What makes you think someone killed her?" I asked in a damping tone, sliding the photos into my file marked LLOYD.

"You can just tell. She doesn't seem peaceful," Gigi said. Her voice dropped to a whisper. "She's not at rest."

"It doesn't get much more restful than that." I kept my tone detached, not wanting to admit the photos had affected me much the way they had Gigi. "Besides, even if she was murdered, it's not my case. That's the CSPD's job. I was hired to find her."

As I talked, my fingers flew over my keyboard and I brought up an e-mail from Aurora Newcastle. My finger hesitated on the mouse, but then I clicked on the attachment and stared at the photo of the beautiful young teen that filled the screen. Defensive brown eyes, a tight smile, cascades of mink-colored hair, and the flawless complexion Aurora had raved about. A full-color, living version of the girl in the morgue photos.

I swung the monitor so Gigi could see it. "Case closed."

5

An hour and a Subway tuna sandwich later, I waited at Designer Touches for Melissa Lloyd to finish with a customer. A
small storefront in Monument, Designer Touches had some
furniture, work areas with computers where customers could
construct their virtual dream room with help from an interior
designer, fabric samples, and a large inventory of accessories
ranging from lamps to clocks to pillows. I read the tag on one
floor pillow. Who buys a dry-clean-only white silk pillow with
tassels to put on the floor? Someone without kids or pets, I
decided. Someone with a maid service.

I sat on a settee—a practical plaid Dacron—and thought
about Gigi dashing to the bathroom to vomit when she saw
Elizabeth Sprouse's photo. I'd hovered outside the door, listening to the retching noises, feeling absolutely useless. Maybe
she'd gotten food poisoning from the butterscotch cake.

"You okay?" I called when I heard the toilet flush.

Gigi emerged, dabbing at her lips with a piece of toilet
paper. "My daughter's only a couple of years younger than
that girl," she said. Without another word, she walked to her

desk and dug in her purse for a breath mint. Popping it in her mouth, she gave Bernie a pat on the head and walked out the door. I stared after her. Was she quitting or merely keeping her nail appointment? I knew which I was hoping for.

"You found her?"

Melissa Lloyd stood in front of me, a look of wary expectation on her face. A large barrette restrained her sandy hair at the nape of her neck, and her minimalist makeup did nothing to conceal the weariness in her face. A pale smudge that might have been spit-up stained the shoulder of her olive green suit jacket. I rose and shook her hand.

"Yes. It's not good news, I'm afraid. Is there somewhere private we could talk?" I glanced around the showroom, my eyes catching on a pair of lamps shaped like flamingoes. No customers, but someone could walk in anytime.

Melissa strode to the door, her heels tap-tapping on the hardwood floor, and flipped over the CLOSED sign. "What do you mean? She won't take the baby back?" A note of panic flared in her voice, and I saw how close she was to the edge. A few days with an infant can unhinge anyone.

"Ms. Lloyd, I'm afraid your daughter's dead."

She stared at me, uncomprehending.

"I was able to trace the blanket left with your—with the baby—and discovered the names of your daughter's adoptive parents. She lived here in Colorado Springs but had run away several months ago, perhaps when the pregnancy became evident. Her father is, by all accounts, a highly religious man." That sounded better than "religious whack-job."

She was still staring at me, glassy-eyed, and I wondered if she'd gone into shock. "Ms. Lloyd, why don't you sit down?"

I put a hand under her unresisting arm and led her to the settee. She sank onto it.

"But she's dead?"

"The police found her body last night. Her parents identified it today." I'd gotten a cell phone call from Montgomery while I ate my lunch. "I'm so sorry."

"Then who will take the baby? I've got to get rid of the baby."

It was my turn to stare. Okay, the woman had never met Elizabeth Sprouse, but the girl was her daughter. Her expression showed no grief, just the drawn brows and thinned lips of someone who's been grossly inconvenienced. I found her reaction rather chilling and selfish. I tried not to let my thoughts show on my face; it wasn't part of my job to judge my clients. Heck, if I only worked for people I liked, I wouldn't be able to afford birdseed for the bear. Instead, I withdrew the photo I'd printed from Aurora Newcastle's e-mail, the live, vibrant Elizabeth, hoping that actually seeing her daughter might evoke a more compassionate response in Melissa Lloyd.

I got a different response, all right. She took one look at the photo, put her hand to her throat, and gasped, "That's Lizzy!" Then she crumpled sideways in a faint.

Shit. I'd never had a client pass out on me before. Unless you counted Bo Remington, who drank so much Wild Turkey and soda the evening I presented him with photos of his wife canoodling with the church choir director—a woman—that he slipped under the table and the bar staff had to pour him into my car so I could drive him home. Divorce work left me feeling slimy, and it's an area I don't go for anymore, unless I'm really, really desperate for income. Like now. As I pulled a bottle of water from my purse to splash on Melissa's face, I wondered how Gigi would do on long stakeouts with a camera. She probably didn't know an f-stop from a bus stop.

I patted Melissa's face gently. She groaned and rubbed a hand over her cheek. I helped her to a sitting position and handed her the water bottle. "Are you okay? Who's Lizzy?"

She gulped half the bottle, her hand shaking so badly that some of it dribbled down her chin. She swiped it away with the back of her hand. "Where's the photo?"

I handed it to her, ready to catch her if she pitched over again. She tapped it with one finger. "Lizzy Jones. She worked for me off and on. She sewed curtains, slipcovers, stuff like that on a per-piece basis. You're sure she was . . . was . . . ?"

I stared at her, watching the implications sink in. "Your daughter tracked you down and persuaded you to hire her," I said. "How long did she work for you?"

She took a deep breath. "I guess she first came in last November. I'd have to check my records."

"Do you have a lot of high schoolers working for you?" It didn't seem plausible to me, not with an interior design business. Maybe if she'd owned a Wendy's franchise.

"She told me she was nineteen, that she was married to a soldier at Fort Carson who was deployed to Iraq and she wanted to keep busy while he was gone, make a few extra dollars so they could afford a down payment on a house when he got back. She brought in several samples of her work. She was a talented seamstress," Melissa finished angrily. "How could I know?"

I eyed her skeptically. "How could a sixteen-year-old named Elizabeth Sprouse cash paychecks made out to Lizzy Jones? Didn't you have a Social Security number on her?"

Melissa squirmed. "I paid her cash."

The light dawned. "Lizzy" was an off-the-books employee. Melissa was probably paying her well below the going rate. The IRS might have a bone to pick with Melissa, but I had bigger fish to fry. "When did you last see her?"

"Maybe six weeks ago. She told me she was taking a few months off to have the baby. She was pregnant."

News flash. "And you never suspected? Not even when Olivia turned up on your doorstep?"

"Why would I? It's not like Lizzy was the only pregnant woman in the world!" Her face flushed. "She lied to me, took advantage of me . . . I gave her a hundred-dollar savings bond for the baby!"

Anger, hurt, and humiliation twisted her face. I could only imagine what she was going through. Somewhat bothered by guilt for giving her child up for adoption, but unwilling to have a relationship with the nearly adult girl, she finds she's had one for months with someone she treated as a casual employee. Lifetime Channel movie material starring a B-list has-been as Melissa and an up-and-coming teen actress as her daughter. In the movie, however, the daughter would reveal herself to the mother and they'd cling together in a tight embrace and raise the new baby together. That wasn't going to happen here.

"Did you never suspect anything?" I asked. "Did Lizzy ever ask questions you thought were strange?"

"I didn't spend that much time with her," Melissa said. "I'd give her material, a pattern or photo of what I needed, and she'd bring the finished product back ahead of the deadline. Wait . . ." She held up one finger as a memory surfaced.

"When she started wearing maternity clothes and the pregnancy was evident, she asked me if I had children."

I knew what she'd told Lizzy.

She paced past me. "Well, I don't! I'm not anyone's mommy. My motherhood was nothing more than a biological accident."

There she went, projecting again. "You don't have to explain it to me," I said. "Do you have an address for her?"

She shook her head. "She came here to pick up work and drop it off."

"How'd you let her know you had something for her?"

She looked at me like I was a moron. "I called her, of course."

"Can I have that phone number?"

She crossed to a desk in the corner of the showroom and clicked through an online contact file. "Here." She wrote it on a yellow sticky and handed it to me.

I could use a reverse directory to get an address. Although I wasn't sure why I wanted one. I'd pass it along to Montgomery. My work was done. Missing person found. I said as much to Melissa, and she stared at me.

"What? But what about the baby?"

"Turn her over to CPS."

"I can't. They'll put her in a foster home. She's my gran—" She cut herself off and massaged her temples with her fingers.

Maybe caring for Olivia had activated some latent maternal hormones or something. Turning her daughter over for adoption hadn't bothered her. Or maybe it had. "Then give her to Elizabeth's parents."

"Right. To the people she ran away from." She bit her lower lip. "You could check them out, see what kind of parents they are. Or, what about the baby's father?" Her eyes lit up. "You could find him. He's the one who should have the baby." She bent over her desk and began to scribble on something.

Yeah, assuming he wasn't a teenager, a rapist, or the married father of one of her friends. Not to be pessimistic, but I had a feeling Elizabeth was on her own for a reason. Still, it wouldn't hurt to look into it, I decided, as Melissa Lloyd ripped out a large check and handed it to me.

"And hurry. I really, really need this settled before Ian comes home. He just wouldn't understand."

What, that she'd gotten pregnant as a teenager? Or that she'd lied to him for years on end? Call me cynical, but I figured chances were good he had something murky in his own past he hadn't fessed up to. Experience—those divorce cases again—taught me, though, that two wrongs didn't add up to long-lasting marital harmony. They more frequently added up to large sums for attorneys and PIs.

And who was I to complain about that?

I returned to the office shortly after five to find it dark and locked like I'd left it when I'd gone to see Melissa Lloyd. However, I'd reluctantly given Gigi keys, so maybe she'd returned but then left again. I unlocked it and crossed to my desk to make the phone call I'd been dreading since Montgomery confirmed Elizabeth Sprouse's identity. Tears choking her voice to a whisper, Aurora Newcastle thanked me for letting her know. I felt like shit: When she'd asked me to hurry up and find Elizabeth, this wasn't what Aurora had in mind. I'd debated not calling her, figuring it might be merciful to let her pass on without knowing Elizabeth was dead, a homicide victim, but she hadn't struck me as the sort who wanted life sugar-coated.

"That poor baby," she said.

I didn't know if she meant Elizabeth or Olivia.

"I'd really like to meet her," she added after a long silence, and I found myself promising to try to arrange for her to meet Olivia.

"No guarantees, though." I couldn't see Melissa Lloyd interrupting her schedule to do a baby show-and-tell in Denver.

"I understand, and thank you." Aurora sounded considerably weaker as we hung up than she had only that morning, and I hoped the news of Elizabeth's death wouldn't hasten her own end. Sometimes this job sucked. I sat for a few quiet minutes before relocking the office and walking down to Albertine's for my free drink. Creole spices, shrimp, and beer scented the cozy room decorated with Mardi Gras masks and beads and populated with a few early diners and Happy Hour hopefuls. My spirits lifted. Sitting alone on a barstool with a Heineken— Albertine was subbing in the kitchen for a chef who hadn't shown up for his shift—I called Montgomery and told him I had some information pertaining to his case. Hearing the bar noises in the background, he told me he was just coming off shift and would stop by and get it in person.

He arrived twenty minutes later, as I was ordering my second beer. Just over six feet tall with broad shoulders and the edgy allure of Clive Owen with silver flecks in his dark hair, Montgomery turned female heads as he threaded his way through the tables to where I sat. He leaned over to kiss my cheek, and the hopeful women turned back to their friends and cosmopolitans, disgruntled. The rasp of his five o'clock shadow against my cheek and the spicy scent of his aftershave stirred something inside me, but I squelched it. Gorgeous men who like to live on the edge are a bad bet. I knew: My ex-husband, the fighter jock, was Exhibit A. As if that weren't enough, I figured, premature gray notwithstanding, he was at least five years younger than me. So I controlled my breathing, passed him the phone number Melissa had supplied, and explained that Elizabeth Sprouse had worked for her as Lizzy Jones.

He thanked me for it, then added, "You're remembering this is a police case, right? You're not poking around in a homicide investigation." His dark eyes met mine as he lifted the bottle to his lips.

The last was an order, not a question. "Of course not," I said. "You have such a suspicious mind, Montgomery." I gave him my wide-eyed Miss Innocent look that hasn't worked on anyone since I was five.

"I've known you a long time, Swift. You're not passing along that number out of the goodness of your heart. You want something."

"You wound me," I said, smiling. "I'm not looking for the murderer," I assured him. "I've got a client who wants me to locate the baby's father."

"The Sprouse girl's baby?" He chucked a handful of peanuts in his mouth.

I nodded. I could see him turning that information over in his mind, trying to decide if he was interested in the baby, if it had any bearing on the homicide. "Just stay out of my way," he finally said, "and if you find out anything that links to the girl's death, you let me know pronto. That includes the father's name."

"You didn't get it from the hospital?"

"Nope. We can't find a record of her giving birth in any hospital in the area." He relaxed against the back of the bar stool, and his sport coat gaped to show the shoulder holster beneath.

Damn. I'd known the police would try to track down the birth records, and I'd hoped he could make my job easier by telling me what was on the hospital form. The hospital certainly wasn't going to give me access to anything more confidential than the public restroom.

"Quid pro quo for the phone number and address: Give me access to the apartment." I'd run the phone number through the online reverse directory I liked and found that "Lizzy Jones" rented an apartment just off Austin Bluffs, an area populated by University of Colorado at Colorado Springs students.

"If it's not the crime scene, I'll see what I can do."

Interesting. Wherever they'd found the body, it wasn't where she was killed. Pretty much ruled out suicide.

Montgomery watched me figure that out, a half-smile crooking his mouth. "So, what's your next step, Super Sleuth?"

"Interview the parents," I said. I debated a third beer and decided it would do too much to undermine my policy against gorgeous men. Montgomery's smile was doing enough to weaken my resolve. "How'd they take the news?"

"The mother, about like you'd expect. Broke down in tears. The father . . . now, he's a strange one. Started ranting about 'the wages of sin is death' and other Bible stuff. I wasn't sure if he was saying that Elizabeth deserved to die or if he was going to kill whoever killed her. He's definitely on my list. Be careful."

"Always." I slid off the bar stool and found myself too close to Montgomery for comfort. A jazz sax sashayed from the speakers, twining its smoky notes around us as if we were the only people in the bar.

His eyes glinted, and he put his hands on my waist, drawing me in between his thighs. I was absurdly conscious of the strength in his hands, the heat of his body. "Dinner?"

I surprised him by leaning forward to plant a kiss at the corner of his mouth, then pulling back beyond his reach. "Sorry. I've got plans. Rain check?" He didn't need to know that my plans included shoveling the ton of lava rock I'd had delivered today into a new rock garden in my yard.

"I must have twenty rain checks already," he said. "If I didn't know better, I'd think you weren't interested." He kept his eyes locked on mine as he swallowed the last of his beer.

"Impossible!" I layered on the sarcasm.

"Exactly." He smiled the smug smile of a man who's made his point and thunked the bottle down on the bar.

(Friday)

Before heading over to the Sprouses' house the next morning, I stopped by the office to give Gigi an assignment. Going undercover at a fast food joint hadn't dissuaded her from working as a PI; maybe some interminably boring surveillance would. I didn't think she was the type who'd be comfortable slouching in a car all day, peeing in a bottle so as not to miss the target if he or she emerged, and keeping a low profile to avoid being spotted. Frankly, I didn't think she'd last four hours with the job I had in mind, one I'd turned down several times because the missing persons business had been brisk. Last night I'd dialed the number from my hot tub and found the client still interested in retaining Swift Investigations. I assured him an operative would be on the job the next day.

I pushed through the office door to find Gigi talking to the ficus as she watered it. Coffee dripped into the carafe on the filing cabinet, and I had to admit it smelled good.

"What a handsome plant you are." She picked off a yellowed leaf. "I hope that didn't hurt." She lifted the swan-shaped watering can in greeting. "Hi, Charlie."

"Morning, Gigi." Today's designer outfit included cropped red slacks under a white tunic top printed with cherries. She looked like an orchard. What sounded like a chorus of sick tree frogs croaked from the small stereo on her desk. I resisted the urge to put my fingers in my ears as I marched to my desk and liberated a Pepsi from the fridge. Ah, cold caffeine made the world look much better.

As I booted up my computer, Gigi plopped into the seat by my desk, crossing her feet at the ankles and displaying red espadrilles with inch-wide laces that wrapped up her fleshy calves.

"Charlie, I don't feel like I'm making as big a contribution as I could to the business," she startled me by saying. Her tone was tentative but determined. "I think—"

"Funny you should bring that up," I said, "because I've got a surveillance job for you."

"Really?" Her eyes lit up. "But I've never done surveillance. I wouldn't know how."

"C'mon, you've got teenagers. Haven't you ever spied on them, read your daughter's diary, listened in while your son talked to his girlfriend on the front porch?"

"No."

Jesus, this was hopeless. This woman had none of the natural instincts of a good detective. No wonder her husband had been able to carry on an affair, transfer all his funds to offshore accounts, and plan a trip to South America without her noticing. "Well, surveillance really isn't difficult. The secret is to blend in. If the target's going to the mall, look like you belong in a mall."

"I can do that!" Gigi put in happily.

"If he's working out, look like you belong at the gym. The key is to never let the target out of your sight and never let him suspect you're tailing him."

"What happens"—Gigi lowered her voice—"if I have to answer the call of nature?"

"You improvise," I said, handing over an empty two-liter soft drink bottle.

She stared at it as if it were an artifact from Mars. "How—"

"Just remember the cardinal rules: Don't lose the target and don't get spotted."

I handed her the photo the client had faxed to my house the night before. "Here's your target."

"She looks nice," Gigi observed, studying the photo.

"So did Ted Bundy. And here's the address." I passed over a slip of paper. "The client thinks his wife, Cheryl, is having an affair, that she's screwing some guy while he's at work. He wants proof. He works a night shift out at Schriever Air Force Base, leaves the house at seven o'clock, so you need to be in place by then. Since you'll be up all night, why don't you go home now and get some rest? Think about having a couple of changes of clothes in the car, maybe a hat or two to change your profile, in case the wife goes out to meet her lover."

I leaned over to pull a digital camera with a telephoto lens out of my bottom drawer and gave Gigi brief instructions on how to operate it. She made careful notes on her steno pad.

"What if nothing happens tonight?" she asked, looking up from the notebook.

I shrugged. "You try again tomorrow night and the night after that, as long as the client's willing to pay."

Gigi shook her head sadly. "I just can't believe that spying on your spouse is the way to maintain a healthy marriage. A good marriage needs trust on both sides! If he has doubts about her fidelity, he should confront her, talk her into going to counseling with him."

"Yeah, that worked a treat with Les, didn't it?"

I regretted the words as soon as they left my mouth. Gigi gave me the wounded doe look and pushed up from the chair. "Should I call you if something happens tonight?" she asked quietly.

"Sure, that'd be great," I said. I started to apologize as she returned to her desk and packed up her saddlebag of a purse, but the words stuck in my throat.

As Gigi walked out the door, I finished my Pepsi and slammed the can into the trash with unnecessary force. The clang of metal on metal jolted me. Shit. This is exactly why I didn't work with anyone. You had to watch what you said, worry about their feelings, make small talk when you'd rather be thinking, and listen to stupid damn tree frog mating songs. I stalked to the stereo Gigi had left on and jabbed the OFF button. The rumble of the Hummer starting up prodded me to the door with an "I'm sorry" on my lips, but the lumbering vehicle was just pulling out of the parking lot as I yanked the door open.

The Hummer! Talk about your conspicuous surveillance vehicles. I'd forgotten to tell Gigi she'd need to find alternate transportation for the night's task, and I didn't even have her cell phone number. A glance at her desk showed a tray with business cards set on one corner. When had she had cards made? I picked one up and saw it through a red mist. The card design matched mine, except under the Swift Investigations logo she had her name, Georgia Goldman, and under that, in small type, the word PARTNER. I methodically ripped the card into so many bits of confetti and sprinkled them around the ficus.

6

~~~

The Sprouse residence, in an unzoned area on the fringe of Black Forest, looked absurdly normal at first glance. With a brick front and white siding, it looked like it'd been built in the seventies and well maintained. The yard consisted of patchy grass ringed by a chain-link fence, and a carport housed a Toyota Tercel and a tan Chevy pickup, neither new. A strange burbling noise puzzled me until I realized it was chickens clucking from the backyard. Maybe the Sprouses had a coop.

When I rang the doorbell, a woman I assumed was Patricia Sprouse answered. Her reddened and puffy eyes and the lank hair straggling to her drooping shoulders convinced me she was the dead girl's mother. The dirty fingerprints of grief clouded her like a window too long unwashed. She wore a long-sleeved cotton knit dress in beige that obscured her figure and ended at ankle height, just above a pair of battered clogs. It was hard to believe this woman had once been Aurora Newcastle's best friend. Aurora, dying of cancer, exuded more energy and personality from her pinkie than this woman had in her whole being. I felt a twinge of guilt intruding on her

sadness, but then I thought of baby Olivia and extended my hand.

"Mrs. Sprouse? I'm Charlotte Swift with the El Paso County Department of Human Services." I handed over the card I'd printed out that morning, complete with the logo I'd lifted off the DHS Web site and my real cell number. "May I say I'm very sorry to hear about your recent loss." I was, too. It's nice to be able to work the truth in occasionally.

She shook my hand limply and invited me into a tiny foyer that opened on a sitting room to the left and a half bath on the right. The kitchen lay straight ahead, something fruity-smelling bubbling on the stove. "I don't understand—"

"I'm here about the baby, your daughter's baby."

She whitened. "There is no baby."

"Mrs. Sprouse, DHS is only concerned about the child's welfare. The police informed us your daughter had recently given birth, but there's no record of the mother or baby receiving postnatal care of any kind. In such cases, it's departmental policy to do a home visit to ensure the child's well-being." Eleven years in the military had given me a good line in bureaucratic bullshit.

"She didn't— I can't— Let me get my husband." She fluttered to the back door and pushed it open. The cackling of the chickens got louder. "Zachary."

I was disappointed by the small man who stepped into the hall after exchanging a few whispered words with his wife in the kitchen. Expecting a towering figure with a Moses-like beard trailing to midchest and eyes that burned with a strange fire, I was confronted by a man who looked like he worked in a cubicle and shopped at Walmart. Short brown hair, thinning, topped a middle-aged face with deeply carved grooves scoring the forehead and bracketing the lips. Big ears that stuck out a bit and a prominent Adam's apple were his only distinctive features. On second glance, the eyes met my expectations: deep-set, blue, and just enough "off" that they set my Spidey sense tingling.

"This is a house of mourning, ma'am," he said to me. "Surely you can respect that."

"I do, and I'm very sorry for your loss," I repeated, "but the welfare of the baby must—"

"Fornication is a sin!" His voice boomed from his small frame, and I almost jumped. "If my wife's daughter was led astray by evil forces, if she fell under the sway of demons and yielded to carnal temptation, if she died without confessing her sins and repenting of them, then she is lost and no daughter of ours."

"No, Zachary—" Mrs. Sprouse bleated.

"Lost! And the child damned." His voice shook on the final word, and he raised his fists above his head.

So much for mourning. It was abundantly clear why Elizabeth Sprouse had run away. What was still not clear was how she could afford to do so. Unless the chickens laid golden eggs, I didn't know where she got the money. Surely, sewing the odd pillow cover or set of curtains wouldn't pay the rent.

I tried again. "Is the baby with its father? If you'll just give me his name and address . . ."

"We don't know who the father—" the pale woman said from the kitchen door, only to be overborne by her husband's fury.

"The devil! Only the devil himself would seduce an innocent virgin and get her with his spawn."

This guy had watched *Rosemary's Baby* too many times. I wondered what my chances were of getting Mrs. Sprouse alone. Not good.

"Does the devil have a name?" I asked drily.

"Beelzebub. Satan. The Beast." He dragged in a deep breath and proclaimed, " 'The dragon is filled with fury because he knows that his time is short. He pursued the woman who had given birth to the child. And from his mouth the serpent spewed water like a river to overtake the woman and sweep her away with the torrent!' " Zachary Sprouse watched my reaction through narrowed eyes. "You are the Serpent's agent," he suddenly declared, advancing on me. Spittle flecked the corners of his mouth. His fingers clenched and unclenched at his sides.

Whoa. This guy was several knights shy of a crusade. I flung up one hand and said in my most sermonly voice, "The wages of sin is death!" Montgomery had told me Sprouse was fond of that line.

It stopped him in his tracks, and the biker-on-PCP look faded out of his eyes. "You speak truly. The wages of sin is death. We are all doomed. We should pray for the power to overcome temptation." He bowed his head.

I backed toward the door, reaching behind me for the knob. "Exactly. Well, nice chatting with you." I slipped out the door and pulled it firmly closed, my heart aching for young Elizabeth, who had lost her father so tragically only to have to accept that nutter in his place. I wondered anew how she had died. If she'd drowned, I knew who got my vote for most likely perpetrator, what with his talk of women getting swept away by serpent-spewn torrents. I made a mental note to ask Father Dan about the quotation, which I recognized from the acid-trip images as being from Revelation. Not for nothing had I grown up with missionaries for parents.

Backing my car past a handsome black chicken, I headed for the local high school, figuring that what Elizabeth's parents didn't know—or wouldn't admit—about her sex life, her friends might.

—⁓⁓—

Finding a parking spot at Liberty High School was damned near impossible since I was neither staff nor student; I ended up leaving the Subaru in a satellite lot outside the stadium and hiked over two blocks. When I presented myself at the office, I was asked to sign in and wear a VISITOR badge. I didn't try to pass off the DHS story at the high school; dealing with so many kids, these people probably knew every caseworker on a first name basis. Instead, I simply asked to see the counselor. As luck would have it, he was pulling lunch duty in the cafeteria. I got directions and headed down a hall clogged with students, some making out in stairwells, others shuffling sullenly in the direction of their next class, one student practicing scales on a trumpet outside a closed door marked BAND. I noted the boys particularly. They were almost universally clad in jeans, some with boxers peeking over the tops of sagging waistbands, others with letter jackets and athletic shoes that cost more than a teacher's daily wage, or a PI's for that matter. You could tell where they stood in the hierarchy of teen coolness by the way they walked, from wall-hugging, eyes-averted slumps to cocky struts down the middle of the hall. I wondered if any of them had fathered Elizabeth's baby.

The hall smelled just like my old high school, despite the fact I was living with Aunt Pam and Uncle Dennis in New Jersey by then; the humidity there should have smelled different from the dry air of Colorado, but the universal scent of raging teen hormones overcame any climatic differences. The mingled odors of sweat, hair-care products, the cold metal of lockers, new denim, tired sneakers, and meat loaf thrust me back into my high school days. The noise in the cafeteria busted me away from wondering what had become of Andrew Meslin, Lancelot in our production of *Camelot,* and the subject of my first crush. I'd heard somewhere he'd dropped out of Rutgers to go on some reality show. I looked around for Jack Van Hoose, whom the secretary had described as "a short Kojak on steroids."

I spotted a bald man sitting at a table near the front of the cafeteria from which he could observe most of the students present and worked my way over to him. He did look a bit like a black Telly Savalas, minus the lollipop. Biceps bulged from beneath the sleeves of his tan polo shirt; I'd've pegged him as a PE teacher rather than a counselor. "Jack Van Hoose?"

He looked up from his turkey sandwich, searching my face with hazel eyes. "Yes. What can I do for you?" His voice was deep and sexy.

I introduced myself and told him I was a PI.

"Like Magnum?" he asked, taking a large bite from his sandwich. I caught the twinkle in his eye.

"Minus the Ferrari and the sidekick with the helicopter," I

said, scooting onto the bench across from him. "I'm here about Elizabeth Sprouse."

He stopped chewing, and his fingers compressed the bread of his sandwich. "I saw the article in the *Gazette* this morning," he said, swallowing. "Do the police know any more about how she died?"

"I wouldn't know," I said, wishing I did. The article had been bare bones: Elizabeth Sprouse, seventeen, found dead near Fountain Creek, police investigating. The smell of pickles from his sandwich was making me hungry. "I'm not investigating her death. She left her newborn daughter with . . . a friend, and I've been hired to locate the father with an eye toward him assuming custody."

"Nuh-uh, Mason," Van Hoose said in a louder voice. I looked over my shoulder to see a tall boy sheepishly tuck a Frisbee into his backpack. I turned back to Van Hoose as he pulled a bag of chips from his lunch box and opened it. "So she had a baby, huh? Have one."

He offered me the bag, and I took a chip. "Yes, a daughter. About ten days ago."

"I must say I'm surprised. She didn't have too many friends, seemed leery of boys. Have you met her father?"

I nodded and twirled my finger near my temple.

"Yes, well, then you can understand why she might shy away from male-female relationships."

"Did he abuse her?" I asked bluntly.

"Not as far as I know," Van Hoose answered, a troubled look in his eyes. "But he forced religion on her, made her wear long skirts to school, wouldn't let her attend dances or try out for any sports team. The only thing he encouraged was her participation in 4-H, where she learned to sew and can and raise chickens. He had a husband all picked out for her, he told me the one time we met, when he came storming in to tell me not to fill her head with college nonsense or encourage her to fill out applications."

"An arranged marriage?" My hand brushed Van Hoose's as we both reached into the chip bag, and I drew back, apologizing.

He gave me a smile that said he didn't mind. I'd originally guessed he was fiftyish, but the smile took off five years. "With some guy from their church congregation."

I shuddered. "A legal form of white slavery. Poor Elizabeth. No wonder she ran. When did you last see her?"

He crumpled the empty chip bag and put it in his metal Batman lunch box. I'd had an identical box with She-Ra, Princess of Power, on the front when I was in middle school. "Before spring break last term, maybe late February? I'd guess it was April before the school realized she wasn't coming back. Look, Ms. Swift—"

"Charlie."

"And I'm Jack. I didn't know Elizabeth all that well. She was a middling student who didn't cause trouble, so I didn't see much of her, especially after Sprouse showed up and made a ruckus about college. The person who might could tell you more is Linnea Fenn. They rode the same bus and ate lunch together more often than not."

He jerked his head toward a thin girl with dyed black hair sprouting from several ponytails, two rings through her right eyebrow, and unremittingly black clothes, including fingerless gloves. She was bent over a thick textbook, and I thought I saw the tip of a tattoo, something green, disappearing under her T-shirt from the base of her neck. She looked like an escapee from a Halloween store display or a Dracula convention. I raised my brows at Van Hoose.

"Tut-tut. Don't let the threads fool you," he said, humor glinting in his eyes. "Linnea's going to end up first or second in her class and already has early acceptance to Stanford." He stood, topping out at about five-ten. "Look, would you like to have dinner sometime?"

The invitation took me by surprise. I passed him my card. "Yes." How long had it been since I'd been on a real date? Not since May.

"I'll call you." He pocketed the card. "My middle initial's *R*—Raymond—if you want to Google me before we hook up." His grin was blinding against his dark skin.

I watched him as he strode across the cafeteria, stopping to talk and laugh with one or two students on the way. His khaki shorts displayed strongly muscled legs, and I wondered if he skied.

Dragging my mind back to business, I approached Linnea Fenn as she stood and struggled into a backpack that looked like it weighed as much as she did. "Linnea? Mr. Van Hoose gave me your name, suggested I talk to you about Elizabeth Sprouse." I introduced myself and held out my card.

She glanced at the card, then studied me for a moment from the corners of her kohl-rimmed eyes. "I've got AP Biology. I'm going to be late." She shouldered past me.

I kept pace with her. "She had a baby, you know. I'm trying to find out who the father is, see if he wants custody."

She stopped dead in the doorway leading to the hall, and a couple of boys with chains dragging down the waistbands of their jeans bumped into us. Cigarette smoke wafted off them as they pushed past. I ignored them, keeping my eyes fixed on Linnea's pale face. Her eyes, an angry green, jumped to mine and she said, "They don't have Olivia? You idiot."

She muttered the last words and I got the impression she was talking to Elizabeth, not me. Her words gave me hope. "Who's 'they'? Do you know who the father is, Linnea?"

"I'm late." With that, she merged into the mass of students roiling the halls. My crumpled card fell from her hand. I took a couple of steps after her, frustrated, but quickly realized this was not the time or place to pursue an interview. No, I'd have to find another time to speak to Ms. Linnea Fenn, some place off school grounds. As I made my way back to the car, idly watching a bunny graze on the pristine lawn of the Mormon temple just south of the high school, I decided now was as good a time as any to scope out Elizabeth's apartment.

—m—

A hundred-dollar bill convinced the manager of the Shady Glen Apartments, a UCCS graduate student named Truman eking out his scholarship with a job that provided a free apartment, to let me into Lizzy Jones's apartment. Skinny, six foot two, and with a mop of dark blond hair, he exuded an attitude so laid-back I was surprised he could stand upright. Slacker with a capital *S*.

"The cops been and gone," he said, plucking the benjamin from my hand. "I don't see why you can't take a look. Like, you could be a prospective renter, right?"

I'd rather live in a cardboard box under a bridge, I thought, smelling a stopped-up toilet and years' accumulation of mildew as we climbed the stairs to Lizzy's third-floor apartment. *It would be cleaner . . . and quieter.* The metal steps rang under our feet, and a baby squawled from the floor above us. *The View* blared from a window on our right, dueling with a noisy game show from a wide-open door on the left.

"Did you know Lizzy Jones?" I asked Truman's back as he climbed the stairs in front of me.

He glanced over his shoulder at me. "Well, yeah, sure. I took her rent money every month. She paid cash."

"Did she ever have visitors that you noticed, a boyfriend, maybe?"

"I don't notice much. It doesn't pay, y'know?" He waggled his eyebrows at me as if we were in on some secret. "Besides, she didn't really do it for me, if y'know what I mean." He winked at me and shoved his master key into the lock of apartment 30B. "Kinda fat. She might've been cute if she knocked off a few pounds."

"She was pregnant." The anger I felt on Elizabeth's behalf surprised me.

"Wow, I guess she looked pretty good for a chick with a bun in the oven." He pushed the door open. "I'd better stay to make sure you don't run off with anything," he said with a belated touch of conscience as I stepped into the living room.

"Sure." His presence wouldn't hinder me.

The apartment was tiny, consisting of a kitchenette with a counter for eating, a living room big enough to hold a sofa, one easy chair, and a small television, and what I presumed was a bedroom and bathroom beyond. The mismatched furnishings were garage sale rejects. The room showed signs of the cops' search with couch cushions askew, drawers left open, and the carpet pulled up in one corner. I pulled on latex gloves and began methodically searching the room, not sure what I was looking for, but wanting to get more of a sense of Elizabeth.

Truman wandered into the kitchen, opened the fridge, and returned with a Coke. It gave a fizzy pop as he opened it. "Want one?"

I threw him a pointed look, and he said easily, "Hey, she's not going to drink it. And I'm saving her next-of-kin the trouble of carting it away when they come to clear this place out. Did you say you worked for her mother? If she could empty this place by the weekend, I could have it re-rented by Monday. I'd get a bonus."

"You must make your mom so proud." In my midtwenties, which I figured he was, I'd been in the Air Force for eight years, served in a war zone, earned a BS in computer science and a commission as a second lieutenant, then been promoted to first lieutenant and captain. Ignoring him, I turned on the TV and saw it was set on the Cartoon Network. Something about that made me sad. I picked up the phone and dialed *69, noting the number that came up. I hung up; I'd call the number later, when I didn't have an audience. Carefully avoiding the kid where he slouched against the doorjamb, I went through the kitchen: nothing but plastic utensils and dish towels in the drawers, spoiled milk and two more Cokes in the fridge, a hodgepodge of dishes and pots and pans, and a family of mice living under the sink. "Ugh!" I jumped back and pointed them out to Truman.

"Cool." He sipped the Coke as he bent his gangly frame to watch the rodents scramble behind a box of dishwasher soap.

"Cool? Isn't it part of your job to get rid of them?"

"How do I know they're not Preble's meadow jumping mice? They're protected." His sly smile said he'd put one over on me.

"How do you know they're not carrying bubonic plague that's going to infect all your renters and get you fired?" I shot back. I headed to the bedroom, leaving him trying to herd the mice into a dustpan he'd found in the gap between the fridge and the two-burner stove.

Bingo! A computer sat on the dresser in a corner of the bedroom. I headed straight to it and turned it on, my eyes taking in the room as it warmed up. A twin-sized bed with a rumpled blue bedspread I'd bet Elizabeth brought from home sat under a window that looked onto the parking lot. A pair of tennies peeked from under the bed, and a clothes hamper stood by the open closet. A pair of maternity jeans, a skirt with an elastic waist, and two blouses hung in the closet. A cracked ginger jar lamp and three books were stacked on the bedside table. The computer reclaimed my attention, and I pulled up Yahoo, wondering if the cops had gotten anything useful off the hard drive. It didn't matter, because I had something they didn't: Elizabeth's e-mail address I'd gotten from Aurora Newcastle. With any luck Elizabeth had checked the box telling Yahoo to always remember her on this computer and I wouldn't need to guess at passwords . . . yes! I forwarded all the e-mails in her INBOX and SENT folders to my e-mail address, listening to whap-whap noises from the kitchen as

Truman apparently tried to dispatch the mice with a broom or mop.

Nothing else on the computer looked interesting—she had no documents or photos stored there—so I turned my attention to the rest of the room and ransacked it quickly but neatly. As I riffled the leaves of the books on the bedside table, something fluttered out of the fifth Harry Potter. I bent to retrieve it and found myself looking at an ultrasound of a fetus. The black-and-white blobs and squiggles meant nothing to me, but tiny text on the bottom of the frame identified the patient as Elizabeth Sprouse and the date as 12 May of this year. Undoubtedly baby Olivia. Ultrasounds were expensive, and I wondered how Elizabeth, living on what she could make from sewing and without insurance, had afforded the prenatal scan.

Pocketing the photo, I checked the clothes in the closet and drawers—nothing—and flipped the lid up on the hamper. The smell of old sweat and something sweetly rotten made me hold my breath. There were no clothes, not even a lonely sock, in the hamper, but something caught my eye. Brownish streaks discolored the sides of the white wicker and spotted the bottom. Blood.

I drew my breath in with a hiss. The police must've taken the hamper's contents for analyzing. Bloody clothes maybe. Had Elizabeth died in this room? My eyes swept it again, but I saw no signs of violence, no stains. Maybe she'd been killed elsewhere in the apartment—with a knife in the kitchen?— and the killer dumped the towels he'd used to clean up in the hamper. I darted into the tiny pink-tiled bathroom. No towels. Bingo.

"Help! No! Get off of me, you motherfu—"

I dashed into the hall in response to the yells, prepared to help Truman fend off whoever was attacking him. When I skidded into the kitchen, I didn't see an attacker, only Truman swatting furiously at himself, his eyes wide with fear, his hair tousled.

"What—"

"Mouse! Get. It. Off meeee!" The last word swooped up into a shriek, and Truman gave a convulsive wiggle. A small mouse dropped from under the untucked tail of Truman's shirt and scampered across the linoleum to squeeze into an impossibly narrow crack beneath the broom closet. Truman continued to shake, a frenetic belly dancer, and hit at his clothes as if they were on fire.

I was laughing so hard tears welled in my eyes. "It's gone," I gasped. When he didn't respond, I yelled, "It's *gone.*"

Slowly, Truman stopped dancing around. His shoulders twitched, and then he stood still, breathing like he'd run a marathon, face flushed, sweat beading his brow. He glared at me as I tried to stifle my laughter. Revenge of the rodents. It sounded like a straight-to-DVD movie.

He didn't seem to appreciate my humor. "I'm locking up now," he said, smoothing his hair down. His chagrin was not so easily smoothed away. "Get out."

I exited the apartment, patting my pocket to make sure I still had the ultrasound photo. Truman locked the door behind us, then clattered down the stairs a full flight in front of me. A young couple held hands at the bottom. The guy called out, "Hey, Tru, is that the empty apartment you said we could use?"

"In a minute, man." Truman waved him away, nervously watching as I crossed to my car.

The buzz-cut youth was having none of it. "I've got the fifteen bucks, dude, but we're in a hurry. Amy has to be back for a three o'clock lab." He kissed the girl's neck, and she giggled. He pulled her up the stairs. "Is it open?"

I raised my eyebrows at Truman as he fought to regain his sangfroid and tossed the keys into the youth's outstretched hand. The slimeball was renting out Elizabeth's apartment for his buddies to have sex. I hoped he'd waited until after the cops had gathered their evidence.

"Are you a business major?" I paused with a hand on the roof of the Subaru. Maybe the MBA program gave extra credit for this kind of entrepreneurship.

"Shit, no. Philosophy. My specialty's ethics." He smirked and flashed me a peace sign as I pulled away. Or maybe he meant it as a V for victory.

━━ ∿∿∿ ━━

It was too late to make it out to Black Forest to catch up with Linnea Fenn where the bus let her off. Damn. Now I'd have to wait until Monday to talk to her. I'd make do with Montgomery. Walking into my blessedly Gigi-free office, I dialed his number. Detective Montgomery was not available, another cop told me. I left a message for him to call me. I needed to let him know about Truman's shenanigans with the apartment, in case he or his buddies had contaminated the scene before the crime scene team got there, and I needed to share the e-mails with him, assuming his team hadn't come up with them.

The e-mails . . . I logged on to my account to view the e-mails I'd forwarded. It looked like Elizabeth only had three correspondents: ANewcastle@earthlink, elfin92@comcast, and stejac1993@hotmail. The notes to Aurora Newcastle were innocuous, describing the pregnancy, Elizabeth's worry about the impending birth, and her refusal to put Aurora in her father's line of fire by accepting her hospitality or money. The notes to elfin92 talked about her pregnancy fears, her financial difficulties, her love for Harry Potter books, teachers and mutual friends, and her plan to escape her parents and Colorado Springs forever once she saw "the deal" through and collected. The text messaging symbols and school talk in these notes convinced me elfin92 was a teenaged friend, maybe Linnea Fenn. If Linnea was Elizabeth's confidante, it seemed more than likely that she'd be able to give me a line on the baby's father. Maybe I could find a way to hook up with her this weekend.

The e-mails to stejac1993 were the strangest and gave the least clue as to the recipient's role in her life. They seemed to be reports on her pregnancy, with her weight recorded each week, her belly measurements, the results of a diabetes test, diet details. One of the e-mails had a scanned attachment of the ultrasound photo. Could these be to her mother, at some anonymous account her father didn't know about? Hotmail and Yahoo were popular e-mail servers for people wanting to keep their real identities hidden or for people wanting accounts their significant others didn't know about. Maybe Patricia Sprouse was not as out of touch with her daughter as she wanted to appear. I definitely needed to talk to her again when the Prophet wasn't there to run interference. I also had to consider the possibility the e-mails were to Olivia's father, but they seemed strangely sterile for a girl writing to her boyfriend, even a boyfriend she might've broken up with. I doodled with a pen on my blotter. Maybe they were to the boyfriend's mother? Now, that idea had potential. The relationship was over, but the soon-to-be-grandparents wanted to keep tabs on the well-being of their son's baby. Hmmm.

With no way to arrive at an answer, I printed out the e-mails, stuffed them into my briefcase, and locked up the office. I felt half guilty at the realization that my workday was ending but Gigi's had yet to begin. I'd forgotten to tell her that staying awake was the hardest part of a nighttime surveillance. Oh well, if she fell asleep, maybe she'd be more willing to admit what was painfully obvious: She just wasn't cut out to be a PI.

7

Gigi slumped in the front seat of the Hummer, her eyes glued to the door of 327 East Primrose Lane. She was frankly surprised that anyone who lived in the run-down cottage could afford a private investigator, never mind the new Lincoln Navigator that gleamed in the driveway. They'd have been better off spending their money on exterior paint or a concrete contractor to shore up the front steps and stoop, she figured. For the hundredth time, she glanced at the photo of her target, although she already had the woman's features memorized. She hadn't seen her in the four hours she'd been parked down the block from the house.

A cold nose nudged her, and Gigi responded to the demand by patting the silky head of her Shih Tzu. "Good boy, Nolan," she said softly. The dog laid his small muzzle on Gigi's lap and heaved a sigh. "I know it's boring, but we've got important work to do."

Dressed in a set of forest green (the closest color she had to black) Juicy Couture sweats, Gigi had figured she'd blend in by taking Nolan for walks. However, she was afraid to get out of the Hummer in this neighborhood. She checked the locks again and patted Nolan absently. Picking up the knitting she'd laid on the passenger seat, she worked on the sweater intended for Kendall's birthday in a month, her eyes still on 327 as her fingers clicked the needles on autopilot. No movement from the house.

Not only was surveillance the most boring job in the world, it gave her far too much time to think. Her thoughts roamed from Les's last communication—divorce paperwork delivered through his lawyer—to the fight that afternoon with Kendall, who wanted to go to a party at a senior's house that night. When Gigi heard there would be no parental supervision at the party, she put her foot down.

"You're only fourteen, honey," she reminded the enraged girl, trying to stroke her silky blond hair.

Kendall jerked her head away. "I'm not a kid. You let Dexter go to parties."

She didn't *let* Dexter go, Gigi thought; he just went. Since his father had gotten him the BMW for his sixteenth birthday, she had virtually no control over his movements. She kept that reflection to herself. "There will be too many older kids there, and you know some of them will be drinking alcohol."

"Oh, Mom, get real! It's not like I've never had a beer," Kendall replied, tossing her hair.

Feeling cowardly, Gigi let that revelation slide. "Besides, you've got the compulsories to get through for the competition Saturday morning. We'll need to be at the rink by seven." Reminding Kendall of her skating obligations usually brought the girl into line; she lived to skate. Gigi congratulated herself on the strategy.

"Skating is ruining my life," Kendall flashed. "Practice, practice, practice . . . that's all I do! Oh yeah, and compete and go to costume fittings and more practice." She glowered.

"That's how you get to the Olympics, honey," Gigi reminded her gently. "You've wanted an Olympic gold since you were three."

"Well, maybe I don't want that anymore." The teenager stormed out of the kitchen and into her bedroom, slamming the door.

Nolan's wet tongue licking her cheeks where the tears were sliding down brought Gigi back to the stifling car and the job at hand. "You love Mummy, right?" she asked the dog.

He responded with a yip, and she laughed, drying her tears with the half-finished sweater. Looking up, she saw a car—she was hopeless with makes and models, but thought it was silver or maybe white—pull up to the curb in front of 327. "Look, Nolan, it must be Cheryl's lover. How brazen! She doesn't even have the decency to go to a motel." She wondered if Les had ever made love to Heather-Anne in their marriage bed. The thought made her want to cry. She readied the camera which she'd been practicing with all afternoon and snapped a picture of the short man in a denim jacket who got out of the driver's seat and strode to the door. The porch light was out, so she couldn't see who answered the door when he knocked, but she took another photo anyway as the man disappeared inside. Charlie had told her the camera had an infrared something-or-other and took clear photos in low light.

She set the camera carefully on the passenger seat and took up her notebook to record the activity. Even as she was jotting down the time of the lover's arrival, he stepped back onto the porch, paced down the cracked sidewalk, and roared away from the curb. "That was fast, even by Les's standards," she told Nolan, penciling in the man's departure. "I guess we're not going to get any proof of infidelity tonight, Nolan. Maybe we should—"

Another car pulled up, this one a blue SUV of some kind. Her eyes wide, Gigi watched a muscular black man hop out and ring the doorbell. He was inside a little longer than the first man, but he, too, left after only a short visit. The scene repeated itself three times in the course of the next hour, with Gigi snapping photos of all the arrivals but never getting a clear look at the woman welcoming them into her home. "Do you think she's a prostitute?" she asked Nolan after the fifth man departed.

"Rrr-row," Nolan growled, putting his small paws on the door to peer out the window. He whined.

"Oh, no, do you have to do your business?"

"Rowf!" the dog affirmed, dancing on the passenger seat, his black-and-white fur bouncing, the tail curled over his back wagging madly.

Gigi glanced doubtfully at the dark street. The blue glow of a television leaked from a window a block away, but that was the only sign of life. Hooking Nolan's leash to his collar, she scooped him under her arm and cautiously opened the door. The only sounds were the swishing of leaves in a light breeze and the rumble of traffic on the interstate, two blocks east. A sudden thought had Gigi reaching back into the Hummer for the camera. Maybe she could get a clear picture of Cheryl with one of her lovers if she was closer. With Nolan as cover—the word made her feel like a spy—she might be able to finagle her way into a better position to observe the tryst. She balked at the thought of becoming a Peeping Tom, but decided she might have a peek in a window if she could work her way around to the back of the house.

Nolan beelined for a tree as soon as she set him on the ground. He lifted his leg briefly, then tugged her to the next vertical object, a mailbox. After letting him relieve himself again, she urged him across the street to the side with 327. He went happily, tail waving, and stopped to sniff a fire hydrant just in front of the shabby yellow house. "Good boy," Gigi whispered, encouraging him to stay put while she checked out the house. The iron bars on the windows told her she was right to be nervous in this neighborhood. She wrinkled her nose at the strong smell of urine. The fire hydrant must be a popular spot with the local dogs. Not having gotten the hang of the private eye thing, Nolan tugged her impatiently down the block, intent on investigating a dried crust of sandwich lying in the gutter.

"Come *on*, Nolie," Gigi said, pulling him away. From this angle, she could see that a privacy fence, in much better repair than the house, protected 327's backyard from potential Peeping Gigis. Discouraged, she started across the street to the Hummer, the leash dangling in her hand. A moment later it zipped out of her fingers as Nolan took off.

"Nolan, come back!" Gigi whipped around in time to see the Shih Tzu dashing after a cat that was sprinting for the fence. As she watched, one hand pressed to her lips, the cat squeezed through a small hole near the gate and Nolan wriggled through after it, dragging his leash behind him.

"Oh, no," Gigi moaned. Instinctively, she started across

the street after her puppy. She had nearly reached the sidewalk when the screech of brakes brought her head around, just seconds before the motorcycle's front wheel struck her hip. She fell.

—~~~—

I skidded the Subaru to a stop on Primrose Lane, two blocks from where an ambulance, a fire truck, and more cop cars than I could count enlivened the night with the red and blue swirls from their lights strobing the seedy neighborhood. Radios crackled, men shouted, and several dogs barked, objecting to the sirens and commotion. EMTs tended someone on a gurney near a motorcycle on its side. Good God, what had Gigi done now? I hadn't understood one word in ten of her hysterical cell phone call. This was a hundred times worse than the Buff Burgers debacle, although I didn't see any flames. I hurried toward the activity, noting the presence of a hazmat team in their safety suits. They moved like moonwalkers from the street to the small yellow house that was the center of all the action. As I drew closer, I realized the figure on the gurney was Gigi and the EMT was splinting her arm.

I saw the moment when she spotted me because her face blanched. "Oh, Charlie, I'm so sorry. I know you told me rule number one is not to get spotted, but I couldn't help it. Nolan got away from me and ran into the yard and then I got hit by the motorcycle and the driver banged on the door and got the people inside to call 911 and then the ambulance and the police and everybody came and—"

"Slow down, Gigi," I said, crouching beside the gurney and gently pushing her back. "Are you okay?"

"She's got a broken arm, ma'am," the EMT, a young woman with her brown hair in a ponytail, told me. "I gave her something for the pain, but we need to get it cast. We'll be on our way if—"

"I can't go without Nolan!"

"Who's Nolan?" Had she brought her son on the stakeout? I looked around but didn't spot any likely contenders.

"My Shih Tzu."

"Shit what?" asked the cop hovering nearby, pad in hand, ready to take her statement. Just my luck—it was Officer Venetti, witness to the Buff Burgers incident.

"Sheet zoo. It's a dog," Gigi said. "His name is Nolan and he's white with black patches and—"

"Would this critter belong to you?" asked another voice I recognized.

I turned to see Montgomery striding toward us, cradling a bundle of fur that was enthusiastically licking his chin.

"Nolan!" Tears leaked from Gigi's eyes.

Montgomery leaned down to place the animal in Gigi's arms, and it sat on her chest, looking up at us from under a fringe of white fur. She hugged it tightly with her good arm, crooning, "You are a bad, bad puppy."

"Rorf," the dog agreed happily, content to be crushed against Gigi's ample chest.

I drew Montgomery aside. "What are you doing here? Please tell me she's not involved in a homicide."

He smiled the lazy smile that always turned my insides to mush. "Nope. But I was at work early when the word came down we had a 911 call from 327 East Primrose Lane. The narco guys've had their eye on this house for months but couldn't get probable cause to bust the dealers who hang here. Apparently a scumbag hoping to score"—he jerked his head in the direction of a scared-looking teen handcuffed in the back of a patrol car—"ran down Ms. Goldman and panicked. He says he ran into the house, grabbed up a phone, and dialed 911 before someone ripped the phone out of the wall. The emergency operator said the call was cut off before anyone said anything, but procedure is to assume someone's in trouble, so we rolled. You'd've thought it was Christmas when the narco team and the SWAT guys got the word." He grinned, looking dangerous in a Kevlar vest with his weapon secured at his hip. "I came along for the ride. It's been months since I saw any real action."

Ooh, boy, if that didn't sound like my fighter-pilot ex . . . "So, did you get the perps?"

He shook his head. "They did a runner, but Ms. Goldman has a camera full of photos of their customers, so I don't think it'll be long before we round them up. And we've shut down a meth lab that put this whole block in danger. The department will probably want to give her a citation. What was she doing staking out this place, anyway?"

Good question. I crossed to Gigi, her face woozy with drugs and the joy of having recovered her dog. "Do you still have the paper I gave you with the target's address?"

She nodded, taking three tries to slip her hand into her pocket and come up with the paper. "Here. Sorry I couldn't get Cheryl in the photos."

I read the slip and rolled my eyes. "This says 327 *West* Primrose Lane. We're on *East* Primrose Lane." I held it out for her to see.

"Oops." Her eyes didn't focus properly, drifting up to Montgomery, who had come up behind me in time to hear our last exchange. I wanted to smack the shit-eating grin off his face. "Is he your boyfriend?" Gigi asked, her eyes going from him to me and a loopy smile decorating her face.

"Hell, no," I said, at the same time Montgomery said, "As soon as she stops fighting her attraction to me." The wicked glint in his eyes sent shivers down my spine, but I ignored them.

Officer Venetti turned his laugh into a cough, Gigi giggled, and I glared. "When hell freezes—"

"The dog can't come," the EMT said, preparing to slide Gigi's litter into the ambulance with the help of her partner.

Her giggles turned to consternation. "What will I do—"

I held out my arms with a martyrlike air, and she scooted the mop-dog to me. "Go on, Nolan. You'll like her."

Nolan looked unconvinced, casting me a suspicious look from under his shaggy fringe, but allowed me to pick him up. "I'll take him over to your house, Gigi, and let your kids know what's up."

A soft snore was my only response, and I realized the drugs had knocked her out. The EMTs secured the door, and Nolan and I watched as they drove off.

"Breakfast?" Montgomery asked, putting a hand on my shoulder. I looked to the east to see the first faintest hint of pink staining the sky.

"Might as well since I'm up," I said ungraciously. "Let me get rid of this furball and I'll meet you. Where?"

"I make a mean omelet," he hinted, his hand sliding from my shoulder down to my waist.

Nolan growled and I laughed, brushing off Montgomery's hand. "Denny's it is, then."

(Saturday)

Over two fried eggs, toast, and a Pepsi, I told Montgomery about my visit to Elizabeth's apartment. He was annoyed by the news of Truman's entrepreneurial activities and accepted my information about Elizabeth's e-mails without comment. "I'll forward them all to you," I said, mopping up egg yolk with a toast triangle.

He waved away my offer with a sausage bit speared on his fork. "Stu, our computer forensics guy, got it all. He's been tracking her Web history—apparently she likes some teen idol named Zac Efron—and going after court orders to get the real names of the people behind the e-mail aliases. That's an uphill battle, though, and it's unlikely we'll get access, not without being able to tell a judge it's key to a murder investigation."

"What about the blood in the hamper?"

"Spotted that, did you?" He eyed me with something close to approval. "She gave birth in the apartment."

My mind conjured what must have been in the clothes bin, and I pushed my plate away. "Poor girl."

"At least it explains why there are no records of the birth," Montgomery said. Unfazed by the topic, he squirted ketchup onto a pile of hash browns and dug in. Cutlery clattered into a plastic tub as a teen bussed the table behind us, and the sound of an argument leaked out of the kitchen when a server shouldered through the swinging door. The closing door cut it off. The omnipresent odor of coffee grew stronger as our waitress came by and refilled Montgomery's cup. I rattled the ice in my Pepsi glass, but she didn't take the hint.

Sated, Montgomery leaned back, his arms stretched atop the booth's padded back, and said, "So, where did you find your new operative? She seems a bit inexperienced, or plain dumb. She's lucky the guys running that meth lab didn't spot her and rough her up. One of the customers we picked up told us he noticed the 'fat granny in the Hummer,' but figured she was just spying on her husband or something. He knew she wasn't a cop."

"Well, that's a blessing of sorts," I said dubiously, then told him about Gigi Goldman's descent into my life and business. "I'm stuck with her," I concluded, "unless I can persuade her to leave."

A knowing smile stretched across his handsome face. "Ah, the penny drops. You sent her on that surveillance hoping she'd screw up, didn't you?"

It sounded mean when he put it like that. I fiddled with my straw and tried to catch the waitress's eye so I wouldn't have to look at Montgomery. "No! Not exactly. I just hoped she'd be so bored she'd decide to take up hairdressing again. I never meant for her to be in danger. I felt really guilty having to tell her daughter she was in the hospital."

The pixie-sized girl with the long blond hair had stared at me, automatically reaching out for Nolan when I handed him over. She had Gigi's blue eyes. It had taken me ten minutes of pounding on the door to summon her from sleep and several more to get my message across.

"She's what?"

"She broke her arm in a collision with a motorcycle. She's going to be fine, just needs a cast. Do you need me to drive you to the hospital?"

"How will I get to the competition?" the girl asked, an annoyed pucker gathering between her brows. "Mom knows I have to be at the World Arena at seven. What time is it?"

"Six," I said.

"Shit, she was supposed to wake me at five thirty. How am I supposed to get my hair and makeup done?" She ran a hand through her blond mane. "This is just typical," she muttered under her breath.

"I suppose I could drive you," I offered reluctantly. I wasn't anxious to spend five minutes with this surly, ungrateful teen, but I felt I owed Gigi something for putting her in the line of fire.

She ignored me. "Dexter! Deeex-ter!" she hollered over her shoulder. "Get up. Mom's flaked out. You need to drive me to the skating competition."

I resisted the urge to teach Gigi's daughter a few manners and turned away as the girl pounded up the wide stairs leading from the slate-tiled entryway to the upper levels without even closing the door, much less a "good-bye" or a "thank you." Why did people have children? They kept you up all night and ruined your wardrobe with drool and spit-up, then grew into teenagers who despised you and ridiculed your every word and idea. Maybe there was a year or two, after kids were done with the spewing formula and filling diapers stage, and before they reached the demonic possession age, when they were polite, affectionate, and fun to be around?

I asked Montgomery, but he held up his hands to ward off the question. "Don't ask me, I don't have kids."

"Do you want any?" I asked, curiosity overcoming good sense.

The corners of his mouth quirked up in a smile and his eyes warmed. "Maybe with the right woman. I'm taking applications . . . interested?"

I rolled my eyes and scooted out of the booth. "In your dreams." I dropped money on the table to cover my breakfast and walked off without a backward glance.

mm

Elizabeth Sprouse's funeral was next on my agenda, but I needed to change first. The jeans and green hoodie I'd thrown on when Gigi called at three o'clock wouldn't cut it for a funeral. There were few things I missed about the air force, but the uniform was one of them. You always knew exactly what to wear to any function. Scrambling over an obstacle course—battle dress uniform. Funeral—service dress. Formal party—mess dress. If you couldn't figure it out for yourself, someone would tell you which uniform to wear. I wasted far too much time now that I was a civilian on deciding what to wear, and all I was aiming for most of the time was clean and appropriate. Decently attired in a black linen skirt that fell straight to my ankles and a matching short-sleeved jacket with white piping, I drove to the Church of Jesus Christ the Righteous on Earth, where Elizabeth's stepfather would conduct her funeral service.

My first glance at the church told me that whatever his gifts as a preacher, Zachary Sprouse didn't have the fund-raising talents of some of his more famous evangelical brethren. When compared to the 7,500-seat New Life auditorium formerly filled by Ted Haggard (before he learned his lesson about trusting gay prostitutes), the corrugated metal warehouse looked modest indeed. I could hear my missionary parents telling me that the presence of God transformed even the humblest dwelling, but my one encounter with Pastor Zach left me doubtful that there was room for his ego and God in the same building.

Inside, metal folding chairs were set up in two sections with an aisle running between them, culminating in a white casket, mercifully closed, that lay parallel to the altar. More than three-quarters of the roughly two hundred chairs were filled when I walked in, many by what looked to be students (wearing jeans) and faculty (wearing business casual) from Liberty High School. Women with long hair and body-obscuring clothes, and men with somber faces and beards, I decided were from the church's congregation. Several of those women clustered around Patricia Sprouse, who had her face buried in a handkerchief. There was no sign of Zachary Sprouse. I spotted Jack Van Hoose on the left and made my way over when he waved. He wore a black polo shirt neatly belted into dark gray trousers and scooted over one chair so I could sit on the aisle.

"Making any progress?" he asked when we'd exchanged greetings.

"Not so's you'd notice," I said.

"Was Linnea Fenn able to tell you anything?"

"Able, possibly. Willing, not." I scanned the crowd and realized Linnea wasn't there. Odd.

"She wouldn't talk to you?"

I shook my head.

"How about if I set you up with her for Monday?"

The bare fluorescent bulbs overhead gleamed off his bare scalp. "Won't you get in trouble?"

He shrugged muscular shoulders. "Maybe, if Linnea complains—but Linnea's not much of one for running to authority figures with her problems. I'll try to talk her into meeting with you, tell her you're only trying to do right by Elizabeth's baby by finding the father."

"Sounds good" was all I had time to say before music tinkled from an upright piano in front and a choir surged into an off-key rendition of "Morning Has Broken." Pastor Zach emerged in a white robe with a hood draped down the back that looked disturbingly Ku Klux Klannish to me and stepped in front of the casket. His sermon rambled for close to an hour and included references to the adulterous Bathsheba, Tamar (who slept with her father-in-law), Jezebel (who was an evil whore eaten by dogs), and Lot's daughters (who got him drunk and seduced him into incest). He recited the lines about the dragon and the drowning woman again and finished with his favorite phrase.

"The wages of sin is death. And we are all sinners, brothers and sisters, all sinners who deserve to die!" He raised his hands straight overhead to the accompaniment of a few half-hearted "Amens."

I couldn't imagine Elizabeth's mother or friends found his words comforting in the least, and I could tell by the jumping muscle near his mouth it was all Jack could do to contain himself. I put a hand on his forearm, and he swiveled his eyes to me, muttering from the side of his mouth, "What's he mean by dishing out a lecture on 'Bad Girls of the Bible'? He better not be implying anything about Elizabeth. The man's certifiable. I hope the police are looking hard at him."

On the words, I glanced back to see Montgomery staring at us, his gaze inscrutable. Without thinking, I sat straighter so I wasn't so cozy with Jack Van Hoose. *Stupid,* I chastised myself. I faced forward for the rest of the service, immensely relieved when it was over and the casket had been carried out to the waiting hearse. The heat had become almost unbearable in the metal building, and smells of perspiration, deodorant, and cloying lilies from the altar coalesced into a smothering fug. As I stood and stretched, making way for people to exit the row, I noticed a woman in the back who didn't seem to fit with either the Liberty High School crowd or the Church of Jesus Christ the Righteous on Earth believers. She had a model's figure and height; her auburn hair was tucked under a cloche hat. Dressed in a black suit that whispered "designer" from every seam and button, she hurried toward the exit on three-inch pumps. The sun streaming through the door as she reached it revealed a slight sagging of the skin around her eyes and jaw that hinted at a woman in her forties, rather than the thirty-year-old she looked from behind.

"Excuse me," I said to Jack, instinct telling me to follow the woman. How had she known Elizabeth? Elbowing my way through the crowd of mourners scurrying out of the incinerator of a church, I squeezed through the door just in time to see her climb into a Lexus sedan.

"Wait!" I trotted toward the car, waving, but she either

didn't see me or chose to pretend she didn't. I scribbled down the license number before she made the turn onto Vollmer Road. My contact at the Department of Motor Vehicles could give me her name and address in exchange for the usual hundred dollars.

Seeing Jack surrounded by a knot of students, and not wanting to spar with Montgomery again, I climbed into the Subaru and headed for home. From the way the mystery woman had driven off, I was sure she wasn't going to the graveside service and I decided to skip it, too. My immediate future held a nap to make up for lost sleep, some hard work in the backyard, and a margarita-enhanced session with Father Dan to pick his brain about Pastor Zach's theology and the likelihood a man obsessed with sinful women had harmed his stepdaughter.

<center>~~~</center>

I found Father Dan at St. Paul's, preparing for a wedding that evening. He wore tan slacks with his black shirt and white collar. Apparently the florist had just left; lilies and carnations decked the altar and draped from sconces, making the room smell eerily like Elizabeth's funeral. I didn't like the juxtaposition and lingered in the hall.

Stooping to pick up a fallen sprig of baby's breath, Dan caught sight of me and smiled. "Charlie. I never thought I'd see you in here," he said, coming toward me.

"I'm not *in* in," I said from the doorway. "Besides, it doesn't count, because there's no service going on." We had an ongoing discussion about my lack of church attendance with me saying I could talk to God just as well on a bike ride or a hike on Sunday morning and Dan trying to persuade me to give the service a try. No, thanks. Given my parents' obsession with the whole Jesus thing, I'd had enough organized religion as a kid to last me until my dying breath. My gaze traveled to the huge plate glass windows that rose to a point behind the altar, framing a stunning view of Pikes Peak and the front range. I had to admit it was a beautiful venue for a wedding.

"C'mon." With his hand at my elbow, he guided me along the hall, down a flight of stairs, and out a set of glass doors leading to the church's memorial garden and columbarium. "What's on your mind?" he asked.

My feet scuffed at the pebbled path as we walked slowly between shrubs laden with yellow or white flowers and the hum of bees. "I've got a case I'm working on that might or might not have a religious element to it," I said. I told him about Elizabeth being found dead and my search for Olivia's father. "My client, the baby's biological grandmother, doesn't want to keep her. And the adoptive grandparents . . . well, let's just say that the new husband rules the roost, and I'm not too sure he didn't do away with Elizabeth. So finding the baby's father might give the baby her best chance at a normal life." I summed up my interview with Zachary Sprouse and the content of his funeral sermon.

Dan was silent when I finished, a gentle breeze ruffling his blond hair. His steps slowed, and he seemed to be studying a viceroy butterfly sipping nectar from a blossom.

"Well, what do you think?" I prodded. "Is he a nutter? Could he have killed his stepdaughter?"

"That's a question for a psychologist, Charlie, not a priest." He pulled me down on a conveniently placed bench and looked at me. Sun glinted off the hairs on his muscled forearm where it lay across the back of the bench. "You met him. What was your reaction to him? Is he capable of violence?"

"Definitely." I stopped to think. "He felt like a volcano, the kind that simmers for a few years, spitting up ash and yuck, and then blows its top, like Mount St. Helens. Not like you. You'd be controlled, premeditated." As soon as the words left my mouth, I knew they were true, that I'd sensed something in Dan from the very first moment I met him, some relic of his life before priesthood, I imagined.

"Like me?" His tone was light, but his eyes were suddenly watchful. "I thought we were talking about Sprouse?"

"Forget it." I swiped the words away with a flip of my hand, backing away from what I might find out about my neighbor if I pushed. Things were comfortable with Dan as they were: We shared beer and conversation, looked out for each other's house if one of us was out of town, argued politics and religion in a way that threatened neither of us. My words endangered the status quo, inviting confidences I wasn't ready to receive. Or, worse, maybe they'd prompt Dan to erect barriers I didn't want to see between us. "You're right. It was silly of me to think you could say anything useful about Sprouse without having met him."

"Those texts he used at the funeral certainly aren't standard funeral material," Dan said, his eyes still fixed on my face, but his shoulders relaxing infinitesimally. "I have to think he was saying something about his stepdaughter. I think he knew about the pregnancy, and condemned her for it."

"Could he have killed her?"

"As punishment for her sins? Maybe. Which doesn't preclude the possibility he was the baby's father."

"Oh, Dan." The thought saddened me. I let my head drop and watched a fuzzy caterpillar undulate along a stick. Reaching the end, he rippled off and disappeared into the grass edging the path.

"If he is, he's convinced himself she seduced him into sin, so she's the one who deserved punishment, not him," Dan added, his expression grim. "I've seen it more than once."

Me, too. "What about the dragon and the drowning woman stuff? Where does that fit in?"

Dan shrugged. "It's part of the apocalyptic vision. In the verse after the ones Sprouse quoted, the woman is saved and the dragon is enraged. He decides to go after her children."

"Baby Olivia?" I asked doubtfully. My mind whirred with the possibility that Sprouse, having killed Elizabeth, might want to harm Olivia to conceal all evidence of his sin . . . and crimes.

"Don't take it so literally. Biblical scholars generally take 'her children' to mean humankind. You can't dismiss the possibility Sprouse was just raving."

As I chewed the inside of my cheek, thinking, he rose to his feet. "C'mon. I've got a wedding to prep for. Wouldn't want to get the names wrong."

"Like that's ever happened," I said with a snort, accepting the hand he held out to pull me up. "I'm sure you've been counseling the young couple for months and have memorized the names of everyone in the wedding party, down to the flower girl. Don't think you can fool me."

The wry half-grin crooked his lips. "Oh, I wouldn't think

that." He squeezed my hand hard, then released it to return to the church. My fingers tingled as I cut through the garden and past the rectory to get to my house. The church is the first structure on Tudor Road, with the rectory two hundred yards behind it, where Tudor Road starts to curve, and my house set back from the road about a hundred yards past the rectory. The rectory is a larger house than mine, clearly meant to house a priest with a wife and two or three preacherkins. Thank God Dan was single. With no fence—just a strip of thin woods—between our properties, I didn't need kids trampling my garden, playing hide-and-seek under my deck, or drowning in my hot tub.

Before changing to work in the yard, I checked my cell phone messages one last time for the week. There was a call from Gigi to say she'd been released from the hospital and to thank me for taking care of Nolan. I deleted it, thinking I should give her a call to see how she was, but knowing I wouldn't. The second caller surprised me: Patricia Sprouse.

"Miss Swift, I need to talk to you. Could you please come to my house tomorrow afternoon? My husband meets with the church elders between two and four. Please." Her voice cracked on the last word, and I got the sense of a woman under a lot of stress. No surprise, really, given that she'd just buried her daughter and lived with Pastor Zach. Interesting that she was letting me know her hubby wouldn't be around. I deleted the message.

8

(Sunday)

I spent Sunday morning hiking part of the Barr Trail up Pikes Peak before coming home, showering, and putting on clean jeans and an orange camp shirt to meet with Patricia Sprouse. The Subaru motored out to Black Forest as if it knew the way, and I pulled up outside the Sprouse home at two twenty. I'd wanted to give Pastor Zach plenty of time to get caught up in his meeting. The tan Chevy that had been under the carport before was missing, so I assumed he was out of the way. As I climbed out of the car, checking to make sure my recorder was in my purse, I spotted another car parked farther down the road in front of a blue-painted home with a horse weather vane on the chimney. I knew that car; in fact, I had its license plate number in my notebook, waiting for Monday to arrive so I could call my DMV contact and get the name of the Lexus's owner. Maybe the car's owner was a friend of the Sprouses after all, and she'd come to pay a condolence call.

The sounds of an argument coming from the backyard as I headed for the front door put paid to that idea.

"I don't know!" Patricia Sprouse sounded close to tears.

"I think you do know. You're hiding her from me." The other woman's voice trembled with rage. "She's mine! If I have to I'll get my lawyers involved. Your husband's church will never survive the scandal—"

"Calm down, Jacquie," a man's voice said as I pushed through the back gate, scattering the six or seven hens pecking at corn nearby. They squawked and half-flew, half-scuttled closer to a weathered chicken coop that was once red but had faded to a rusty pink.

"Hi, Patricia," I said brightly, my eyes on the auburn-haired woman and her male companion. Her husband? She wore black slacks with a cream silk blouse and turquoise earrings, bracelet, and belt buckle. A large diamond sparkled on her hand as she hitched her purse higher on her shoulder. The man was equally well turned out, but in a less showy way, the subtle plaid pattern on his sport coat meeting flawlessly at the seams and his neat beard well barbered. He stood half a head taller than his wife and looked to be ten or fifteen years older, putting him in his midfifties, I'd guess. A large hand rested on his wife's shoulder. Comfort or restraint?

Completely ignoring me, he told Patricia, "Two days, Mrs. Sprouse. That's all I'm prepared to wait. That baby is ours." Without waiting to see Patricia's reaction, he strode toward the gate, sizing me up with a glance as he exited.

His wife paused to say, "Please," with a pleading look at Patricia before following him. Fastidiously picking her way around the clots of chicken poop, she brushed past me without a word and stalked out the gate. I pushed it closed as a fat white chicken tried to escape.

"Are you okay?" I asked Patricia, who stood unmoving in the middle of the yard, a pail of chicken feed forgotten in her left hand. "Who was that?"

My words broke Patricia's trance, and she stared at me with troubled eyes. "The Falstows, Jacqueline and Stefan."

When she didn't continue, I said, "I saw her at the funeral. Was she a friend of Elizabeth's?"

"Oh, no." She hesitated, as if unsure how much to tell me. Then the words burst from her. "She says Elizabeth's baby is hers! She says Elizabeth signed a contract with her and her husband to let them adopt the baby. They paid her. If we don't give them the baby within two days, they'll sue us."

Her words knocked me back a step. Pieces of the puzzle clicked into place in my mind, and I knew I'd found the source of the money Elizabeth planned to use to escape her home. I didn't know how much a teen could make on such a deal— wasn't selling babies illegal?—but I suspected there were some under-the-table ways to profit, like college athletes accepting cars and bogus jobs and such from team boosters. It might add up to a lot of money, at least by a teenager's standards.

A black chicken pecked at the feed pail, recalling Patricia to her task. She scooped up seed with one hand and scattered it across the yard, inciting a mad flutter of wings and some vicious pecking as the chickens converged on the food.

"Are you going to give the baby to her?" I asked. "The DHS—"

"I know you don't work for the Department of Human Services," she said, her voice stronger. Her faded blue eyes met mine as she upended the pail, dribbling the last seeds onto the ground. "Aurora Newcastle told me who you were."

So much for my cover. "Is she doing okay?"

"She's dying," Patricia said flatly. "She was too ill to travel down for the funeral. I'm going to drive up to Denver this week, have lunch with her. I want to see her one more time before . . . I don't care what Zachary says. She was—is—my best friend." Her eyes stabbed defiantly at me, as if I were the husband who had detached her from the friendship.

"Why did you call me, Mrs. Sprouse?"

"Come in." She led the way across the yard, away from the scratching chickens, to the back door of the small brick house. Inside the kitchen with its white appliances it was cooler. "Would you like some iced tea?"

"Sure." I settled into one of four wooden chairs around a Formica-topped table.

A gust of cold air filtered across the room as she opened the fridge to retrieve a pitcher of tea. I wondered if Elizabeth had sewn the pleated curtains veiling the window over the sink with a cheerful pattern of farmyard animals on a pale blue background. They looked freshly laundered; the whole kitchen was sparkling clean, despite such signs of age as a gouge in the porcelain sink and linoleum curling back from where it met the cabinets.

"Thanks," I said as Patricia handed me a glass and sat across from me. It wasn't Pepsi, but it was cold and caffeinated, and I realized I was thirsty. I took two long swallows as Patricia gathered her thoughts.

"Aurora told me you were looking for Elizabeth on behalf of a client. Who is your client?"

"I can't tell you that, Mrs. Sprouse." I could tell by her quiet acceptance of my answer that she hadn't expected me to divulge the name.

"Is it Elizabeth's birth mother? Elizabeth started searching for her not long after I married Zachary and we moved down here from Denver. Did she find her, make contact? Is that who has the baby?" She sat in her chair, as if anticipating a blow, and I knew it must hurt her unbearably to think her daughter, the girl she'd raised from infancy, had entrusted her own baby to another woman. Worse, to the woman who had given her up.

"Who is the baby's father?" I countered.

"I don't know," Patricia said. "When she told me she was pregnant, she wouldn't say anything about who the boy was, not even when Zachary took the strap to her to make her tell us the truth."

"He whipped a pregnant teenager?" *And you let him?* I left the second question unsaid.

"Zachary believes in strong discipline to rebuke the sinful," she said, not meeting my eyes. "It's God's way. Look at how he punished David and Bathsheba for their sin—he killed their child. And Jonah, and Lot's wife." She reached desperately for examples I was sure her husband had paraded in front of her and Elizabeth time and again.

"I heard that your husband had arranged a marriage for her. Could that man have fathered the baby?"

She stared at me in dismay. "How did you know— No, Elizabeth was resistant to that betrothal, much to Seth's disappointment. I'm sure they hadn't . . . that he didn't . . . ."

"What's Seth's full name?"

"Johnson. Seth Johnson. He's a godly man, a pillar of the church, one of our elders."

"How old is he?"

"Maybe forty-three. The poor man's been a widower for three years now." She twisted the plain gold band of her wedding ring.

Call me cynical, but when a man in his forties tries to marry a sixteen-year-old, I know just what "pillar" is driving him.

"What happened after your husband beat Elizabeth?"

"She left the next day," Patricia said, despair darkening her eyes. "I never spoke to her again."

I let the unutterable sadness of that lie between us for a moment.

"So why are you interested in finding the baby?"

"She's all I have left of Elizabeth," Patricia said. "I owe it to her. I want to do better this time."

"You don't get do-overs with raising children," I said. Not if you dump them with relatives so you can travel the world saving sinners, not if you run off to Costa Rica with your personal trainer, not if you marry perverts who molest them. I drained my glass and set it on the table, leaning forward to catch Patricia's eyes. "When you say you owe it to 'her,' do you mean Elizabeth or Olivia? Because, frankly, even though I'm not really with the DHS, I'm not sure this house is the best place for Olivia. Look what happened to Elizabeth."

"That wasn't my fault!" she cried, tears springing to her eyes. "Zachary—" She stopped.

"Zachary what? Would he be willing to submit to a DNA test to check paternity?"

It took her a full thirty seconds to grasp my meaning, and

when she did, bright circles of red stained her cheeks. She used both hands to fan herself. "He would never . . . Zachary didn't . . . you have a filthy mind!"

I probably did, the result of too much time as an OSI agent and too many cases like this one. In fact, it was a molestation case that had finally driven me out of the Air Force. Didn't mean Zachary hadn't raped his stepdaughter. "The simplest way for your husband to prove his innocence would be to offer to donate a DNA sample, Mrs. Sprouse," I said more mildly. "I'm sure DHS would look more favorably on your request for custody, too, if he were to do that." I had no idea if that was true or not, or even if DHS would be involved in deciding who got custody, but it sounded good.

"Can I just see the baby?" she pleaded. "Does she look like Elizabeth?"

Hell if I knew. I hadn't studied her that closely. I was sure Patricia would see a resemblance to her daughter, however. I felt sorry for this woman, mourning her daughter, maybe blaming herself for marrying the man who beat her or worse, yearning to see her granddaughter. Yet I couldn't imagine how she could stand by and let her husband drive her daughter away.

"I've been hired to find the baby's father—nothing more," I said, rising from the table. "I can't tell you who my client is, but I'll pass along your desire to see the baby."

"Thank you," Patricia said, clearly used to making do with half a loaf.

"How did the Falstows expect you to contact them?" I asked.

Patricia looked confused by the change of subject, then

pulled a business card out of her pocket. It read RUSSELL ZIEGLER, ATTORNEY-AT-LAW and offered several phone numbers. I wrote them all down.

Conscious of passing time and of the possibility of Pastor Zach returning with all his Old Testament bombast, I crossed to the door. Patricia Sprouse remained seated, her head in her hands, the picture of defeat.

"Look," I said, pity for her overriding my usual policy of noninvolvement, "I've got a lawyer friend who specializes in custody cases. Maybe if you gave her a call she could help you."

She looked up, a shadow of hope in her eyes, and I recited Valerie's number. Patricia repeated it several times, committing it to memory, and I wondered if she was afraid of Pastor Zach's reaction if he found the number written somewhere.

"God's peace be with you," she said as the screen door banged shut behind me.

Back at you, I thought. If there was a God and he had extra peace to pass around, these people needed it more than I did.

I drove home pondering my progress on the case. As far as I could tell, I had one strong candidate for Olivia's father, Zachary Sprouse, and one maybe, Stefan Falstow. I'd only gotten a quick look at him, but something about him—the crinkles at the corners of his eyes, his work-hardened hands?—said "virile" with a capital V, and the way he said *"our"* when talking about the baby made me wonder if he meant *"mine."* I reined in my speculations. Where could Elizabeth have met a man like Falstow? Maybe he had a teenager at Liberty. I resolved to check.

A third possibility for baby Olivia's daddy was Elizabeth's wannabe fiancé, Seth Johnson, with some high school boyfriend I didn't yet know about sliding into fourth. I hoped tomorrow's interview with Linnea Fenn would give me more info on that front. I considered calling Montgomery to see if he had any leads on the girl's death—keeping in mind that whoever killed her might not have fathered the baby—but decided to let it go until tomorrow. With no leads I could pursue on a Sunday afternoon, I headed for home and a regrouting job in the shower I'd been putting off for weeks.

(Monday)

The sight of Gigi polishing Bernie's plastic nose with a damp cloth greeted me when I arrived at the office Monday morning. Her lime green blouse and tiered skirt clashed with the pink cast on her arm. When she turned to greet me with a cheery "Good morning," I saw she wore a strand of fat beads and button earrings that matched the cast. Even her shoes were the same Pepto-Bismol pink. I could just see the headlines in *Vogue*: CASTS ARE THIS SEASON'S MUST-HAVE ACCESSORY. I shut my eyes and made my way blindly across the room to my desk, reaching for a Pepsi like a drunk with a hangover.

"How's the arm?" I asked, for the first time feeling grateful she was my "partner" and not an employee—at least she couldn't file a workmen's comp claim.

"Not too bad," she said, settling into her chair. Considering she'd been sideswiped by a motorcycle, she looked pretty good, her hair styled as usual and makeup mostly concealing a small bruise on her forehead. "Although I don't know if I'll be able to do any fieldwork for a while."

Thank God.

"What are you going to do today?" Gigi asked.

"Talk to a girl who was a friend of Elizabeth's and see what I can get from the lawyer representing the Falstows." I hadn't been able to find an address for them online, only a Web site for Falstow Construction, and would have to rely on my Department of Motor Vehicles contact to supply me with one. On the thought, I dialed his cell phone number. He hated it when I called him on his work phone, convinced the DMV recorded its workers' conversations. Maybe they did. "Curtis, I need—"

"Don't use names!" His reedy whisper sounded more frantic than usual. "Wait a minute."

The sounds of people talking in the background, computer keys clicking, and a fan whirring reached my ears as I waited for him to return. It got quieter, and I realized he must have walked out of the office. The sound of a flushing toilet told me where he'd gone.

"Did you know people can intercept cell phone conversations with equipment they buy at Radio Shack?" he hissed. "Not just the National Security Agency or something, but regular people? I saw it on the Discovery Channel."

"Yeah, well, those people are more interested in getting credit card numbers than listening in on your conversations with your mother, Curtis," I said, amused by his paranoia.

"You can laugh," he said. "It's not your job on the line. I'm having to raise my price."

That ended my amusement. "Curtis—"

"No names!"

"Mr. Deep Throat, you already charge a hundred bucks for something that takes you two seconds." I wondered if he was really as paranoid as he made out or if he just wanted justification to hold up his clients—I was sure half the PIs in Colorado Springs had his number on speed dial—for more money.

"Yeah, well, the risks have gone up, so my price has gone up. A hundred and twenty-five. Take it or leave it."

I fumed, envisioning the middle-aged man with his argyle sweater vest and comb-over. "Fine. The name is Jacqueline Falstow." I spelled the last name for him and added the license plate number. "I need the info today."

"I'll e-mail it to you. I've set up an anonymous account, so don't think it's spam or a virus or something when you get an e-mail from CaptainAmerica6771. That's 1776 backwards," he explained.

"Very patriotic," I said drily.

"Hey, buddy, you gonna be all day? You're not the only one's gotta take a crap, you know."

I hung up as Curtis responded to the bathroom heckler.

"Who was that?" Gigi asked, her eyes wide with curiosity.

I explained, adding, "Prices are going up all over. It's getting hard for an honest PI to make a buck."

"You bribe government officials?" Gigi sounded simultaneously amazed and disapproving. "Shouldn't you report them? I mean, we're taxpayers."

"Contacts are important for a PI," I said, impatient with her naïveté. "We don't have the official resources that the police or the feds do. Bribes are just part of the cost of doing business, only you have to be creative with how you deduct them because it's not like you get a receipt."

"I still think honesty is—"

"How did your daughter do Saturday?" I asked. I wasn't actually interested in the spoiled blonde's performance, but I was tired of the ethics lecture.

Her face relaxed into a glowing smile. "She qualified for regionals, in October. I just know Kendall's going to earn a berth on the Worlds team this year."

I was sure every mother at the competition thought the same about her own sequin-spangled little Dorothy Hamill. "Super," I said mechanically as my computer signaled I had an e-mail. Curtis had come through with Jacqueline and Stefan Falstow's address and phone number. Something about the number rang a bell. Where had I seen it before? I flipped through my notebook, scanning all the notes I'd taken on this case. There it was: the number I'd gotten when I dialed *69 on the phone in Elizabeth's apartment. I rocked back in my chair and grabbed another Pepsi. The Falstows had just surged into the number one spot on my interview list, edging Seth Johnson by a nose. As I was MapQuesting directions to their house, the phone rang again, and Jack Van Hoose told me Linnea Fenn had agreed to talk to me over lunch.

"We've got an open campus, so there's no problem with her leaving. She says she'll meet you at the Pikes Perk at eleven thirty." His deep voice sounded just as good over the phone.

"Thanks, Jack. I owe you a dinner."

"Friday night?"

"You're on."

I hung up, smiling slightly, and Gigi asked, "Was that another bribe?"

"No, that's a date."

I was almost positive there was a difference between the two.

—*m*—

Gigi, focused on her computer screen, barely waved as I walked out. I had the directions to the Falstows' and would cruise by there after meeting Linnea. I paused at the door. "Do you want me to bring you back some lunch?" I asked, surprising myself. "It must be hard to drive with that cast."

She looked up and smiled. "That's very kind of you, Charlie, but Albertine has invited me down to try her gumbo. She wants to sign my cast." She waved her pink-plastered arm in the air.

"Fine." So she and Albertine were going to be best buds now? Fine, just fine. I stalked to the Subaru and pulled the door closed with unnecessary force.

—*m*—

Linnea was waiting at a corner table of the small coffeehouse three blocks south of Liberty High School when I walked in. A bored barista behind the counter was texting someone, thumbs tapping rapidly; other than that, Linnea and I were the only ones in the place. The hoops through her eyebrow had disappeared, but her left ear now sported at least eight earrings, including a purple skull that dangled almost to her shoulder. A nose stud glinted from one nostril, and her clothes looked like the same ones she'd had on when I met her in the cafeteria: black jeans, black T-shirt with three-quarter-length sleeves, and black-painted fingernails. In my pin-striped blouse and navy slacks, I knew she must think I was as uncool as her parents. I could be this girl's mother, I realized with a jolt, pulling out the chair that faced hers. Shit, I was getting old.

"Hi, Linnea. Thanks for meeting me."

"Yeah, well, Mr. Van Hoose said if you could find the baby's father, maybe it would be better off. When he said that she might have to live with Beth's parents if you couldn't find him, well, I thought I should try to help because anything would be better than that." She took a swallow from the stainless steel mug in front of her, and aromas of chocolate and cinnamon wafted out.

I started out with a softball. "Did you know Elizabeth found her birth mother?"

Her eyes widened, making her look younger and less sophisticated. "Really? No *way*! I knew she was looking, but I thought she'd given it up. She didn't tell me . . ." A hurt look flashed across her face before she hardened it to blasé again. "Recently?"

I didn't want to intensify her hurt. "I'm not sure when. Had she been trying to find her for a while?"

"God, yes. She was obsessed when we first met in eighth grade, after her mom married the church guy. I asked her once if she thought her birth mom was going to ask her to live with her or something—I mean, I didn't really think that was likely, and I didn't want Beth to be disappointed—but she just laughed and said she didn't want to meet her 'biological maternal unit'—that's what she always called her—for that."

"Why did she want to find her, then?"

Linnea shrugged.

Conscious of Linnea's lunch half hour ticking away, I moved on to what I really needed. "Did Elizabeth have a boyfriend?"

Linnea shook her head, setting the skinny ponytails bobbing in all directions. "Not really. Not a real boyfriend." She hesitated, her eyes slipping from mine to study the napkin holder on the table. "I mean, it's not like she was a virgin, although I'm sure her parents thought she was."

She said "virgin" as if it were synonymous with "total loser" or "scummy creepizoid." Despite that, I got the feeling she was one. There was just something innocent about her, despite the black eyeliner, stony face, and wardrobe from Vampires "R" Us.

"They'd kill her if they knew. There were a couple of guys last year . . . well . . . I really think she hooked up just to get the attention, you know? With her dad dying and her stepdad being a jerk, I think she just wanted to make some guy love her. I tried to tell her that sex wasn't love and that these guys were just using her."

I was in favor of giving this girl her own call-in radio psychology show. She knew more about relationships than half the men I'd dated.

"Maybe she listened, because I don't think she was . . . you know, doing *that* anymore." She pushed out a deep breath, and her green eyes fixed on mine again. "Her parents had a man picked out to be her husband, though."

"Seth Johnson."

She nodded. "Yeah, that's the name. She told me that he

tried to kiss her once, in an empty Sunday school classroom, and she told him she was a lesbian." Linnea grinned, revealing a beautiful smile that completely canceled out the darkness of her attire.

"Resourceful girl," I said. "How did Johnson take that?"

"He said he was man enough to help her overcome her evil desires. Beth said he undid his pants right then, started to pull it out, but she pushed him over when he had his jeans around his ankles and ran out."

"He was going to rape her?"

Linnea shrugged. "Who knows? Beth could be a little melodramatic."

"Did she tell her parents?"

Linnea raised an eyebrow. "What would be the point?"

Indeed. I tried another line of questioning. "Did she say anything to you about making a deal with some couple to give them her baby?"

Linnea looked down, studying a scratch on the tabletop. "She was going to be a surrogate mother for this couple that couldn't have their own children."

I rocked my chair back on two legs, staring at her. "A surrogate? Good God, how'd she come up with that?" I tried to dredge up what I knew about surrogacy. Not much. I thought the surrogate mother underwent in vitro fertilization and then birthed the baby for some desperate, rich couple.

"She saw a show on *Oprah* and thought it would be a good way to make some money. I told her it was a dumb-ass idea," she said finally. Her eyes met mine. "It's a form of prostitution, you know? Selling your body is selling your body, and I told her she was too smart for that, that she could get a regular job and save up to move away. But she said that working at Mickey D's or something would take too long, that she needed to get away *now*."

"Why now?"

"I think because her stepdad was pushing really hard for her to marry the guy from church. She was afraid he'd force her into it. She thought the guy had promised her stepdad a big donation for the church and he was desperate to get it. He wanted to get into television ministry to 'reach out to more poor souls in need of salvation.'" Her face twisted in distaste.

My dislike for Pastor Zach continued to grow. Warm air burped into the room from the opened door as a pair of young moms, each pushing a stroller, walked in. The barista took their orders and set a couple of machines to hissing.

"How much was she getting?"

"Fourteen thousand dollars, plus all her medical expenses," Linnea said, a trace of awe in her voice despite her opinion of women selling their bodies.

I was less impressed, having a better idea than the teenagers of the cost of funding an apartment, food, utilities, and other necessities of life. Fourteen thousand wouldn't have lasted long. I wondered where the money was now and made a note to look into it. "Do you know how she found this couple, the Falstows?"

"Some Web page. I don't know which one. She was really psyched about the money, though."

"She wasn't worried about having to give up the baby?"

Linnea hesitated. "Not at first. Then, well . . . you know she was adopted?"

I nodded.

"I think she was having second thoughts. That's why she decided to not go to the hospital to have the baby."

"You talked to her after she had the baby?" I straightened, my antennae on alert. Linnea must have been one of the last people to see Elizabeth alive, since she seemed to have disappeared very shortly after depositing the newborn on Melissa Lloyd's doorstep.

"I was there," Linnea said, her pale skin going blind-cavefish white at the memory. "I helped her have the baby."

I stared at her. "You were at the apartment? You helped with the delivery?"

She nodded, fidgeting with the dangling skull. "Yeah. She called me on a Saturday night, told me she thought she was in labor and asked me to come over. I borrowed my mom's car and drove over there at about midnight. She was in pain, but not like later. Before it got too bad, I looked up home births on the Internet and ran out to Walgreens to get some supplies. The baby came at about six Sunday evening. I cut the umbilical cord," she said matter-of-factly, "with sewing scissors I sterilized in boiling water."

"You're a very brave girl," I told her, "and a good friend." I'd accompanied an Air Force friend to an abortion clinic once and sat with her while she cried all night, but that wasn't on a par with this. I hadn't been sixteen, either.

"I thought it would be gross," she said, "but it wasn't. I mean, yeah, it was bloody and everything, and the baby was all slippery and sticky, but when she opened her eyes and looked up at me while I was sponging her off—she seemed so serious—it was like fireworks went off in my head. I've always planned on being a doctor, and now I know I want to specialize in obstetrics."

Conviction rang in her voice, and I had no doubt she'd succeed. "What did you do then?"

"Went home. Was my mom ever pissed about my keeping the car out so long!" She batted at the skull earring and set it swinging.

One of the young mothers seated several tables away got up for a refill, and her baby flung his rattle across the room. The kid had an arm. It rolled to a stop five feet from me, and I picked it up, noticing Linnea's bulky backpack under the table and a pair of incongruous flip-flops on her feet. Black, of course. I handed the Elmo rattle to the exasperated mother. She thanked me and returned it to the baby who promptly flung it again. This time, when she picked it up, the mother tucked it into the diaper bag. The little Cy Young wailed.

"I've got to get back to class," Linnea said, slipping her arms through the straps of her backpack and shrugging into it. It bowed her slim shoulders forward.

"Do you want a ride back to school?" I asked, thinking the SPCA would get a call if anyone made a pack mule carry that much weight.

"Nah. I'm in good with Mr. Anderson, my calc teacher. He won't care if I'm late."

"Look, I've still got some questions," I said. Like, why did Elizabeth leave the baby with Melissa Lloyd? How did she get along with the Falstows? Did her father ever abuse her? "Can I call you at home later?"

She looked reluctant. "My mom would have a cow if she knew about all this."

"Well, how about if you call me? Would that be okay?" I gave her one of my cards.

She studied it for a moment, then nodded. "I guess."

We walked to the door together and stepped out onto the sidewalk. She turned to me as the sunlight glittered into our eyes and said, "Elizabeth asked me to be Olivia's godmother."

I wasn't sure what sort of response she was looking for, so I said nothing.

"I don't even believe in God, but I said yes. How stupid is that?" She held my eyes for a moment, then turned away, her flip-flops thwapping as she headed north to the high school.

9

The Falstow home was faux Mediterranean or something similar. Architectural styles are not my forte, but this house was tan stucco with a tile roof and a terra-cotta courtyard brimming with flowers that were definitely not native to Colorado. A small fountain splashed in the middle of the courtyard, attracting twittery sparrows. The smell of newly mown grass hung in the air, and a lawn mower buzzed from across the cul-de-sac. Parking my car on the street, I walked up the circular driveway, already feeling the heat of a late August day. Melodious chimes sounded when I pressed the doorbell, but no one came. Damn. That was the problem with my preferred tactic of not warning someone by calling ahead—sometimes I wasted a trip.

I backed up close to the fountain, the cool water misting my bare arms, and craned my neck to either side. A wrought-iron fence ringed the backyard, allowing glimpses of an emerald lawn that undoubtedly sucked up more water than Colorado's reservoirs had to spare, and a pool. I spied a gate's hinges and headed to the left.

"Hello?" I called, swinging the gate open. I thought I heard music coming from the back and followed the stone path around the side of the house to an oasis with a kidney-shaped pool surrounded by blue tile. A woman wearing a broad-brimmed sun hat sat in front of a laptop computer on a poolside table. Long, tanned legs descended from a pair of tobacco-colored shorts, and a coral bandeau allowed her shoulders and chest to soak up more sun. "Hello?" I said again, keeping back so as not to make her feel threatened.

She looked up, startled, and pulled ear buds from her ears, turning off the MP3 player lying on the table. "Who—"

Despite the Jackie O sunglasses she wore, I recognized the auburn hair. "Mrs. Falstow, I'm Charlie Swift. We met briefly at Patricia Sprouse's?" Okay, "met" was stretching it, but I wanted to establish a connection.

"Oh, oh yes! You must be here about Roberta. I knew that woman was lying when she said she didn't know where she was." A midwestern twang of some kind stretched her vowels. "Where is she? When can we have her?" As she spoke, she stood, topping my five foot three by at least six inches.

"Roberta?" What the hell was she going on about? Then it clicked. "You mean Olivia?"

Her salon-shaped brows drew together. "The baby's name will be Roberta. Roberta Justine, after my father and Stefan's."

"I am here about the baby," I conceded. Maybe not in the way she was hoping for, but I wasn't lying. "May I sit down?"

"Of course. Coffee?" She gestured to a cafetière on the table, seated herself, and refilled her mug.

"No, thanks." I pulled out a webbed chair and sat. "Mrs. Falstow—"

"Please, call me Jacqueline. Would you like to see the nursery?"

Before I could answer, she sprang up again and headed for French doors. Either she'd had enough caffeine to rev up a Formula One vehicle, she was the poster child for ADD, or she was nervous about something. I pushed back my chair and followed her. She was halfway up a grand staircase of some exotic wood, sunglasses in her hand, before I caught up with her.

"In here," she said breathlessly, pushing open the door to a fairy-tale bower. A round crib, big enough for quintuplets and lined with pink satin, occupied pride of place in the middle of the room. Dressers, a changing table, a diaper pail, a wipes warmer, and every other infant accessory available to people with too much money lined the walls. A rocking horse awaited a young rider in one corner, and fairies frolicked in a wood-land mural. Pink gauze hung from a ring on the ceiling, muting the light from the large window. I knew if I looked in the bureau drawers or opened the closet I'd find enough precious princess clothes to outfit every female infant between here and Pueblo.

"Isn't it splendid?" Jacqueline asked.

"I've never seen anything like it."

"You can see we love Roberta already," she said, turning a pleading face toward me. "I can't wait to hold her." She mimed rocking a baby in her arms and hummed a snatch of lullaby.

This was a woman who really, really wanted a baby. I didn't want to be around if she found out she couldn't have Olivia. I suspected a judge would end up making that decision.

"Actually," I said, "I'm a private investigator, and I've been hired to find Olivia's father. I understand that might be your husband?"

"What? How dare you!"

She went from loving mommy to Mommy Dearest in a heartbeat. The fury in her face pushed me back a step.

"Stefan has always been completely faithful. He would never— Especially not with a teenager young enough to be his daughter. Get out!" She pointed a rigid finger toward the door.

I held up my hands in apology. "I'm sorry. Please wait. Someone told me that Elizabeth had agreed to be a surrogate mother for you and your husband. If—"

"A surrogate?" The flush of anger slowly faded from her cheeks. "Who told you that? She was pregnant when we met her. Our lawyer set up the introduction, arranged for the private adoption. We signed a contract with Elizabeth, but it was for an adoption, spelling out how we'd cover the medical costs and some incidental living expenses—"

Yeah, fourteen thousand dollars of them, if Linnea was right.

"—and she'd turn the baby over to us when she was born."

"I'm sorry for the misunderstanding. If Elizabeth was pregnant when you met her, I don't suppose you know who the father was?"

She looked ten years older as her eyes narrowed and her mouth tightened. "Do I know who the semen contributor was? No. Stefan and I are her parents. That baby is legally ours. We have a contract." She rushed out of the room again, bare feet slapping on the wood floors, and darted into a door on the left. Feeling like Alice trying to keep up with the White

Rabbit, I found her in an office, flipping through folders in a file cabinet. "Here," she said triumphantly, thrusting a sheaf of papers at me. "The contract."

I didn't reach for it. "I really have nothing to do with that," I said, "but is a contract signed with a sixteen-year-old legally binding?"

Alarm flared in her eyes. "Sixteen? She told us she was nineteen!"

"Your lawyer didn't ask for proof of age or identity or anything?"

"How would I know? Stefan handled all the legal stuff." She tore around the room, her movements so agitated I thought the bandeau top might lose its grip. "He did the paperwork, set things up with the insurance company and the hospital—"

"Look," I said, holding up a calming hand. "What made you consider a private adoption?"

Jacqueline sank into a club chair positioned by the window. "I had to have a total hysterectomy in my twenties. I can't have biological children of my own."

Although she spoke matter-of-factly, I heard the underlying sadness. Sitting in a matching chair, I asked, "How did your lawyer locate Elizabeth?"

She took a deep breath. "Russell found Elizabeth on a Web site where prospective parents can meet girls—mostly teens— who want to have their babies adopted. We liked her photo, liked the fact she was here in Colorado Springs. We invited her over for dinner, and she seemed nice. Really, she was very businesslike, and that's part of what I liked about her. She kept in touch throughout the pregnancy, e-mailing us with details of the baby's development. We went with her for the ultrasound, and I got to hear the baby's heartbeat." Her eyes lit up but then darkened. "So when she went off and had the baby on her own, instead of at Memorial like we had planned, well, I was terrified, afraid she was going to tell us she wanted to back out of the contract, keep Roberta herself."

She took a ragged breath, as if reliving the ordeal. "Then she called Sunday night two weeks ago to tell us about the birth and make arrangements to deliver the baby to us. I was overjoyed! Everything was going to work out just fine. But she didn't show up on Monday like she said she would, and when we called her, she never answered. When I saw the death notice in the paper, I was stunned. I read every word, scared there'd be something about the baby dying, too, but there wasn't. Stefan and I didn't know where she lived—she always came to us—and I was frantic with worry about the baby."

I was pretty sure this woman was frantic more often than not. "Then what did you do?"

"I went to the funeral and saw Elizabeth's parents. I knew then they must be hiding the baby from me, and I confronted her mother." She glared at me defiantly, daring me to question her behavior. "You can tell her that if it's a matter of money, we'll happily pay her the money we still owed Elizabeth."

"How much was that?"

"None of your business." She moderated her instinctive response. "Of course, we'd pay you a finder's fee if you can locate the baby and deliver her to us."

I shook my head, rising to my feet. "Sorry, but that would be a conflict. I'll let my client know about your interest and pass along your name and number."

"Thank you. Please help us bring Roberta home." She brushed a strand of hair behind her ear.

We descended the stairs, me in front for once, eager to get away. In the foyer, we shook hands. Her hand was cold and bony. I gave her one of my cards and told her I was sure my client would be in touch. I felt her gaze searing into my back as I cut through the courtyard to reach my car.

<center>~~~</center>

My tummy grumbled as I drove away from the Falstow house, and I was in dire need of a Pepsi. Dialing Montgomery's number, I told him I'd buy lunch if he'd meet to share information.

"Get something to go and we can meet up at America the Beautiful Park."

I zipped into Pita Pockets and got us both fragrant gyro wraps dripping with cucumber sauce and yogurt. I sucked down half my Pepsi waiting for the clerk to bag our pitas. My whole car reeked of spiced lamb by the time I pulled into the parking lot fronting the park with its huge circular fountain and wading pool. Just across from an artists' commune on the west side of downtown, the park was an easy drive for Montgomery coming from police headquarters on South Nevada.

His unmarked car pulled up alongside mine as I got out. Wearing suit pants and a white button-down shirt, he greeted me with a kiss on the cheek that went straight to the pit of my stomach. I wrote the feeling off as hunger. Food would fix it. Handing him the bag with his gyro in it, I cut across the grass to a spot near the fountain and settled cross-legged on the ground. Misty droplets spangled the air around the fountain and lent a fresh smell to the small park. Kids ranging in age from barely walking to obnoxious ruffian splashed and squealed in the fountain. Parents offered varying degrees of supervision from neurotic—"Put on more sunblock! Wrap up in the towel so you don't catch cold!"—to negligent as they chatted with friends, munched on picnic lunches, and smoked cigarettes.

Finished with his lunch, Montgomery stretched out on his back, hands tucked under his head, and watched me from beneath drooping lids. The sun gilded the smooth olive skin on his face and firm curves of his lips. He looked ridiculously young relaxed like this. I had a feeling the sun was not so kind to me: It was undoubtedly spotlighting the faint crow's-feet I'd been noticing recently around my eyes.

"Don't fall asleep." I prodded his calf with my foot. "I bought you lunch; now you've got to put out."

"Willingly," he said, inviting me into his arms by stretching them up toward me.

I fought the temptation to let him pull me down against his hard chest. "No, no, you have to give me something I *want*," I said, pressing my lips together to keep from smiling.

"You *do* want me," he said with conviction but sat up, brushing at blades of grass on his shoulders. His voice shifted from seductive to businesslike. "The autopsy results are back."

"And?"

"Let's just say they're equivocal. Her neck was broken, possibly in a fall."

"It was an accident?" All my theories went up in smoke.

He held up his right hand, and the garnet in his University of Colorado class ring shot red sparks. "Not so fast. She might have fallen, she might've been pushed. There are no signs of manual strangulation. But . . . livor indicates she was moved after she died, so we have to assume she was with someone."

"Maybe they just found her, already dead."

"Then why move the body? Why not just call 911?"

Montgomery had been through this with his team, I could tell. "When did she die?"

"You know the pathologist doesn't want to commit to a time, especially since the girl was dead better than a week before we found her. Ballpark figure, she died sometime on Sunday or Monday two weeks ago."

The day she had the baby, or the day after. "Did you find any prints in her place?"

"Plenty, but none of them are in the system. She wasn't killed in the apartment—"

"How do you know?"

"She struck the back of her head, just where it meets the spine, on a hard edge of some kind." Montgomery's hand snuggled up under my hair, and two fingers made a slow circle on my neck to demonstrate. "There's no trace evidence of any sort on her kitchen counters, her bathtub, any likely surface, and no indication anybody tried to clean up." His hand lingered, kneading my neck muscles, and I forced myself to lean away. It felt too damn good.

"Got any leads?"

"How about you?" he countered.

I let him get away with not answering my question—for the moment—and told him about my interviews with Patricia, the Falstows, and Linnea Fenn and gave him my impressions. "Pastor Zach could well be the baby's father," I said. "I think the mother suspects something but can't admit it to herself. Or he could've killed Elizabeth in a fit of rage if she told them she was pregnant. I'm sure he laments the day stoning disobedient kids went out of fashion."

Montgomery grinned at my vicious humor.

"And the Falstow woman . . . well, she definitely wanted Elizabeth's baby. Still does. But Elizabeth was already committed to giving them the baby, so I don't see any motive for them to kill her." I paused, reviewing my impressions of all the people I'd talked to about this case. I wondered why Elizabeth had lied to Linnea about the pregnancy. Maybe because she was ashamed. Or maybe because she didn't want questions about the baby's paternity. Both of those items pointed to Pastor Zach, as far as I was concerned.

"I need the name of your client, Charlie," he said. Montgomery's expression and voice told me he'd be pissed if I ducked the question. PIs in Colorado have no legal standing when it comes to protecting clients' confidentiality unless they're working for a lawyer and are covered by attorney-client privilege.

"No can do. My client's into discretion."

He glared at me from under dark brows. "I can charge you with second degree kidnapping."

I grinned at his bluff. "Uh-uh. I've had nothing to do with the baby. And the mother voluntarily left the kid with my client—she's got a note—so I don't think you could even scare her with a kidnapping charge."

"Obstruction of justice?" Montgomery offered, but I could tell he wasn't going to press the issue.

"Get a court order and I'll spill it all," I suggested, pretty sure he wouldn't go that route, at least not yet. "I'm not exposing my client to your Gestapo tactics without one."

"Damn, and I left my jackboots at home this morning," Montgomery said, pretending to study his shined shoes. "Have you figured out who the dad is?"

I plucked a blade of grass and began systematically shredding it. "Lots of possibles, but no one admits to it. Too bad we can't just DNA-test 'em all, figure it out."

"And you called *me* the Gestapo." He grinned. "Ever heard of a thing called probable cause?"

"Yeah, it was overrated in the OSI, too." I pushed to my feet, swatting grass off my butt. "Those of us not mooching off the city's dime have to get back to work."

Montgomery stood. "Too bad we can't spend the day like that." He nodded at the kids dashing in and out of the fountain's spray, gilded with sun and water and the joy of summer.

I gazed at them for a moment, trying to absorb some of their carefree attitude. "I *do* have a bikini I didn't get to try out this summer," I mused with a sidelong look at Montgomery.

"You're torturing me, Swift," he said.

The heat in his eyes almost made me jump in the fountain to cool off. I beat a hasty retreat to my car, telling Montgomery I'd call him if I learned anything pertinent to his homicide investigation. Like who fathered Elizabeth's baby. Like who killed her.

I dialed the number to Designer Touches to warn Melissa the police were working hard to find her and got an answering machine that told me the shop was closed for the day. Hmm.

Maneuvering around a van doing ten miles under the limit, I dialed her home number. A man's voice answered with an impatient "Hello?"

Her husband must be home early. "Is Melissa there?"

"She's busy. She'll call you back." Without even waiting to get my name or number, he hung up.

I debated calling back but decided that a drive out to Melissa's house might prove more fruitful. I pointed the car north on I-25 to Monument, the small town adjacent to Colorado Springs. The exit was almost twenty miles up the highway, and I cruised along at just over the speed limit. Passing Uintah, I remembered my wine supply was low and crossed two lanes of traffic to exit. My favorite wine store, CoalTrain, sat just off the access ramp, in the shadow of the highway overpass. I wondered idly if Aurora Newcastle had ever considered opening a Purple Feet in Colorado Springs. I liked the store but wasn't prepared to drive an hour to Denver every time I needed some zin or pinot grigio. A screech of brakes and a blare of horns behind me made me check my rearview mirror. A gray SUV with the distinctive Mercedes hood ornament had taken my example and jumped off the interstate at the last moment. It barreled up Uintah as I swung into the parking lot.

With several bottles of chardonnay rattling in a box, I got back on the highway. Another call to Melissa's number netted nothing, not even an answering machine. A faint twinge of worry niggled at me, and I sped up. Fifteen minutes later I was about to make the turn onto Scottswood Drive, Melissa's street, when I noticed a familiar silhouette cresting a hill as I climbed the next one. *Don't be silly,* I told myself, dismissing the notion I was being followed. SUVs, even Mercedeses, were a dime a dozen in this area. Still, this one was the same gray as the one that followed me off at the Uintah exit.

I'd survived as a cop in a war zone by trusting my instincts, and I decided to heed them this time. Passing Scottswood, I made a quick left at the next street in front of oncoming traffic, trusting the Mercedes, if it was really following me, would have to wait to make the turn. With no one in sight behind me, I pulled into the second driveway I came to, one partly obscured by lodgepole pines. Sure enough, the gray SUV zipped past the driveway entrance moments later. Gotcha, amateur. I backed out of the driveway and followed the Mercedes from a distance of a couple of blocks. It drove slowly, hesitating at a cross street, before going straight. When the driver gave up and pulled into a driveway to turn around, I quickly closed the distance between us and used the Subaru to block the driveway.

Adrenaline coursed through my system, and I was out of the car, pounding up the driveway, before the startled driver realized his predicament. I really needed to start carrying my gun, I thought, pounding on the tinted driver's window with my fist. I could just make out the shape of the driver inside.

"What in Sam Hill is going on out here?" a querulous voice called from the direction of the house. A small man old enough to get a salute from *Good Morning America* on his next birthday, with white hair wisping around his head like cotton candy, and wearing a pair of old jeans with the waistband hiked up to his armpits, stood quivering behind a half-open storm door.

"Call the police, sir," I yelled. "This man was following me."

"Is he one of those stalkers you hear about?" Curiosity had replaced fear in the man's quavery voice, and he took a step out onto the stoop.

"Probably," I said, yanking on the door handle. Locked. "Sir, the police?"

The engine revved, and the car backed up a foot. For one moment, I thought the driver was going to try reversing over my Subaru. Then the engine cut out and the window buzzed down a couple of inches. I found myself looking into the frightened and defiant face of Jacqueline Falstow.

"You followed me!" I said.

She nodded, brushing a strand of auburn hair off her forehead.

Damn, I was losing my touch. She must have followed me from her house to the park, waited while I lunched with Montgomery, and then trailed me here. "Why?" I asked, although I suspected I knew the answer.

"I thought you'd lead me to Roberta," she whispered, her gaze meeting mine for a fraction of a second before she fixed her eyes on the steering wheel.

And I would have, I realized, if I hadn't needed wine and broken fifteen traffic laws to exit on Uintah. As it was, I'd led her damn close to my client's house. Annoyance at myself made me scowl.

"Don't call the police," Jacqueline pleaded, misinterpreting my expression.

I knew she was worried about how an arrest would look to

a judge if the courts ended up deciding who got custody of Olivia.

"Are you going to cut this shit out?"

Dark circles under her eyes attested to sleepless nights as she said, "Yes. I'm sorry. I didn't mean to scare you. It's just that . . . Does she live on this street?" She looked left and right, as if hoping to see the baby in the window of the yellow house next door or in an infant swing in the yard across the street.

"Go home, Mrs. Falstow," I said, irritated with the woman, but feeling unwanted sympathy for her, too.

"Hey," said a voice at my elbow. "That's a girl. I didn't know they had girl stalkers these days."

The homeowner was peering suspiciously from Jacqueline to me, his eyes bright blue in a face with more wrinkles than a litter of Shar-pei puppies. His head only came up to my chin.

"Thank you for being concerned," I said. "My friend and I just had a misunderstanding. We won't bother you anymore." I gave Jacqueline a meaningful look and she nodded. I shook the man's callused hand and walked back to my car. Making a U-turn, I waited for the Mercedes to precede me down the street. When we reached the intersection with the main road, she turned right and sped off in the direction of the interstate. I went left and tooled around the side streets for twenty minutes before deciding the coast was clear and I could backtrack to Melissa's.

10

~~~

The Lloyds had a small house set back from the road on a couple of acres of forested land. Aspens and the ubiquitous lodgepole pines crowded around the house. A thicket of shrubs with glossy dark leaves nudged up against the porch that ran half the length of the house, and a flower garden, most of its blooms spent, nestled under a picture window facing the road. Wind chimes of ceramic, metal, and wood clanged and rattled as I rang the doorbell. The din of the chimes would make sitting on the porch with a Pepsi or glass of wine about as appealing as dining on the interstate, drowning the sounds of birds and wind. On the thought, a magpie landed on the porch rail, his black feathers gleaming iridescent as he cocked his head to study me. The opening door startled him, and he flew off with a loud caw.

"Yes?" A man stood framed in the doorway, a look of impatience on his face. Wearing a paint-spattered pair of cargo shorts and a black T-shirt, he looked to be about my age. A paintbrush tipped with sage-colored paint dangled from his left hand, and he kept his right hand on the door. He was obviously primed to announce he didn't need Girl Scout Thin Mints or Boy Scout popcorn or marching band chocolate bars.

"I'm Charlie Swift. I'm looking for Melissa. Is she here?"

"You're the PI?" A faint look of interest replaced the impatience in his brown eyes.

"Yes. You must be Ian. I thought you were working in Arizona." I extended my hand, and he shook it, leaving a smear of paint on my thumb.

"I am," he said with a thin smile. "I rearranged a couple of meetings and flew up for the day to see how Mel was getting on with the baby. She's not used to infants. Neither am I, for that matter. C'mon in." He pulled the door wider. "Excuse the mess. Mel had to take the baby to the doctor, and I thought I might as well get some stuff done." He gestured to the living room just off the entryway. Blue plastic tarps covered the furniture and most of the floor, and a ladder stood in one corner, a small bucket balanced precariously on the top step. The paint smell cleared my sinuses.

"I hope Olivia's okay," I said.

"Just the sniffles. But Mel was convinced she had meningitis or bubonic plague or something equally unlikely, so she hauled her off to the doctor." His voice held the disparaging note of the superior male who thought taking an aspirin was tantamount to tattooing WUSS on his forehead and wouldn't visit the ER unless he'd severed a limb in a manly woodchopping accident or been mauled by a puma, preferably while hauling a field-dressed elk out of the woods. "Mind if I keep working?"

Without waiting for my answer, he climbed up the ladder

and dipped his brush into the bucket. I had to crane my neck to look up at him as I said, "I just stopped by to let Melissa know she should expect a call from the police."

The brush clattered to the floor, spraying sage-colored paint on the ladder and the wall. I picked it up gingerly between two fingers and handed it up to him. He had freckles on his hands.

"The police? Why do they need to talk to us? To Melissa? I suppose it's about Lizzy," he answered his own question. "Mel told me she'd hired you to find out who the baby's father is. She told me about the baby being Lizzy's and Lizzy turning up dead. What a shame."

"Elizabeth worked for your wife and left the baby with her," I pointed out, circumspectly not mentioning the closer relationship between Elizabeth and Melissa. I didn't know if Melissa had come clean with her husband. I suspected not. "Since she was killed not long after leaving the baby here, the police just need to talk to Melissa. I didn't give them her name, but they'll probably come up with it."

"It's too bad. What happened to Lizzy, I mean," he said, brushing paint onto the wall in choppy strokes. "She was a sweet girl." His profile looked pensive.

"You knew her?"

"I met her once or twice. As you said, she worked for Melissa."

"What was she like?"

"Really pretty, with a great smile and—"

Great tits, I filled in mentally when he paused.

"Her husband was in Iraq or Afghanistan, and she was counting the days until he got back so they could leave

Colorado. I got the feeling she'd had a bad experience here. Her dad died, she said, and her mom remarried some jerk she couldn't stand."

"Where were they going?" I asked, knowing there was no "they."

"She talked about Virginia," Ian said. "I remember because she said she wanted to go to the University of Virginia and study psychology. Melissa said she was a great little seamstress, but I guess she had bigger plans."

"It was nice of you to take time to draw her out," I said. His back was to me now as he painted up into a corner. I maneuvered closer to see more of his face, almost tripping on a drop cloth.

"She seemed lonely. We got to talking when she came to install those curtains she made." He jerked his head in the direction of ruby-colored velvet drapes half closed against the westerly sun.

"When did you first meet her?"

"I don't know . . . late last year? Not too long after she started sewing for Mel."

"Was she already pregnant?"

He laughed uneasily. "I hope so, since her husband was already deployed. She wasn't showing, though, if that's what you mean. Why?"

Before I could answer, my cell phone rang. "Excuse me," I said, stepping into the hall.

Gigi's excited voice bounced over the line. "Charlie! There's another PI here. She said she's the one you're looking for."

"What?"

"You posted a question on some online bulletin board,

right? Well, this woman says Elizabeth Sprouse hired her to find her birth mother. I think she carries a gun," Gigi added in a whisper, and I assumed she meant the strange PI.

"Tell her I'll be right there."

I flipped the phone closed, ducked my head into the living room to say good-bye to Ian Lloyd and remind him to tell Melissa the cops would come calling, and gratefully escaped the paint-scented confines of the house for the fresh air in the yard and my car parked in the driveway.

∼∼∼

I walked into my office to find Gigi holding a gun. Déjà vu all over again. Another woman, with short salt-and-pepper hair, wearing black leather pants and a matching vest that showed off smoothly muscled arms, was showing Gigi a two-handed shooter's grip. The pink cast got in the way.

"Cup the bottom of your right hand with your left. Like this." She demonstrated, and the gun, a small .22 that looked like a Halloween prop in Gigi's hands, took on a silky air of menace.

"Oh, Charlie," Gigi said, catching sight of me in the doorway. "This is Frieda Vasher. She's showing me how to hold my gun."

Bending, Frieda tucked the gun into an ankle holster before turning to greet me. "Swift," she said, shaking my hand with a grip that would mash aluminum cans, "I've heard a lot about you. The way you tracked down the Olson kid . . . whew!" She shook her head. "That story in the *Denver Post* about it was great advertising, I'll bet."

"I got some business from it," I admitted. The lines in

Vasher's face suggested she was in her late forties or early fifties, but she was as fit as a twenty-year-old. She wore no makeup, but a tattoo that looked like a Celtic bracelet girdled one rock-hard bicep. Her eyes were a light gray, almost silver, under strong black brows. She studied me for a moment, and I got the feeling she saw more than most people.

"Let me tell you what I know about the Sprouse girl," she said, pulling forward the straight-backed chair and straddling it backward.

I propped my shoulders against the wall and nodded: I was listening. Gigi rolled her chair around the desk and leaned forward, elbows on her knees, chin in her hands, her expression suggesting she had front-row seats to a Broadway premiere.

"She contacted me a year ago May—"

"How'd she get your name?"

"My Web page," Vasher said with a grin that showed one front tooth slightly overlapping the other. "I notice you don't have one. You might want to think about designing one; I get better than half my business off the Internet these days. Anyway, she came to see me and said she wanted to find her birth mother. She was obsessed." Her brows drew together. "She'd been saving money for years to afford a PI, squirreling away every dime of her allowance and the money she made sewing. Can you imagine?"

Gigi nodded. "That poor girl. How awful not to know who your mama is."

Frieda gave her an approving look. "Exactly. It didn't take me long to track down her mother's maiden name—she had the correct date of birth and the name of the hospital—but it took longer to find the marriage certificate and her current location. She got married in Syracuse," she said, "where her husband's from."

"How did she react when you gave her the information?" I asked.

Frieda hesitated. "I've done a lot of work like this, finding the birth parents of adopted children, or vice versa. In almost all cases, the person searching is full of hope, and maybe a little fear that the truth—or the parent or the child—won't be what they've dreamed about for years. Still, they're hopeful, excited, and they've planned out the reunion in their minds a hundred times. First I'll say this, then he'll say that . . . you know?"

Gigi and I both nodded. I'd played that mental game waiting for my parents to come home from Kigali or Montevideo or wherever, hoping that this time they'd hug me like they'd never let go, tell me how much they missed me, say they were never going to leave me with Grandy and Gramps again. It never worked out that way until after Grandy died and they started dumping me with Aunt Pam and Uncle Dennis instead. "But Elizabeth didn't react like that?"

Frieda's emphatic headshake set her short hair swaying. "No. She just said, 'Now we'll see,' with a funny little smile, paid me, and left. I guess," she said, her eyes settled on the middle distance as she thought, "she was missing the hope. It bothered me a little. I even felt a little bad about giving her the info."

"Did you see her again? Did she call, like after she made contact with her mother?" I asked.

"Nope. Never heard from her again. It all came back,

though, when I checked the bulletin board and saw your query. And then the obit." She heaved a sigh, pushing the chair away to stand. "She was too young to die."

She shook hands with me again, refused payment for her time, and handed me her card, telling me she did bodyguard work, in addition to investigations. I promised to call her if I ever needed her expertise, and she left. Not on a Harley as I might have guessed from her attire, but in a cream Nissan Sentra.

"Now, she looked like a private eye," Gigi said admiringly. "Tough."

"And what am I?" I headed for the fridge and my Pepsi fix.

"A businesswoman," Gigi said.

I was tough, damn it. I felt a twinge of irritation at her assessment, and it must've shown on my face.

"That's good," she assured me. "I've been reading some PI magazines"—she opened her bottom desk drawer and fanned a handful of magazines on the desk—"and they all mention how important it is to be professional and businesslike. Maybe Frieda's right about a Web page, though. I'll bet we could really increase our bottom line if we had a good one."

We? My ears started to itch, deep inside where I couldn't scratch, the way they do when I get angry. If there weren't a "we" in this office, my bottom line would be just fine.

"Actually," I said, "a good way to increase our cash flow would be to do some process serving. A lot of PIs do it to have a steady income stream." I'd always steered away from it, preferring real investigations to handing unsuspecting women divorce paperwork or upstanding citizens notice that they were being sued. However, needs must when the devil drives, as Grandy used to say, and process serving was less distasteful than photographing adulterers. Best of all, a cast wouldn't pose much of an impediment to process serving.

"What's that?" Gigi asked.

"You know, tracking down people and handing them court paperwork, saying, 'You've been served.' "

"I wouldn't know how to track anyone down," Gigi said dubiously.

"Mostly you just get the address off the paperwork and ring the doorbell," I said. "Occasionally, you might have to wi— be a bit more creative." I bit off the words "wing it" as Bernie glowered at me from the corner.

Before she could protest further, I called my lawyer friend Valerie and got us set up to deliver a summons for her the next day. Then I handed Gigi the Yellow Pages and suggested she call every lawyer listed to pitch them on our ability as process servers. She looked appalled but gamely started dialing. This would be perfect: Not only would it bring some money into the agency, but it would be such tedious work—driving around town, waiting for people to come home—that Gigi would run, not walk, back to her Broadmoor mansion and dial up a new lawyer who could pry more money out of the larcenous Les the Lecher.

~~~

A tan pickup blocked my driveway when I arrived home, and I wondered if it was a lost St. Paul's parishioner, looking for Father Dan. Parking on the street, I approached the truck, prepared to direct the driver to the rectory next door. The door swung open, and Pastor Zach stepped out, his face contorted with fury. The late afternoon breeze had no effect on his Bryl-creemed comb-over, but his blue tie was askew and his short-sleeved shirt crumpled. I wondered how long he'd been waiting for me.

"What gives you the right?" he yelled, stomping toward me.

I held my ground, refusing to give way on my own property, as he came to within an arm's length. He exhaled stale beer breath into my face along with his anger. "You don't have the right to cozy up to my wife and drip your poison into her ear!"

Ah, Patricia must've told him about my visit. I doubted she'd told him that she'd initiated our conversation. "Look, Mr. Sprouse—"

"No, you look." He wagged a trembling finger half an inch from my nose. "You have poisoned my house and my marriage with your evil insinuations. I would not defile myself by any congress with that harlot. I would not! I am a man of God, and I do not consort with evildoers." His Adam's apple bobbed convulsively.

"Really? How do you 'save' them if you refuse to consort with them?" I knew my flippancy would stoke his fires, but I couldn't help myself. His self-righteous blather pushed all my buttons. At least my parents hadn't held themselves above the people they hoped to convert.

"You may scoff, you whore, but I will not tolerate your libel—"

"I think you mean slander."

"—or your turning my wife against me." Before I could read his intention, his arm flashed up and he slapped me across the face.

My head whipped to the side. Damn, that stung. The pent-up anger that had been simmering inside me since I found Gigi sitting in my office surged to the forefront. My eyes narrowed as I turned to face him, his face glowing with triumph.

"That's assault," I told him, my voice flat and cold. "Your wife and daughter may let you get away with it, but I will prosecute."

My words didn't faze him. He was tripping on the power, and his eyes burned with lust for more. He stepped toward me again—just as I wanted him to—his hands balling into fists.

"You want a crack at the other one?" I asked, turning my face to show him my unmarred cheek. Even as he shifted his shoulders, putting all his weight into a blow aimed at my face, I ducked under his arm and plowed my fist into his midsection, right below his sternum, just like the Air Force taught me. His breath woofed out and he tried to grab me, but I danced away.

"And that's self-defense," I instructed him, hoping he'd come at me again.

"You will be punished, just like that other whore was punished," he gasped. He straightened up, attempting to reclaim his dignity. "You cannot escape the consequences of your sins. Fire and brimstone rained down on Sodom and Gomorrah, and your fate will be even worse."

"Worse than Elizabeth's? Why'd you kill her, Zach?"

"She deserved her fate, but I had nothing to do with it. The wages of sin—"

"Yeah, yeah, you're repeating yourself." My muscles relaxed as it became clear he wasn't coming after me again, and the breeze chilled my flushed skin. I caught the scent of beef charring on a mesquite grill.

The light of madness drained out of his eyes, and he was suddenly an ordinary-looking middle-aged man, maybe a little scrawnier than most, his shoulders slumped with the weight of a wife mourning her daughter, unpaid bills, and dreams of evangelical fame unlikely to come to fruition.

"You stay away from my wife," he said more quietly, squeezing his face with his fingers and pulling the flesh down. "She's a grieving woman, and you are doing nothing but adding to her pain, just like that daughter of hers did with her disrespectful mouth and her whorish ways. It was a blessing when she left our house, but my Patricia didn't see it that way."

I didn't imagine many mothers would.

"You leave her in peace." He trudged back to the truck and fired it up, reversing so quickly I had to jump out of the way. As it was, bits of gravel peppered my legs. His brake lights flashed at the corner of Tudor Road, and then he was gone.

My muscles trembling slightly as the adrenaline leached away, I pulled my Subaru forward into the spot vacated by Sprouse. Then I trudged into the house and splashed water on my face to relieve the sting in my cheek. That side of my face was puffy and red, and I lightly patted it dry with a towel. A soft dusk was settling as I changed into a pair of shorts and the yellow T-shirt that brings out the gold flecks in my brown eyes, scuffed into a pair of sandals, grabbed a six-pack of beer, and followed the scent of barbecuing beef to Father Dan's patio. I was too damn worn out to cook for myself.

Dan sat in an Adirondack chair, reading a book by porch light. I breathed in the aromatic smoke wafting from the grill as I came up the walkway. Dan looked up at the sound of my sandals slapping on the cement. Concern clouded his eyes, and he closed the book.

"I've come for dinner," I said, lifting up the beer, my contribution to the meal.

"Should I ask what the other guy looks like?" Dan stood and moved toward me. He gently touched his forefinger to the tender spot on my cheek. He wore a Hawaiian shirt with yellow hibiscuses—hibisci?—on a turquoise background and shorts that showed off his muscular legs. His feet were bare. Suddenly way too conscious of his scent—soap and an aftershave with a hint of lime—I stepped away, resisting the impulse to lean my face into his large palm.

"His bruises won't show," I assured him, appropriating his second chair. I pulled a bottle of cold beer from the six-pack and held it against my cheek. "Aah." I took a swallow.

After another moment of scrutiny, Dan apparently decided I was going to live and helped himself to a beer. Using the tongs dangling from the grill, he poked at the meat. "Who hit you, Charlie?" he asked, replacing the tongs and turning to face me.

"A man of God," I intoned.

His face remained impassive, his gaze steady. When I didn't amplify, he asked, "The one fond of quoting Revelation?"

"One and the same." I raised my beer in a salute and drained half the bottle. I hadn't realized how much the stress of this case and of having Gigi around was piling up.

"Did you file a report with the police?"

I gave him a sheepish look from under my lashes. "I told him I was going to," I said, "but when it came down to it, I felt kind of sorry for the guy. I don't know why. He came off like he was really trying to protect his wife."

"Charlie—"

"I know, I know," I said. "If he lifts a finger against me again, if he even looks at me funny, I'll file charges. Okay?"

"No, not okay." A thread of anger ran through Dan's voice. "Abusers and bullies count on their victims' silence. That's how—"

"I know the stats. Anyway, I'm not a victim. I gave as good as I got. I'm not here for pastoral counseling." I glared at him. Discovering my bottle was empty, I set it down with a hard clink on the patio.

"What *are* you here for?" Curiosity and something else colored his voice, and I found it hard to meet his intense gaze.

"Dinner."

"I'll set another place."

As he turned away, I noticed the two place settings on the glass-topped patio table. "Are you expecting someone?" I jumped to my feet, almost knocking over my beer bottle. "A date?"

"Just a friend," Dan said. "You're welcome to stay."

"A he-friend or a she-friend?"

"A woman."

"Oh, my God, I'm crashing your date."

"You don't have to—"

The sound of a car pulling up in front galvanized me. Grabbing another bottle from the six-pack, I swung my legs over the low stone wall surrounding his patio. "Keep the beer. Have fun. See you around."

I tossed the words over my shoulder as I navigated the

uneven terrain between our yards, blundering into a low shrub in the dusk. It scratched my legs, and I cursed. The low murmur of voices followed me as I climbed the stairs to my deck. Damn. I couldn't even soak in my hot tub since I didn't want to eavesdrop, even accidentally, on Dan's date. Feeling aggrieved, I yanked open the door and stomped into my kitchen. Still unmotivated to cook, I ate tuna from a can and munched an apple from the fridge. I went over my notes from the Lloyd case until my eyes started to blur, then went to bed, pretty sure I hadn't heard Dan's visitor drive away yet.

11

(Tuesday)

Seth Johnson, Elizabeth's wannabe fiancé, owned a ranch—a large one—east of Colorado Springs on the Big Sandy River near a small town called Wild Horse. I'd called ahead when I woke up and been told he could spare me fifteen minutes that morning. Giving Gigi a call at the office to let her know where I'd be—and gritting my teeth at the necessity—I headed east on Woodmen Road into a blinding sunrise and a sky so clear I could see to the far side of Kansas. I happened to notice that no strange cars cluttered Dan's driveway as I drove past.

I'd done a quick Internet search and made a couple of calls about Johnson before setting out and unearthed some interesting details. He was from a well-off ranching family in eastern Colorado and, through innovative breeding practices and good management, had turned the respectable family fortune into a large one. He'd picked up a master's in agriculture science at Colorado State University and interned in a lab in Pennsylvania doing genetic engineering before returning to

Colorado to run the ranch when his father died. He'd gotten married for the first time at the age of thirty. His bride was only eighteen, I'd noted with interest, and they'd divorced three years later. No children. His second wife, also eighteen when they married, died in a hiking accident five years into the marriage. Also no children. His third wife, twenty to his forty, lasted less than two years before going the way of wife number one. Still no little Seths. Elizabeth would have been his fourth wife. In addition to marrying frequently, he made large contributions to political campaigns but, aside from one disastrous run for the state senate, he remained a behind-the-scenes power broker.

An hour of driving through increasingly flat vistas brought me to the entrance to Johnson's spread. Ten minutes later, I arrived at the house and a grouping of barns, silos, sheds, and other ranch buildings I couldn't identify. Three or four pick-ups and a Lincoln Town Car were parked outside a building with a neatly lettered sign reading OFFICE. I pulled up alongside the other vehicles and got out to the smells of dust, hay, and a whiff of cow dung. A stiff breeze stirred my hair and sent the dust spiraling in little eddies. Anxious to escape the wind, I pulled open the door and found myself in a room with an empty desk, a watercooler in one corner, a wall of photos of prizewinning bulls on my right, and a door leading to an inner office from which came male voices.

About to knock on that door, I started as a voice came from my left. "Help you?"

I whirled to see a middle-aged woman, her face stiff with suspicion, emerge from a small bathroom I hadn't noticed earlier. Dressed in a denim skirt and a Western shirt with a yoke and snaps instead of buttons, she dried her hands on a paper towel and sat behind the desk, obviously more comfortable with its bulk between us. Squirting lotion from a bottle into her hands, she massaged them together, her pale blue eyes looking a question at me.

"I'm Charlotte Swift. I have an appointment with Mr. Johnson." I handed her one of my cards.

"I'm afraid he won't have time to see you this morning after all," the woman said, not sounding apologetic. "There was an emergency and he's running behind schedule, and he's got to be in Denver by noon. So—"

"Look," I said, trying to repress my irritation, "I only need a couple of minutes. If you'll just tell him—"

The door to the inner office opened as the word "no" formed on the secretary's lips. A man I took to be Seth Johnson, tall and gangly and with gingery hair and mustache, wearing a well-cut suit and cowboy boots, shook hands with a shorter, squatter man in a sheriff's uniform. "Thanks, Carl. I appreciate your taking care of it personally."

"Of course, Mr. Johnson," the sheriff said. "Rustlers are a plague on all of us."

Tipping his hat to me and the secretary, he left, letting in a blast of wind that gleefully spun a stack of papers off the desk. As the secretary bent to retrieve them, I took advantage of her distraction. "Mr. Johnson? I'm Charlotte Swift." I held out my hand, and he shook it, looking down at me with sharp eyes. Patricia Sprouse had been kind: I'd put his age at closer to fifty than forty. "Do you have a few minutes to talk about your fiancée?"

He looked at me blankly as the secretary gasped and

dropped the papers she'd just finished collecting. "Elizabeth Sprouse?" I prompted.

He forced a laugh. "I wasn't engaged to Elizabeth. I don't deny I had some discussion with her father, but it came to nothing. I was saddened to hear about her death, however."

"Not sad enough to attend the funeral," I said. I'd've noticed him if he'd been there. In addition to his height and coloring, he had an indefinable air of command that set him apart.

"I was out of state on business," he said, narrowing his eyes. "Who did you say you were again?"

"Charlotte Swift. Call me Charlie."

"Mr. Johnson, I'm so sorry! I told her—"

Johnson waved his secretary to silence. "It's okay, Jean. I've got a few minutes before I need to leave for Denver. Walk down to the barn with me, Charlie." He held the door, and I ducked out into the wind, resisting the urge to send a triumphant smirk Jean's way.

"We lost fifteen head of cattle this week. We're not sure exactly when," Johnson said, speaking close to my ear to be heard over the wind. He put a hand to my elbow to steer me toward the large barn. "Rustlers."

The word conjured images of the Old West, of greasy-haired desperados in black hats cutting cattle from a herd and hiding them in an arroyo or box canyon or some such feature of western geography. The theme music from *The Good, the Bad and the Ugly* whistled in my head. "Is rustling still a problem for ranchers?"

"Hell, yeah. Rustling is high-tech now, with the thieves using ATVs to round up the cattle and load 'em into a semi. They truck the cattle to market on the other side of the country before you even know they're missing. Every rancher I know counts his rustling losses in the tens of thousands of dollars each year."

Who knew? I wondered briefly if this might be a new line of work for me. I could expand the agency's portfolio from finding missing persons to tracking missing cows. I could see it now: photos of cows' faces on milk cartons. How apropos. Somehow—maybe because I suspected the victims ended up as hamburger before anyone could trace them—the idea didn't resonate with me, and I didn't pitch it to Johnson.

We crossed the threshold of a barn large enough to hangar a 747, and the ammonia smell of cow urine stung my nose and made me blink. Dust motes danced in the shafts of sunlight penetrating the dim space, and cows lowed from stalls marching horizontally across the barn. Grandy and Gramps had kept two cows for milk, and the feeling in this barn, though much larger and more modern, blasted me back to the time I first crossed the threshold of the shed housing Buttercup and Lulu. I couldn't have been more than three or four, but I still remember Grandy solemnly introducing me to the cows and telling us how much we'd like each other. Not so different from what Delicia Furman had said to Gigi, now that I thought about it.

Seth Johnson didn't offer to introduce me to any of the cattle currently inhabiting his barn. He read notes posted on clipboards on the front of each stall, cast an eye over the inmate, and moved on. All he needed was a white lab coat to impersonate a doctor on rounds. With no clue what he was looking at, and less interest, I felt my time with him slipping away and decided to wrest his attention away from the bovine world.

"So, what are the chances you're the father of Elizabeth's baby?" I asked in the tone I'd use at a cocktail party to inquire about someone's job or hobbies.

He didn't turn a hair, or even look up from the clipboard he was studying. "Zero."

"Really? I understand you got pretty cozy with her in a Sunday school classroom."

That brought his head around to me, and his eyes were flinty as he said, "Your sources are ill-informed."

I considered the possibility Elizabeth had lied to Linnea about the encounter, especially since she'd misrepresented the nature of her dealings with the Falstows. "Possibly," I conceded. "Are you saying you never had sex with Elizabeth?"

"That would be illegal," he said smoothly. "It's called statutory rape."

"So you'd be willing to give a DNA sample for comparison with the baby's?"

"Get real," he said. "My lawyer would have a coronary."

"Otherwise, of course, you'd cooperate."

"Of course," he said with a smile as false as my own.

A caramel-colored cow stuck its head toward me, and I absently scratched her between the ears. She rewarded me with a slurp on my hand with her sticky tongue. Johnson laughed at my dilemma: wipe cow drool on my tan wool-blend slacks, or let my hands air dry with a film of spit.

"Here." He handed me a handkerchief, which I took gratefully.

"Thanks. So, why is an obviously successful, attractive,

and *mature* man like yourself interested in marrying a sixteen-year-old? For that matter, why do you attend the Church of Jesus Christ the Righteous on Earth when, I'm sure, your generous donations would get you the front pew at any church between here and Denver?"

"Pastor Sprouse speaks God's truth. His ministry is based on the Lord's word. I know he can reach millions of sinners with the right backing." Johnson shot back the cuff of his pinstriped suit. "I've got to go."

He started for the barn door, and I trotted to keep up with his long strides. "So, you're buying in? What do you get from your investment? Certainly not money."

His profile was unrevealing, but a muscle jumped near the corner of his mouth. "The Lord has blessed me with an abundance of money," Johnson said. "I am privileged to use it to do his work."

A nearby cow snorted, and I felt like doing the same.

Johnson continued, "Some men give millions to see their names blazoned on a hospital wing, or an engineering school at their alma mater, or a library. I'll leave a legacy of salvation, not a building of stone and sand that will crumble to dust."

I took a shot in the dark. "If you're so big into legacy, it must really piss you off that there's no Seth Junior to carry on when you're gone."

He spun to face me, a white line rimming his lips. For a moment I thought he was going to strike me, but he breathed in twice through his nostrils, exhaling forcefully. "You don't want to mock me, Charlotte Swift." He leaned down until his face was inches from mine, and I could see the flecks of amber in his hazel eyes, deep pores in the grooves of his nose, and a few gray brow hairs growing longer than the ginger ones. "I don't take that kind of sass from U.S. senators, never mind third-rate private investigators or smart-ass teenagers."

He held my gaze for another moment, to make sure I wouldn't venture a reply, then turned on his heel and strode out of the barn, getting into the backseat of the Lincoln that was waiting to take him to Denver.

I let my breath out, not aware until then that I'd been holding it, and let Johnson's crumpled hankie fall from my hand. The wind caught it before it hit the floor and chased it into a pile of straw and dung. Apparently I'd hit a sore spot. Maybe Johnson's young wives were no more than brood mares and he discarded them when they didn't produce offspring. Shades of Henry the Eighth. Hadn't Henry's second wife, Anne Boleyn, lost her head to the guillotine, when her princely hubby decided he stood a better chance of getting an heir from Jane Seymour? A dark thought wormed its way into my mind: I wondered if there'd been any witnesses to the second Mrs. Johnson's hiking accident.

—*m*—

As I made the long drive back to Colorado Springs, wondering what Elizabeth could've said to Johnson to merit his comment about "smart-ass teenagers" and wishing I'd had a snappy comeback for his remark about third-rate investigators, my cell phone rang. I didn't recognize the number.

"Ms. Swift? Charlie?"

"Yes?" The female voice was familiar, but I couldn't place it.

"This is Linnea Fenn. You wanted to finish our conversation, and I thought I'd let you know I could meet you during track practice right after school. Coach is out sick, and we're just supposed to be working out on our own. No one will care if I take a break in the stands."

"I'll be there. Thanks for calling."

I hung up, wondering if it'd be worth my time to track down one of the former Mrs. Johnsons and see what she had to say about Mr. Legacy. I decided to wait until after I'd talked to Linnea; unless I thought there was a good chance Johnson had fathered Elizabeth's baby, then it wasn't worthwhile finding his ex-wives. Anyway, given his apparent obsession with having a child, wouldn't he have claimed Elizabeth's baby was his if he had, in fact, fathered it? Even if he'd have to face down some scandal to do so? Or—I tapped my fingers on the steering wheel—maybe he was only interested in having a son, and Olivia, a mere girl, didn't make the cut.

With my cell phone still out, I called information and got a number for Russell Ziegler, the adoption lawyer who'd apparently matched up Elizabeth with the Falstows. It was remotely possible Elizabeth had confided in him about the father of her child. Even if she hadn't, he might know something that could point me in the right direction. His secretary informed me he was in court all day and asked what I was calling in reference to. I told her nothing, thanked her, and headed for downtown Colorado Springs and the courthouse. I figured I could talk with Russell Ziegler during a break in the court action and still make it to the high school track in time to talk with Linnea after school. I called Gigi to update her on my whereabouts, but the answering machine picked up at the agency. Good . . . I hoped that meant she was out delivering summonses and beefing up our bottom line.

12

~~~

Gigi tucked the summons paperwork Valerie Driscoll's para-legal had given her into the depths of her capacious purse, wedging it between the pepper spray and the plastic container of sanitary napkins she couldn't afford to leave home with-out now that her period—once as punctual and regular as the *CBS News with Walter Cronkite*—stayed away for two months and then arrived without warning in a flood of Niagara pro-portions. Once, menopause had looked attractive because it meant she and Les could stop fussing with condoms and sper-micides and their lovemaking could be more spontaneous. Now, with no Les and no sex, menopause had no upside that Gigi could see.

"How'd you break your arm?" the paralegal, an intense woman in her midthirties with her corkscrew curls corralled by a headband and wire-rimmed glasses, asked.

"Drug bust," Gigi said.

"Oh, it must be exciting being a private detective."

"Well, I've only been doing it for a bit more than a week," Gigi said, pleased by the interest lighting the woman's eyes, "but so far it's been more than I expected." *And less,* she added to herself, returning to the elevator. She pushed away memories of Charlie's lukewarm welcome—how could anyone object to a coffeepot, for heaven's sake?—and the disquieting thought that her partner would be happy if she up and quit. She wouldn't, though. She couldn't. Not with the bills for Kendall's skating to pay. And the maintenance and taxes on their house. At least Les had had the decency not to sell it out from under her. And college expenses looming in the future, assuming the kids managed to earn grades high enough to get admitted anywhere. She didn't figure Les was planning on sending tuition checks from Costa Rica. And insurance, and . . .

The elevator dinged open in front of her, and she forced herself to plan a strategy—or was it a tactic?—for delivering the summons. The paralegal had assured her it would be easy. She'd handed Gigi the address and told her the woman, Connie Padgett, should be home after she'd dropped off her kids at Mountain View Elementary and Challenger Middle School until time to pick them up again in midafternoon.

"This should be a piece of cake," the paralegal said, striking superstitious fear into Gigi's heart.

Hiking her skirt to clamber into the Hummer, Gigi headed toward the Pine Creek subdivision on the north side of town. Twenty-five minutes later she pulled up across the street from a large house with a stone front and huge picture windows and contemplated her next move. Finding no reason why she shouldn't just ring the doorbell and hand over the summons to whoever answered, she crossed the street, devoid of traffic at midday.

The doorbell played a snippet of something classical Gigi didn't recognize. After a moment, the tap-tap of heels on tile told her someone was approaching. Shifting nervously from foot to foot, she bit her lip as the door swung open.

"Yes?" A woman a few years younger, but with similarly expensive hair and an immaculate manicure, dressed in a Betsey Johnson dress no one over twenty-five should have attempted, stood in the doorway, an enquiring look on her face. Before Gigi could open her mouth, the woman said, "Look, my kids are selling those Gold C books, too. Sorry."

"But I don't have—"

"And we've got a pantry full of Girl Scout cookies, so I'm afraid—"

"I'm not selling anything," Gigi cut in, flustered. "I've got paperwork to serve you from—"

"That bastard," the woman said, tears welling in her brown eyes. "He really filed? He's throwing away eighteen years of marriage to set up house with Reed's orthodontist? I can't believe it!"

"I really don't know the nature . . ." Hampered by the cast, Gigi fumbled in her purse for the envelope, reluctant to look the poor woman in the face.

As Gigi dragged the packet free, Connie Padgett suddenly whirled and sprinted into the depths of the house, yelling, "I won't take it. You can't make me."

Without thinking, Gigi plunged into the house after her, following the clicking of the woman's heels. A door slammed, and Gigi skidded around a corner into the kitchen in time to see Connie Padgett taking the stairs down from her deck two at a time and racing across the backyard. Gigi followed, grateful she was wearing her low-heeled Joan and David pumps and not the Stella McCartney vegan sandals she'd considered when dressing that morning. Clutching the rail, she made it down the deck stairs and started across the yard, lifting her royal blue skirt to midthigh as she hurdled down the shallow terraces to the open gate in the back fence. She paused for breath at the opening, her head swiveling from side to side.

The smooth green expanses of the Pine Creek golf course lay before her, dotted with golfers and carts. A commotion from the left caught her attention, and she started in that direction, pretty sure Connie must have run afoul of the four-some in the middle of the nearest fairway. An octogenarian golfer was shaking his 9-iron in the direction of a figure disappearing from view over a hill. Gigi trotted after her target, her breath coming in gasps. She really needed to get back to her cardio step classes; yoga was just not keeping her fit enough. Coming level with the irritated golfer, now lining up his shot, Gigi got an idea.

She paused respectfully to let him hit the ball—Les just about took her head off when she made a noise during his backswing—and then darted toward the empty golf cart. "So sorry," she said, climbing in and depressing the pedal. "It's an emergency." Before the startled golfers could react, she sped across the fairway, the two sets of clubs in the back of the cart threatening to fall out with every jounce. Cresting the hill, she saw Connie running pell-mell down the middle of the fairway, now carrying her shoes in her hands.

Gigi pointed the cart downhill and floored the pedal. The breeze generated by the cart's movement tossed her hair, and she felt herself flush with the thrill of the chase. Or maybe it was another hot flash. As she gained on the fleeing woman, exhilaration coursed through her. She felt like an olden-times posse chasing an outlaw, or a U.S. Marshal pursuing a fugitive— like the character Jennifer Lopez played in the movie where she got to make out with George Clooney. Gigi wondered if J-Lo had done the movie for free, just for the opportunity to kiss Clooney. She would. Not that anyone would hire her as an actress. J-Lo's bum was trim compared to hers, and just look how much grief the media gave her about it. *Out of Sight,* that was the movie.

Gigi's quarry looked over her shoulder and cut toward a pond. Was she going to swim to freedom?

"Connie, stop," Gigi called.

In response, something thudded onto the roof of the cart, and Gigi ducked. What was— A second shoe came flying at Gigi, landing in her lap. A blue python Jimmy Choo. The woman was really desperate.

"It's not worth this, Connie," she said, almost abreast of her, the pond to their left. Geese honked at them, and tur-quoise dragonflies skimmed the surface of the water. A ball plopped into the murky depths, and an irritated "Shit!" came from the parallel fairway. Connie held up her middle finger and jogged on, but she was losing steam. Gigi kept pace with her until she slowed to a walk. Climbing out of the cart, Gigi descended the incline sloping toward the pond and put her good arm around the now crying woman.

"It'll be okay, sugar," she said. "My husband did the exact same thing to me, and I survived it."

"He did?" Connie looked up, black streaks on each cheek where mascaraed lashes had bled.

Gigi nodded. "Only he went to Costa Rica with his personal trainer, not an orthodontist. Left me with nothing but the kids, the house, and his Hummer."

"That bastard," Connie whispered, struggling to her feet.

"They're all bastards—"

Connie's startled scream cut her off. Gigi turned to look in the direction of Connie's stabbing finger. The golf cart, previously parked at the top of a slight rise, was trundling toward them, gaining speed as it came. The two women leapt aside as the cart hurtled past, spewing clubs from the bags strapped in the back, and drowned itself in the lake.

Gigi lay on her stomach, heart thudding and arm aching, stunned by her narrow escape from the runaway cart.

"Goose shit!" Connie wailed.

That struck Gigi as a strange expletive until she pushed herself up and surveyed the splotches on her St. John top and skirt. It was too gross, as Kendall would say. Her suit was ruined, her arm hurt, she'd failed in her attempt to deliver the summons, and she'd probably be sued by the golf course for borrowing the cart and letting it commit suicide in the water hazard. Gigi felt like following its example but bit back her tears, used her good hand to haul Connie to her feet, and began the long walk back to the clubhouse under the amused or appalled gazes of assorted golfers, homeowners, and triumphant geese.

⁓⁓⁓

I was mounting the stairs to the courthouse, a rosy brick building with a clock tower surmounted by a cupola, before I realized I had no idea what Russell Ziegler looked like. I asked a guy in a lawyerly three-piece suit if he knew him and got "The dude ain't representin' me" in return. Oops. Who knew it was so hard to tell the lawyers from the criminals?

I got luckier the second time around, asking one of the uniformed security guards about Ziegler. "Medium height, buzz-cut hair, glasses," she said. "Try Courtroom Four."

I thanked her and slid into the courtroom, scanning the crowd. Apparently the judge had just declared a late lunch recess, because the few people in the room were straggling toward the door. I returned to the hall and snagged a man fitting the guard's description. "Russell Ziegler?"

"Yes?" He squinted at me as if trying to place me. Wearing a stylish four-button suit with a yellow shirt and tasteful tie, he was younger than I'd expected, in his midthirties.

I handed him a card. "I'm Charlotte Swift. I spoke with Jacqueline Falstow yesterday, and she told me you arranged their private adoption with Elizabeth Sprouse?"

"Yes?" A guarded look came into his eyes.

"I've been hired to locate the baby's father. Do you have a few minutes?"

He made a show of looking at his watch. "A couple. We only have a half hour break. Judge Garmin thinks we'll conclude our cases faster if we're hungry. This way."

I followed him down the hall, noting he had a slight limp. He paused in a room with vending machines and bought a Payday and a Mountain Dew. Lunch in hand, he led me out of the courthouse and took off at a brisk pace down the sidewalk, not slowed by the limp. "A walk clears my head," he said, taking a bite of his candy bar.

Downtown's tall buildings buffered us from the wind, and

the sun was comfortably warm; I wasn't averse to a walk after all my time driving. I let Ziegler chew and swallow, then asked, "Can you tell me how you met Elizabeth Sprouse, paired her up with the Falstows?"

From the way he screwed up his face, I knew what was coming. "No can do. Privilege, you know."

"What could be privileged about how you hooked up with Elizabeth? Never mind," I said, waving the question away before he could turn on his heel. "Can you at least tell me when you met her?"

He considered the question, then said, "January. I can talk about her, but not the Falstows. They're my clients."

"Did Elizabeth have her own lawyer?"

"Not that I know of."

"So she had no one looking out for her interests?"

He shrugged. "I don't know that she needed anyone—she seemed like a really sharp cookie."

Right. The sixteen-year-old didn't need advice entering into a legal contract. I bit my tongue.

"Lots of the teenagers come to see me with their folks, their moms, at least. A few come with the baby's father. Not her. It didn't seem to bother her to be alone, and she was really savvy." He glugged half his soda.

"How so?"

"She'd obviously done some reading about private adoptions."

"Did she tell you she was adopted?"

He turned his head to look at me. Light glanced off the lenses of his glasses. "Was she? No."

We jaywalked across Tejon Street to get to Acacia Park.

Mature trees cast pools of shade over the walkways, and a loud crowd of kids gathered around the Uncle Wilber fountain, where the tuba-playing figure of Uncle Wilber emerges on the half hour to play his tune. Faint oompahs drifted our way as we stepped aside to give joggers the right-of-way.

"What did she tell you about the pregnancy?"

"Virtually nothing. She saw a doctor, of course, one I recommended, to make sure she and the baby were healthy. Then, after I matched her with Jacquie and Stefan, I was pretty much out of the picture."

I wasn't sure I bought his noninvolvement, but I couldn't see how it mattered. "How pregnant was she when she came to you?"

"Completely," he said with a small smile.

I rolled my eyes. "How far along?"

"Six weeks."

I counted back to late November or early December. "Did she say who the father was?"

"Sorry." Ziegler shrugged and shot his empty soda can into a trash barrel. "Two points!"

"Don't you ask for that information? Don't the adoptive parents want to know the baby's health history?"

"Sure. But what can I do? If the girl doesn't want to tell, I'm not getting out a rubber hose to beat it out of her. You've got to understand . . . this is a hard time for these girls, Ms. Swift." He stopped and faced me, his eyes serious behind the thick lenses. "They're scared. Sometimes of their parents, sometimes of actually giving birth. Some of them are scared they'll be pariahs at school or with their friends. Some are worried that having a baby will tube their chances to go to college or have a career. I don't add to their pressure. When I represent a teen mother trying to find a home for her baby, it's my job to make things easier for her, match her up with a loving family she can feel comfortable giving the baby to, help her out logistically, if necessary."

It sounded like a rehearsed spiel, as if he were hawking vinyl siding or time-share condos. "Did Elizabeth need 'logistical' help?"

"Like I said, she wasn't my client, but I don't think so. She was still living at home, she said."

I wondered exactly when Elizabeth had run away from home and moved into the grotty apartment. The timeline probably didn't matter.

I tried one last time as Ziegler picked up his pace and headed back across the street to the courthouse. Savory smells from a sidewalk hot dog vendor followed us and made my stomach rumble. "Did she say anything at all that might help me find the father? Refer to a boyfriend? Anything?"

Dodging a panhandler without making eye contact, Ziegler said, "Well, I'm not sure why, but I got the feeling she was extra nervous about discussing the guy. She completely clammed up whenever I brought the subject up and got this look in her eye. Not the gooey 'I'm so in love with him' look some of the girls get. A wary look. Maybe the guy was married, or prominent in some way, like a TV personality or athlete. One seventeen-year-old I helped was pregnant by the father of the kids she babysat. His wife brought the girl to see me." He gave a mock shiver at the memory.

"Could Elizabeth have been raped or sexually abused?" I asked, lowering my voice as a chattering herd of twenty-something women swarmed around us.

"Always possible," he said. "That would certainly explain why she didn't want to talk about it." The sun winked on his glasses, and I couldn't read his expression. He handed me his card. "Call me if you know any pregnant women who might want to go the adoption route."

I put a hand on his arm as he started to turn away. "Could Stefan Falstow have been the father?" I don't know where the question came from. Maybe the surrogate idea had jarred it loose, or maybe it was the way Ziegler avoided talking about how he met Elizabeth.

His eyes went blank-TV-screen dead. "I'd advise you not to repeat that as a question or an accusation, Ms. Swift, unless you're looking for a slander action." He jerked his arm away from my hand and limped into the courthouse.

Hm. A sensitive spot, maybe. Moving thoughtfully back to my car, I checked the messages on my cell phone. Two calls I'd return later and then one from Gigi. I listened with growing incredulity to her babbling about stealing a car—was that possible?—and then about a drowning. Since I hadn't gotten any calls from the police, I decided Gigi must not be under arrest, and clearly she wasn't the one who'd drowned, so she was just going to have to cope on her own. I didn't have time to fix whatever new catastrophe she'd orchestrated before meeting Linnea. I called Gigi's number, hoping to encourage her to work things out, but she didn't answer. I left an upbeat message, affirming my faith in her ability to get the situation straightened out, and told her I'd meet her back at the office after interviewing Linnea.

—*mm*—

I didn't immediately spot Linnea when I arrived at the Liberty High School stadium. Built primarily for the hordes of football fans who descended on Thursday, Friday, and Saturday evenings in the fall, it had seating for several thousand and a track that circled the football field. I wished I'd brought a jacket as anvil-shaped thunderheads piled up and the wind, which had been blowing all day, ushered in a new chill to nip at my bare arms. People say that if you don't like the weather here, just wait ten minutes, and today looked like it was proving them right.

No one challenged me as I walked onto the track. It didn't look like the girls were busting their butts in the coach's absence. A few of them jogged at a warm-up pace while others stood in small groups talking. A figure separated herself from one of the groups and came toward me. Linnea's outré hair and makeup looked incongruous in the red tracksuit, but her long, slim legs promised speed.

"Let's sit on the bleachers," she greeted me, heading for a concrete ramp.

We settled onto the front row bleacher. The metal was still warm from soaking up the earlier sun, and I pressed my palms against it. Linnea watched as one of her teammates ran. "She's a pronator," she observed. "See how her feet slant in?"

She could be a Terminator or an alligator, for all I cared. I touched Linnea's arm lightly to recall her attention. "Linnea, you said that Elizabeth told you she had been hired as a surrogate parent, but the couple adopting her baby said she was already pregnant when they met her."

"Really?" Linnea didn't look too surprised. "Elizabeth always was something of a drama queen. I guess choosing to become a surrogate sounded better to her than admitting she got careless. You'd think with how easily you can get condoms from drugstores or in restroom vending machines, that everyone would use them. But no."

Linnea's voice had a bite, and I could see why Elizabeth might not have fessed up to an unplanned pregnancy.

"Give me a name, Linnea."

"A name?"

"Since we know Elizabeth's pregnancy wasn't the result of a surrogacy in vitro procedure, who's your top candidate for the baby's father? What's the first name that comes to mind?"

"Wes Emmerling," she said finally. "They hooked up a couple of times. He spread rumors about doing her. Maybe he really did."

Sounded like a great guy. "He's a student?"

She shook her head. "Not anymore. He graduated in June. I think he works for his dad's landscaping company. Unless he's already left—he got a scholarship to some school in Virginia, UVA or William and Mary or somewhere."

My pulse quickened. Virginia. That's where Elizabeth told Ian she wanted to move. "Do you know the name of his dad's company?"

"Sorry."

"No problem." I could find it easily enough. "After you helped deliver Olivia, what did Elizabeth do?"

"Well, that's the thing. She called those people—the couple

she was doing the surrogacy for—oh, I guess it wasn't a surrogacy but just an adoption, and told them she'd changed her mind."

Whoa. "You overheard this conversation?" That certainly didn't jive with what Jacqueline Falstow had told me about Elizabeth calling to arrange delivery of the infant.

"Oh, yeah. She said she wanted to keep Olivia. I was in the kitchen, and I could hear them yelling through the phone."

"Him or her?"

"I couldn't tell. Maybe both. Elizabeth was panicky when she hung up, worried they'd take Olivia. She wanted me to hide her at my house, but my folks would've had a cow. I told her she should go to the police."

"Did she?" I knew the answer to that one.

"I don't think so. Before I left, she looked calmer, said she had a better plan, thanked me for everything and gave me a hug. That was the last time I talked to her. I called her every day, left messages on her cell, but she never called back." A bleak, lost note sounded in her voice, and she turned her gaze back to the infield. I thought she was blinking back tears.

"I'm really sorry for your loss," I told her. I wanted to hug her, but she didn't strike me as the touchy-feely sort. "It's hard to lose a friend, especially when you've been through something like that." I paused for a beat, then said, "This is really important. Who would Olivia have asked for help, besides you?"

Linnea brought her thumb to her mouth and gnawed on a cuticle. The black nail polish had chipped, leaving a Dalmatian dog effect on her nails. "I should have helped her," she said.

"You did help her. You did more than many adults could or would do for their friends."

My conviction glanced off her like an arrow off armor. "Yeah, right. Maybe she called her birth mother?" she offered after a moment's thought. "You said she found her. Or maybe Mr. Van Hoose."

"What?" A fat drop of rain plopped onto my cheek, and I looked up. The clouds were swollen to breaking point, pregnant with rain and hail. Lightning zigzagged across the sky in a burst of eerie blue-white, and the girls on the field stampeded for cover.

"He's the counselor," Linnea yelled over the rumble of thunder. "Beth spent a lot of time with him last fall, thought he was the bomb."

Could Jack— I didn't want to go there. "C'mon, we've got to get inside," I said, nudging Linnea off the bench. Metal bleachers were not where I wanted to be in an electrical storm.

Rain began falling in earnest as we scurried down the ramp, but Linnea stopped me short of the tunnel that led to the locker rooms. We huddled under a shallow overhang. "Do you think the Falstows killed her because she wouldn't give them Olivia?" she asked, her green eyes troubled. She looked young and confused and wet, no longer the doctor wannabe capable of coping with a medical emergency. "If I'd told someone . . ."

"It's not your fault," I said. "No way. You should call the police, though, and tell them what you know. It might help with their investigation."

Her face registered "unconvinced," and a second later she was dashing away from me, legs pumping hard. She spun into the center of the field, lifting her arms as the rain sluiced down, washing over her.

13

~~~

"Please tell me you didn't really steal a car and drown some-one," I said to Gigi as I walked into the office half an hour later, drenched to the bone. I immediately kicked off my pumps and stripped away my sodden knee-high stockings; barefoot was better than squelching. I wanted a snifter of cognac but made do with a Pepsi.

Gigi looked, if anything, worse than I did. Grass and some squishy greenish substance speckled her expensive knit suit, and her coiffure looked like someone had been at it with a hay baler. Her eyes, though, sparkled in a new way, and she rolled her chair over to my desk as I plunked into my chair, inhaling Pepsi.

"It was a golf *cart,*" she said, hitting the *t* hard, "and I didn't really steal it—just borrowed it."

She launched into a tangled report of serving Connie Padgett with her summons, and I became lost in the tale of the golf cart chase, enraged golfers, and malevolent geese. It seemed, though, that Gigi had managed to serve Padgett in the end.

"So after I talked the golf course manager out of suing us over the cart," Gigi finished her story, "I took Connie home and made her a cup of tea, and we talked—and before I left I gave her the summons and the name of the best divorce lawyer in town!" She flourished her pink cast in the air triumphantly.

"Yours?"

"Les's."

"Good work, Gigi," I said. I felt a twinge of guilt over what Gigi had gone through and suggested, "Why don't you take the rest of the day off? And get your suit dry-cleaned at the agency's expense. We can write it off." I sniffed. "What have you got all over it, anyway?"

"Goose poop," Gigi said, her enthusiasm fading somewhat as she surveyed herself.

We both wrinkled our noses, and Gigi gave me a tentative grin. Before I knew it, we were laughing.

"Go home," I said. "I've found it pays to keep a change of clothes in my car. If you're going to stay in this business, you might want to think about having a gym bag with extra clothes here, too."

"Good idea," Gigi said. "I'll put one together tonight."

I was pretty sure the bag—probably Louis Vuitton—would weigh fifty pounds by the time she chucked in some designer shoes, a five-hundred-dollar sweatsuit, enough makeup to last the Rockettes a year, and moisturizing lotion made from rare sea snails and the petals of an exotic flower only found in the Andes (or something equally expensive). Still, she was trying; I had to give her that. I didn't want to burst her bubble by telling her Padgett was effectually served when she opened the door. Maybe tomorrow I'd let her know she could've just said "You're served" and dropped the papers in the foyer.

As Gigi walked out, I flipped a quarter to determine whether my next call should be to Montgomery or Jack Van Hoose. Heads—Montgomery, tails—Van Hoose. It came up tails. I called Montgomery.

"We got a complaint about you today, Swift," he said when he heard my voice.

Seth Johnson moved quickly. "Look, Johnson's a—"

"You must have pissed off a lot of people. It wasn't someone named Johnson. It was Zachary Sprouse. He said you assaulted him. He wants a restraining order."

That dickhead. My ears itched ferociously. "*I* assaulted *him*? Did he tell you he was trespassing on my property? Did he tell you—"

"Calm down, Charlie," Montgomery cut off my sputtering. I could tell he found the situation humorous. "I talked him out of filing charges."

"Big of you," I said grudgingly. This was what I got for giving into a compassionate impulse. "I owe you a beer."

"You owe me dinner. Your place. Six o'clock."

"Nice try. Margarita at Pine Creek." I named the restaurant a stone's throw from my house. "Six thirty. I need to change. And we're doing the bar menu on the patio." The restaurant also offered a five-course meal inside its quirky, multiroomed dining area for a set price, and I didn't want Montgomery thinking he'd done me that big a favor.

"Done."

He hung up. It was already almost five thirty. My conversation with Jack Van Hoose would have to wait until tomorrow.

Feeling equal parts relief and guilt about not confronting him today, I locked up and headed home for a hot shower and a dress designed to make Montgomery regret that I was completely unobtainable.

———

"So, this Fenn girl says she heard Sprouse tell the Falstows she was keeping the baby?" Montgomery asked. "Damn, this is good." He spooned the last bit of lime panna cotta from the dish.

I leaned back in my chair, enjoying the twinkling lights strung in the trees over the patio, the cool night air against my shoulders bared by a halter-top sundress, the quiet conversations of other diners, and the crisp sauvingon blanc I'd ordered with my ahi tuna. The sight of Montgomery across the table, his dark eyes sweeping over me appreciatively, added to my enjoyment. "Yep. Sounds like a darn good motive, to me."

"Killing her didn't get them the baby," Montgomery pointed out.

"Well, you said her death could've been an accident. Maybe they didn't mean to kill her. Maybe they didn't know she'd already stashed the baby with Melissa Lloyd."

"Or maybe they had nothing to do with it."

I shook my head, feeling my hair swish against my neck. "You didn't see how obsessed this woman was with getting hold of Olivia. She even followed me, hoping I'd lead her to the baby."

"Which you almost did." Montgomery's grin gleamed white in the gathering darkness. He'd liked that part of my story. He stretched his long legs to the side of the table and crossed them at the ankles.

"Elizabeth had a pseudo-boyfriend, too, at least at one time. A high schooler named Wes Emmerling. I'm talking to him tomorrow. He's a possible. And Seth Johnson . . . there's something weird about him," I said. I swirled the wine in my glass, took a sip. "He stopped short of actually threatening me, but I could see him terrorizing Elizabeth."

"Why?"

"I don't know. But Linnea said Elizabeth told her he almost raped her in a classroom at the church."

"Hearsay."

"I'm not suggesting you throw him in jail, damn it, just that he's worth talking to. He keeps trading in his wives for younger models, and one of them died in a hiking 'accident' where he was the only witness." I'd looked up newspaper accounts of the death on my home computer. "Also, he called me a third-rate investigator."

"Ah-hah. Now I know why you want me to roust him. Not going to happen. He may be everything you've said, but he's also the governor's buddy, and we have no evidence whatsoever that he committed any crime or that he even had any contact with the Sprouse girl after she left home."

"Contact . . . what do her phone records tell you?"

"Her cell phone—if she had one it must have been one of those pay-as-you-go deals—is missing, and the only calls on her landline are to the punk managing her apartment complex—"

"She probably wanted him to do something about the rodent infestation."

"—and Melissa Lloyd's numbers, and since she worked for Lloyd, there's nothing to follow up on there. The most recent call was the Friday before she had the baby."

"Okay, then who do you like for it?" I challenged him. The server unobtrusively removed our dishes and left the check at Montgomery's elbow. Sexist. I slid it over and put my credit card on it.

"I'm leaning toward the stepfather," he said. "I think the girl went to her mother after the baby was born, looking for help, and her dad lost it. But, unless the mother cracks, we're not likely to put him away for it. And, frankly, I've got other cases that are higher priority than what may just be illegal dumping of a body. My team'll be burning the midnight oil on the body that turned up in the trunk of that car on Constitution. We haven't even ID'd the vic yet."

"You'd better get back to work, then," I said, rising.

"Everyone's got to eat." He stood, too, draping his arm casually across my shoulders as we walked to the exit. His warmth and closeness made me stumble on the uneven flagstones of the patio. He'd shed his sport coat, draping it over his arm, so there was nothing between me and his skin but the fine cotton of his shirt. The realization made every inch of me supersensitive, and I tried to squirm out from under his arm. His grip tightened.

"I'll drive you home," he said, his breath warm against my ear.

"That's okay. I walked," I said, fighting to keep my voice level. "And you've got to get back to work."

"It's only eight thirty. Midnight oil-burning doesn't start for almost four hours." From the way he smiled, I knew he knew the effect his closeness was having on me. Damn the man. I did not want to ruin an extremely useful professional relationship, or get emotionally entangled with a man five years younger (who reminded me way too much of my ex-husband), to satisfy a temporary physical urge. Summoning all my resolve, I pulled away.

"Really, it's a short walk."

"A gentleman always escorts—" His cell phone rang, and he looked at the number before cursing and answering it. "Montgomery."

He listened for a moment, his body language segueing from seductive to alert. "Fifteen minutes." He snapped the phone closed and gave me a rueful look.

"Duty calls?"

"Exactly. Otherwise . . ." He leaned over and pressed a hard kiss against my lips before I could back away. "Dinner's on me next time."

"What makes you think there'll be a next time?" I called after him as he strode to his car. My voice lacked conviction, and he just laughed, lifting a hand in farewell as he put his car in gear.

I set out to walk the two blocks home, heading north on Pine Creek Road past the large carrot sculptures at the entrance to Margarita. By the time I made the turn onto Tudor Road, the clanking and conversation from the restaurant had faded, and I listened to the whisper of the wind in the grass and the scurryings of night creatures in the underbrush. Passing St. Paul's, I noticed a dark form moving on the far side of the parking lot. A metallic clang sounded loud in the stillness, and I jumped. Was someone breaking into the church? A car approached from behind me, and its headlights swept the parking lot, illuminating the ursine figure snuffling at the Dumpster. My bear! I paused, something about seeing the huge predator in this semiurban environment catching at me. Another car passed, and the bear turned his head toward me, eyes gleaming red, long muzzle working the air as he sniffed. I kept walking, hoping he was too engrossed in the treasures to be found in the trash to follow. The rectory was dark as I passed, and I wondered if Dan was out on another date. Not wanting to analyze my annoyance at the thought, I marched up the steps to my porch and unlocked the door. Safe inside, I might have shut the door more firmly than necessary, but there was only the bear to hear.

(Wednesday)

Melissa Lloyd hovered outside my office when I drove up the next morning. Dressed for work in a peach skirt and coordinating blouse, she was babyless this time and shifted from foot to foot as I got out of my car. I scanned the parking lot but didn't see Gigi's Hummer. Maybe she'd slept in.

"Good morning," I greeted Melissa.

"Hi. Look, Ian said you stopped by. Then the cops came. Olivia's on antibiotics for an ear infection, I've got a huge design order pending, and I'm at my wit's end."

One look at her had told me that. Her skirt hung from her hipbones as if she'd lost weight, and her skin had a sallow cast that spoke of too many sleepless nights and not enough exercise. Or maybe peach just wasn't her color.

"Are you any closer to finding her father? Ian says I should just give her to Child Protective Services, but I can't bring myself to do that because . . ."

"You haven't told him about your relationship with the baby?" I unlocked the door and actually missed the smell of the coffee Gigi usually had perking by now. I offered my client a Pepsi and helped myself to one when she refused.

She wandered to the window and looked out into the parking lot. "I just can't. When he came home unexpectedly because he thought I sounded stressed—so sweet of him!—I was going to, but then Olivia got sick, and he's so fed up with the time I spend with her that I just . . . I *did* tell him the baby was Lizzy's and that since Lizzy had died unexpectedly I felt responsible for her."

I handed her a note with Patricia Sprouse's and Jacqueline Falstow's phone numbers. "Both these women would kill"—unfortunate turn of phrase—"to get hold of that baby. If you can't cope with her, give one of them a call. Or do like your husband suggested and turn her over to the authorities. I'll keep looking for the father, and the legal outcome will likely be the same no matter whose custody the baby is in."

"Maybe I'll do that," she said, turning to accept the slip of paper. She massaged her temple with two fingers wearily. "Caring for a baby is so hard," she said. "I don't know how single parents do it, especially teen mothers. This—having Olivia—confirms for me that I made the right decision in giving Lizzy up. It's been good that way." She nodded decisively, but her eyes slid to the window again, and her fingers plucked at the fabric of her skirt.

I wondered if she continued caring for Olivia as a kind of

punishment for the guilt she still felt about giving up Elizabeth. I'm no psychologist, but she seemed to wear the burden of the baby like a hair shirt, accepting the itch of sleepless nights and the irritation of having no time for herself and her husband as a retribution she deserved. It seemed kind of hard on Ian since he had to share in the punishment without understanding why.

As if she'd heard my thoughts, Melissa said, "Ian's headed back to Arizona today—he's got to get back to his customer. He said the baby has to be out of the house by the time he gets back for good."

"When—"

"This weekend."

I couldn't tell if the look she sent me was a plea or an ultimatum. I told her the case was my top priority and saw her to the door just as Gigi descended from her Hummer, wearing a floral wrap dress that displayed a lot of pillowy bosom and matched her cast.

"Good morning," she trilled.

I introduced her and Melissa, and Gigi's eyes filled with sympathetic tears. "I am so sorry for your loss," she consoled Melissa with a pat on her hand. "Your daughter's passing—"

Melissa jerked her hand back. "I don't have a— She wasn't my— Please."

She directed the last word at me, and I knew it was a plea to find the baby's father quickly. I watched her rigid back as she returned to her car, ignored Gigi's "I didn't mean to upset her," and dialed Jack Van Hoose's number. He was booked up all day but agreed to meet me at Albertine's for a drink after work. I held out small hope that a beer would help my questions go down any easier. When I hedged about telling him what I wanted to talk about, his rich voice carried a grin through the phone line as he said, "Just couldn't wait until Friday to see me, huh?"

"Something like that," I replied and hung up. I so hoped he wasn't the father of Elizabeth's baby and that my questioning him about it wouldn't doom our fledgling relationship from the start.

I needed to track down the Emmerling kid. It made more sense to think of Elizabeth getting it on with a fellow student than with the counselor, right? Flipping open the Yellow Pages, I zeroed in on Landscapers, quickly locating Emmerling Landscape Installation and Maintenance. A phone call netted me the address of the house where Wes was installing a sprinkler system. No time like the present. Telling Gigi I'd be back in an hour or so, I headed east on Woodmen, out past Powers, aiming for the Meridian area, where Wes was supposed to be working. I couldn't believe how many buildings had sprung up since I last drove out this way. What used to be pronghorn terrain was now a mélange of housing and shopping areas. I shook my head as I drove, lamenting the loss of the open prairie. My mind turned to work, however, when I rounded a corner and saw a pickup truck with EMMERLING stenciled in green on the doors and an open trailer filled with yard equipment hitched to the rear. Several men were digging trenches and unloading sod in front of a nondescript two-story house.

"Wes Emmerling?" I asked the first person I came to after exiting my car, a barrel-chested Hispanic man with a thick mustache.

" 'Round back." Without a hint of curiosity, he returned to digging a hole for the young spruce sprawled on the sidewalk, its roots bound in a ball.

I hadn't realized I had a preconceived notion of what Wes Emmerling would be like until I pushed through the gate and saw him laying PVC pipe in the trenches crisscrossing the backyard. Based on Linnea's comments and his job as a landscaper, I'd imagined he'd be bare-chested, rippling with muscles, bronzed by the sun. I saw him with a strut and the cocky attitude that kissed and told. As he turned to face me, brushing mud off his hands, I saw a slender kid of medium height, not quite filled out yet, with soft brown hair that fell into his eyes. He wore an emerald Emmerling Landscape T-shirt and jeans, both crusted with dirt and grass.

"We'll be another couple of hours, Mrs. Denton," he said with a shy smile, "but it's going great."

"Huh?" I looked behind me. No one.

His brows drew together in confusion. "Don't you live here?" He nodded toward the house. "Aren't you Mrs. Denton?"

"No. I'm a private investigator, Charlotte Swift. Call me Charlie." I passed him one of my cards. "I'd like to talk to you if you're Wes Emmerling."

"That's me." He shook my hand, his grip firm, a puzzled look on his face. "Why—"

"It's about Elizabeth Sprouse."

To his credit, his eyes didn't drop from mine. He heaved a sigh that seemed combined of resignation and sadness. "What about her? She died."

"Look, is there someplace more comfortable we could talk? I'd be happy to buy you a coffee or a soda."

He looked around the empty backyard, at the rutted earth and the pile of sprinkler piping and heads. "I don't know. I've got a lot of work . . ."

"Twenty minutes," I promised. "We'll zip up to that Mickey D's on the corner."

"All right." He tramped to a hose coiled near the deck and rinsed off his hands and boots before following me out of the yard. "I'll be back in twenty, Manny," he told the man out front.

He was silent as he climbed into my Subaru, and I didn't try to get him to open up until we were seated at a sticky table at the McDonald's with our sodas.

"So, tell me about Elizabeth," I suggested.

"She was okay." He pleated the paper casing from his straw.

"Okay? I heard you guys were pretty close." That wasn't exactly what Linnea had said, but it sounded less confrontational than "I heard you screwed her a couple times."

"I was sad to hear she'd died," he offered, swiping his bangs out of his eyes. They were a warm brown, and I could see how a troubled girl like Elizabeth might find his sensitivity appealing. "I wanted to go to her funeral, but . . . My dad's pretty strict, and he didn't know . . . I had to work."

Wes looked defensive, but an underlying sadness made me like him. He pulled the straw from his soda and began to bend it into a triangle.

"You were really into her, weren't you?" I asked gently.

"She was smart and beautiful," he said.

I liked that he put "smart" first.

"But she . . . she had issues, I guess you'd say."

"Like?"

"Like she was really hung up on finding her birth mom, but in a weird sort of way."

"How so?"

He shrugged, seeming more like fifteen than eighteen. "I dunno. It was like she was mad at her or something. But she'd never met her, so that doesn't make sense, does it? And she hated her stepdad."

"Did he abuse her?" My pulse quickened, but I kept my voice even.

"She didn't say so, not in so many words. But I wondered. After we . . ."

Sensing his embarrassment, I stepped in. "Had sex?"

He nodded. "Yeah. She talked about him. Said he played mind games with everyone, said he'd brainwashed her mother—Mrs. Sprouse, you know—so she wasn't even the same person. It made me sad to listen to her."

"Did you use protection?"

He caught my meaning immediately and blushed under his tan. "She was on the pill."

Hmm. I was tempted to give him the "condoms are your friends" lecture, but decided it wasn't my place. "Did you know she was pregnant when she ran away? That she had a baby?"

"Really? No, I . . ." His eyes widened, and I saw all the possibilities flash through his mind. "Was it—"

"Yours? You tell me."

"We only did it three times. She was on the pill," he reiterated. "She said."

"You could take a DNA test," I suggested. "That would—"

"My dad!" He blanched.

Clearly Papa Emmerling was a forceful figure. I wondered what he knew about his son's dallyings with Elizabeth.

"Are you eighteen?"

"Next month," he said. "The twelfth."

"Then your dad wouldn't have to know. Think about it."

"I'm leaving for college next week. In Virginia. I got a scholarship to UVA." A trace of pride sounded in his voice. As if suddenly becoming aware of the straw he was mangling, he dropped it on the table.

"They have labs in Virginia," I pointed out drily. "Think about it."

"I will," he promised. He hesitated, and I saw his throat work. "Miss Smith—"

"Charlie."

"Is it a boy or a girl?"

"A girl. Olivia."

He bit down on his lower lip. "I don't know what my dad would—"

"Did your dad—your folks—ever meet Elizabeth?" I asked when he didn't continue.

"Once." His tone said the meeting was not a success.

I didn't press it. "Did you hear from Elizabeth after she left school? When was the last time you saw her?"

"February. But we didn't date after November. She broke up with me around Thanksgiving, and I only saw her around school after that."

"Did she say why?"

"Not really. She didn't have time, she said. She'd gotten a part-time job. It took up a lot of her time, she said. Look, I gotta get back to work." Wes pushed back from the table.

"Did you get the feeling she was seeing someone else?" I persisted.

"Maybe. Probably. Elizabeth was the kind of girl who needed to always be with a guy. I think it was her way of proving she was pretty and . . ."

"Lovable?" How sad.

"Yeah. She even flirted with—" He pressed his lips closed and headed for the door, chucking his empty cup into the trash with unnecessary force.

Why did I get the feeling he was going to say "my dad"?

After dropping a subdued Wes back at work, I drove to the office, thinking about what he'd said. I knew women like Elizabeth, women who got their sense of self-worth from attracting men. Each new conquest bolstered their self-esteem, made them feel worthwhile or likable. The feeling never lasted, though, and they'd move on to another man, needing to prove and re-prove their desirability. I didn't get it, but I'd noticed those women frequently had strained relationships with their fathers. Elizabeth certainly qualified on that front, with her birth father unknown, her adopted father dead, and her stepfather screwier than a hardware convention. From my point of view, it made finding Olivia's father that much more difficult since Elizabeth might have had a series of casual partners.

I parked myself at my desk when I got back to the office

and popped a Pepsi. Fresh out of brilliant ideas, I pulled a legal pad out of a drawer and made a list of possible candidates for Olivia's father, roughly in order of likelihood:

Wes Emmerling
Zachary Sprouse
Seth Johnson
Jack Van Hoose
Stefan Falstow
Unknown boyfriend/rapist/other

I surveyed the list with dissatisfaction. Wes had admitted actually having sex with Elizabeth, so he had to get top billing. Sprouse seemed the next likeliest candidate, based on proximity and access, if nothing else. Johnson also seemed possible; he'd known Elizabeth for some years, apparently had a thing for young girls, and had (maybe) tried to seduce her in a classroom. Jack Van Hoose seemed unlikely, but I couldn't discount him. Linnea seemed to think Elizabeth had feelings for him; maybe he'd been flattered by her attention and one thing led to another. Stefan Falstow was a ludicrously long shot. I'd started thinking Falstow was the father when Linnea told me the surrogate story, and even the news that Elizabeth had been pregnant when she met the Falstows didn't completely knock the idea out of my head. Maybe she and Falstow had some sort of prior relationship. I realized I didn't know anything about the man and had no idea whether or not his path might have crossed Elizabeth's. I starred his name.

I stared unhappily at the last line. If I couldn't jolt one of the named men on the list into admitting his paternity, I was left with Mr. Other, and I didn't know where to begin to look for him. I supposed I could ask around the high school, see if Elizabeth had confided in anyone besides Linnea, but it seemed unlikely, especially since she'd run away almost a year ago and apparently Linnea was the only one she kept in touch with. Maybe she'd made new friends at the apartment complex. Returning to the seedy development to do a house-to-house (or a door-to-door, in this case) would probably be a waste of time, but I needed to do it. I made a new list:

> Interview "Lizzy's" neighbors
> Interview Stefan Falstow
> Track down Johnson's ex-wives and interview them
> Meet Van Hoose

"So," Gigi interrupted my thoughts, "what's next?"

I looked up to see her leaning forward, chin in palm, at her desk. Her eyes were fixed on me like a dog hoping for a Milk-Bone.

"I've contacted all the lawyers in town," she said, thumping the phone book, "to let them know our agency wants to do process serving. A couple of them said they might give us a call, but they don't have anything until next week. What did Melissa want?"

Our agency. Grrr. "For me to find the baby's father," I said. "Now. ASAP. Pronto."

"I'm surprised she doesn't want to keep the baby," Gigi said. "I know if Kendall had a baby—heaven forbid!—no power on earth would make me turn it over to a stranger to raise."

"Not all women are the maternal type," I said. I was pretty sure I wasn't. Not positive, but pretty sure. Every now and then I heard a faint tick-tick that might have been my biological clock but was probably just the creaking of my joints as I aged. I ripped the page off the legal pad and tucked it into my purse. "I'm headed back to the apartment complex where Elizabeth had the baby. With any luck, one of the neighbors might have noticed her visitors, or she might have confided in someone out there."

"If I came, too, it would only take half as long," Gigi said. "I could talk to some of the neighbors while you talked with the rest. You could tell me what to ask," she added, forestalling the objection hovering on my lips. She pulled out her steno pad and waited.

"Okay," I caved. "Let me print some photos"—the ones of the live Elizabeth from Aurora—"and I'll tell you what to cover."

Forty minutes later we pulled into the parking lot of the Shady Glen Apartments. As on the last time I'd visited, a handful of cars occupied spaces around the lot, and I figured we'd find at least a couple of neighbors home. Also like before, the sounds of crying babies and television programs drifted from open apartment windows. The door to apartment 30B was propped open, and what looked like a father-and-son duo pulled boxes from a small U-Haul trailer, lugged them up the stairs, and deposited them in Elizabeth's old apartment. Had the Sprouses cleared out her stuff, or had Truman stuffed it into a Dumpster or, more likely, sold it?

"Let's start with her next-door neighbor," I told Gigi, motioning upward. We climbed, Gigi puffing several steps behind me and letting out a ladylike "fiddlesticks" when the heel of her pump slipped through the wire grating of the stairs. I waited for her to arrive on the landing before knocking on the door of apartment 30A.

"No one's home." The older of the two men moving stuff into the adjacent apartment, the one I took to be the father, balanced a box on the balcony rail. The tiny landing was crowded with the three of us. "Lady left half an hour ago."

"Thanks," I said. I tucked one of my business cards, with a note saying *Please call* between the door and the frame.

Gigi and I knocked on two more doors before finding someone home. A petite woman in her early twenties with dark hair falling to her waist and Oriental features opened her door a crack. When I showed her the photo of Elizabeth, she said, "Oh, yeah, I've seen her around. You're not bill collectors, are you?" She looked suspiciously from me to Gigi.

"She's dead," I said. "The apartment's been re-rented." I nodded at the men trekking past us with their boxes.

"Oh, yeah, I noticed them. What'd you do to your arm?"

How could she find a pink cast more fascinating than the news of her neighbor's death?

"I broke it—"

"Did you ever notice if Lizzy had any visitors?" This woman hadn't even realized her neighbor had been missing and was dead, so I didn't have much faith that she'd've seen anything useful.

"Sorry." She closed the door.

"Goodness," Gigi said, "that wasn't very polite."

"Get used to it. She behaved like Miss Manners compared to the way lots of folks respond to strangers at their doors," I said. I pointed across the complex. "Why don't you start over there? If you find anyone you think I should talk to, holler."

I knocked on seven more doors, exhausting my half of the building, without getting any useful information. Elizabeth had kept to herself, it seemed, and although several people said they knew who she was—and two mentioned they'd heard she died—no one had taken note of her visitors or heard anything unusual from her apartment at any time. I rejoined Gigi in the parking lot. "Get anything?"

"There's a ten-year-old boy, Mike Lacey, in that apartment." She pointed to a second-floor door. "He's home-schooled, and he says a man in a Lincoln Town Car came to visit Lizzy. At least, he's pretty sure he came to see Lizzy. Mike saw him go up those stairs." She motioned to the stairway leading to apartments 30A and 30B.

Seth Johnson had a Lincoln Town Car . . . "When? Why does Mike remember this?"

Gigi consulted her notes. "Lizzy used to give Mike Starbursts sometimes, so he kept an eye out for her. He says the Lincoln was here 'a long time ago,' and he remembers because he was hoping she'd come out with the man and he could 'accidentally' bump into her and she'd give him some candy. He's really cute, and smart as a whip," Gigi said. "He reminds me of Dexter when he was that age."

"Did you try to pin him down on when 'a long time ago' was?" I pushed my hair out of my face and moved off the asphalt into the shade of an aspen tree. Gigi followed me.

"Uh-huh," she said proudly. "I asked him when his birthday is, and he said June tenth, and I asked him if it was before or after his birthday. He said 'after' and then got to thinking and decided it was after the Fourth of July, too, because he remembered watching the fireworks from a friend's roof not too long before he saw the Lincoln."

"Good work," I said. I meant it. Gigi beamed as if she'd won an Olympic gold medal as we crossed to the car.

So Seth Johnson had visited Elizabeth Sprouse at her apartment a month or so before she had the baby . . . funny he hadn't mentioned that. I foresaw another meeting with the enigmatic Mr. Johnson in my near future. First, though, I would see what kind of ammunition I could get from one or more of his ex-wives.

14

The databases I subscribe to yielded their treasures with little prompting, and I had basic facts about both of Johnson's surviving ex-wives within an hour of returning to the office. Courtney Robinson, wife number one, now thirty-six years old, had remarried a contractor who was currently running for city council. I'd seen his ads—featuring the whole family, including two towheaded kids (suggesting to me that the failure to produce offspring rested with Johnson and not his wives)—and didn't plan to vote for him. Contractors and developers are intent on building on or paving every square inch of Colorado Springs, and I'm against it. Wife number three, Larissa Davern, was twenty-eight and lived in Manitou Springs, a small arty community west of Colorado Springs. She owned a shop called Twinkle and had not remarried.

I dialed Courtney's number.

"Hello?" Her voice was throaty, very Lauren Bacall.

When I told her I wanted to talk with her about Seth

Johnson, she was quiet for fifteen seconds, then said, "I can't talk about Seth. I signed a confidentiality agreement along with the divorce papers."

"A young girl died last week, and I'm trying to find the father of her baby. All I need is a few min—"

A choked laugh cut me off. "I doubt Seth is your man, and that's all I'm going to say. My husband is running for office, and Seth is a powerful man in this state. Please don't call again." She hung up.

I stared at the phone, convinced I'd heard real fear in her voice. Without much hope, I punched in Larissa Davern's number.

"Twinkle!" This voice was light and fluty, the vocal equivalent of a wind chime. "Come by the shop any time," Larissa said when I told her what I wanted. "I'm here from nine till five every day except Sunday. Poor Seth! I haven't seen him in years . . . how is he?"

"He seemed fine when I saw him yesterday," I said. Poor Seth? This woman certainly had a different take on Johnson than anyone else I'd talked to. "I'll be there in half an hour, if that's okay."

Gigi emerged from the bathroom, a damp paper towel plastered across her forehead, as I hung up.

"Headache?" I asked.

"Hot flash." She fanned herself with her good hand.

"Here." I tossed her a Pepsi from my fridge, and she gratefully rolled the cold can against the back of her neck as I headed for my car.

—*m*—

I found on-street parking at a meter in Manitou Springs—no mean feat in a town that lets ecologically friendly vehicles park for free—and walked uphill a block to Twinkle. Blinking strings of lights in white, lavender, and blue festooned the outside of the store, making it easy to spot. Maybe the store sold Christmas lights. I pushed open the glass-paned door and found myself in a dim grotto with hundreds of foil, fabric, wood, and metal stars hanging on fishing line from the ceiling. Some of them glowed. A delicate floral scent twined around the racks of hand-printed cards, local art, books, and jewelry—all with a star theme. Gregorian chants—not "Twinkle, Twinkle, Little Star"—played from hidden speakers.

"Please let me know if I can help you," said the voice from the phone.

The woman behind the cash register was wraith thin and dressed in swirling clouds of blue gauze and chiffon. Strawberry blond hair trailed down her back in tiny corkscrew ringlets. A teardrop-shaped amethyst pendant hung from a heavy chain to midchest, and a silver anklet set with bells tinkled when she floated around the counter. She was barefoot. "You must be Charlotte." She held out a long-fingered hand for me to shake.

"Yes, how did you know?"

"You have a sense of purpose about you," she said with a smile. Her skin was so translucent a tracery of veins showed at her temples. Not a line marred her face, and I reminded myself she was not yet thirty. "Can I offer you some water or tea?"

I knew the tea was likely to be caffeine-free—why bother?—and probably steeped from twigs and wildflowers picked at the vernal equinox, or some such thing. Water seemed safer.

Larissa disappeared into a back room through a clacking beaded curtain and returned with two bottled waters. "Passion fruit or guava?" she asked, lifting both bottles.

What's wrong with plain old tap water flavored with chlorine, fluoride, and sediment? I reached for a bottle at random. Perching on the velvet-topped stool she pulled forward, I filled her in on Elizabeth's death and my reason for wanting to know about Seth Johnson, including his attempt to marry Elizabeth. Larissa listened attentively, her head slightly cocked. Every now and then she reached up a hand and drew her fingers through the silky curtain of her hair.

"Marrying Seth was necessary for me to shed my former self and emerge in my present form," she said, "but he was not my ultimate destiny."

She talked like she thought she was a damned butterfly. "Can you tell me why the marriage broke up?"

She considered. "At the ashram, where I went to heal my spirit after the division of our souls, I came to see that Seth had let himself be defined by his inabilities, not his gifts. So sad. Who knows what he could have become if only he was more accepting of the body's limits." She gazed out the window at passersby on the street.

"Huh?" She'd completely lost me with her New Age–speak. "In English?"

Her gaze returned to me, her irises such an unusual purple I wondered if she wore contacts. "He was impotent, yet obsessed with having a biological child."

Aah. "The man's a geneticist, for heaven's sake. Surely he considered in vitro?"

She was shaking her head before I finished. "Such manipulations were against his faith. Are you familiar with the Church of Jesus Christ the Righteous on Earth?"

"Oh, yeah. Elizabeth, the girl who died, was the pastor's stepdaughter."

"Pastor Sprouse was single when I married Seth," Larissa said. "Anyway, the church forbade any kind of medical intervention, especially for procreation. If God didn't bless you with children naturally, it was probably because you were either unfit to be a parent or because he had other work for you to do."

"And Seth bought that?"

"Oh, yes. You wouldn't believe the vile things he had me do to . . . to . . ."

"Help him get it up?"

Larissa's face became a mask of sadness, and I knew what she'd look like when she was old. "I am still a virgin," she stated simply. "Since being released from my covenant with Seth, I have discovered that my spirit expands only in the company of women."

I suspected I knew what she meant and didn't ask her to translate. "So there's no way Seth fathered Elizabeth's baby."

"None."

"So why did he want to marry Elizabeth?" I didn't realize I'd spoken the thought aloud until Larissa answered.

"Hope. I think he chose very young women to marry because we were not quite grown into who we would become and he was able to mold us more easily. When we began to resist, he divorced us, threatened us."

"Why aren't you scared of him?" I asked. "His other wife refused to talk to me."

217

"He can't hurt me anymore," she said. "I refuse to cede him that power. I have no husband or children he can threaten, and the type of people who shop at Twinkle"—she gestured around the tiny store—"have mostly never heard of Seth Johnson. I own the store outright—I bought it with the divorce settlement—so he can't have me evicted." A small smile of satisfaction curved her lips. "He is truly impotent here."

<center>~~~</center>

After my talk with Larissa, I was chomping at the bit to have another go at Seth Johnson. Even though it didn't sound as if he could be Olivia's father, his visit to Elizabeth at the apartment suggested he knew more than he was telling. I dialed his number from my cell phone, but Secretary Jean took great pleasure in telling me he had left instructions not to put me through or grant me another appointment.

"I suppose he left orders to shoot me on sight if I just show up?"

"Arrest you for trespassing," Jean said with satisfaction.

I hung up. Drumming my fingernails on the steering wheel as I fought rush hour traffic back to my office, I tried to think of a way to maneuver Johnson into talking to me, but came up empty.

I was in a grumpy mood when I stalked into the office, and the sight of Gigi plugging in a lava lamp with turquoise blobs floating in garish pink ooze almost drove me around the bend.

"No," I said simply, marching to my desk.

"But I got it on eBay," she said. "Look, it really brightens the place up, don't you think?" She stood back to admire the effect.

218

"No."

"I suppose Kendall might like it," she said, unplugging it and wrapping the cord around it. "It's a bit too pink for Dexter, don't you think?"

"Absolutely." I grabbed a Pepsi and drank it absently, trying to shake my surly mood. If only I could think of a way to get to Johnson . . .

"You look like you've had a hard day," Gigi said. She leaned forward with her elbows on the desk, good hand cupping her chin. "What's wrong?"

I almost told her to mind her own business, but couldn't stand hearing the answer I was sure I'd get: Swift Investigations *was* her business. So I told her about the meeting with Larissa and my frustrated attempts to talk to Johnson again, feeling some relief at venting.

"Well, I know where Seth Johnson'll be tonight," she said when I finished.

"What?" I spun my chair to face her directly.

"At the Wild West Casino Night—it's a benefit for the Fine Arts Center. He's on the board of directors. So was Les." Her happy smile dimmed. "I've got tickets, if you want to go. We bought them before Les . . ."

"You do?" My grandpa always said it was better to be lucky than good, and right now I believed him. "We could both go." She wasn't the ideal date, but they *were* her tickets.

"Thanks, Charlie, but I've got to help Dexter with his English term paper tonight. If he doesn't turn it in tomorrow, he's going to fail English."

I knew what "help Dexter" meant: She was going to write the damn thing for him. I felt a niggle of annoyance at the way her kids took advantage of her. "Well, thanks," I said. "Maybe I can talk Jack into going. What's the attire?"

"Festive Western—"

Whatever the hell that was.

"—or period Western costume. You know, like dance hall girls or gunslingers. I was going as a madam—like Miss Kitty in *Gunsmoke*?—and Les had a marshal's costume." She sounded wistful. "You could borrow my costume, too," she said helpfully. "The waist is elastic. I'll run home and get it and the tickets."

Before I could tell her I was more a boots and jeans kind of cowgirl than a saloon hostess, she'd bolted. Oh, well. Maybe she'd bring Les's costume, too, and Jack could play Marshal Dillon.

Gigi wasn't back yet when I wandered over to Albertine's to keep my appointment with Jack Van Hoose half an hour later. I found him deep in conversation with my friend. The crowd was scarce on a Wednesday night, and New Orleans jazz playing over the speakers filled the silent spaces. Albertine, clad in a zebra-striped tunic that fell to her knees over black leggings, laughed as I walked in. "Get away with you," she said, giving Jack a playful push on the shoulder. He grinned.

"I'll have whatever you guys are having," I said. A martini glass with less than an inch of green slush remaining sat in front of each of them. I slid onto a bar stool beside Jack.

"One margaritatini coming up," Albertine said.

"A what?"

"It's a margarita made with vodka," Jack said as Albertine

busied herself with bottles. "Without salt." Wearing a red golf shirt with khaki shorts displaying his strongly muscled legs, he only needed a whistle strung around his neck to pass for a football coach.

Skewering a wedge of lime and a cherry on a tiny plastic sword, Albertine set the drink in front of me. "Voilà!"

I took a cautious sip. Strange, but somehow refreshing. I took two more swallows, then set the glass down on a bar napkin. Albertine wandered off to serve a couple in their sixties who settled in at the end of the bar, and Jack swiveled to face me, his knee brushing mine.

"So, lady detective, how's your case coming?" A smile tugged at his broad lips.

"So-so," I said. "I've got a couple of possibilities for the father, but no one's owning up to it or handing over voluntary DNA samples. You told me Elizabeth's stepdad came to see you once. What kind of vibe did you get from him?"

Jack finished off the dregs of his drink. "Intense. He seemed jittery, edgy, like some of the kids get before a big game . . . on the brink. Only I got the feeling he was always like that. It was almost like he was high on something, PCP or meth, not a drug like marijuana that mellows you out."

"High on God."

"Frankly, the way he came off, I'm surprised Elizabeth wasn't home-schooled." He signaled Albertine for a glass of water. "Liberty was not much better than an opium den or bordello, to hear him tell it."

I ran my fingers up and down the stem of my martini glass, putting off the questions I didn't want to ask. "Did you know Linnea helped deliver Elizabeth's baby?"

"You're shitting me!" After a moment's thought, he nodded. "I guess I can see it. That girl's got one cool head."

"She told me she's going to be an obstetrician. She also told me"—I took a deep breath—"that Elizabeth might have called you after the baby was born. Maybe to ask for advice?" I looked a question at him.

"Me?" He looked genuinely surprised. "Why would she call me?"

"Elizabeth thought you were 'the bomb,' according to Linnea. It would be natural for a young girl to turn to a counselor she trusted in a time of crisis," I said, "especially if, like Elizabeth, she couldn't count on her parents for help."

"I wish she had, but she didn't," Jack said, a tight look descending on his face. "I hope you're not implying there was anything improper in my relationship with Elizabeth."

"I'm not implying anything," I lied. "Just trying to do my job."

"Since your job is finding the baby's father, forgive me if I get a little pissed off here!" He put his glass down with such force that water sloshed over the sides.

Albertine sent us a sideways glance from her position near the cash register.

I kept my voice low. "Look, Jack, I don't think you're Olivia's dad, but I've got to cover all the bases. You knew Elizabeth before she became pregnant, and, as far as I can tell, you're one of very few men she liked and spent time with."

"In my office with the door open! Jesus! Do you realize what you're suggesting, what that kind of accusation would do to my career?" He tossed back the rest of his water as if wishing it were straight vodka.

I held up my hands placatingly. "Okay, okay. I'm not making any accusations. I had to ask. My instincts have been wrong before."

"Oh, so your instincts told you I wasn't a child molester? Is that supposed to make me feel better?" He stood, careful this time not to brush against me. Slapping a twenty-dollar bill on the bar, he stalked away.

"Are we still on for Friday?" I called after him, already knowing the answer. He shoved the door open with a rigid arm. Sunlight poked into the dim room before the closing door strangled it.

I pivoted on the stool to face the bar again. Glumly, I swallowed the last of my margaritatini.

"Damn, girl, that was one mighty fine lookin' man," Albertine said. She stood in front of me, shaking her head slowly from side to side. "Mighty fine. Why'd you have to go and piss him off?"

"It's a gift," I said.

"More like a curse, I'd say. How long's it been since you had a date?"

"I suppose this doesn't count?" I gestured at Jack's abandoned glass.

"Nuh-uh. Not even close."

I considered. "About an eon or two. Roughly since triceratops walked the earth."

"Well, I can see why, if you go around accusin' all the potentials of being child molesters." She placed our glasses in a tub filled with soapy water and swabbed at the bar's polished surface with a damp rag.

"His words, not mine. Wait, I paid Montgomery off for

some info with dinner last night. Does that count as a date?"
I looked up hopefully.

"Gettin' warmer," Albertine admitted. "Did you let him get
to first base?"

"We didn't even get into the ballpark." I pushed away the
thought of Montgomery's hard kiss as he left.

"Girl, there is no hope for you." Responding to a signal
from the pair at the end of the bar, Albertine rang up their tab
and waved good-bye as they left. She drifted back to me.
"Why did you accuse that gorgeous hunk o' man-flesh of im-
proprieties, anyway?"

I filled her in on my search for Olivia's father, toying with
the plastic sword I'd filched from my drink.

"So, did the baby look like her daddy was black?" Albertine asked when I finished.

I sucked air in through my teeth and sheepishly admitted,
"I didn't look at her that closely. You know how I am with
babies. I think her hair was dark."

Albertine rolled her eyes. "And you call yourself a detective. Girl, you are hopeless." She flicked the bar rag at me.

I was halfway tempted to agree with her and order another
margaritatini when my phone rang. Albertine drifted over to
the cash register as I answered.

"Swift."

"Is this Charlotte Swift of Swift Investigations?" The voice
was halting and female.

"Yes."

"My name is Mina Downey. I'm calling because you left
your card in my door today with a note asking me to call?"

Curiosity colored her voice, and I envisioned a UCCS coed happy to postpone studying by making a phone call.

I straightened on the bar stool, plugging my left ear with a finger so I could hear better. "Yes, Ms. Downey, thanks for calling. It's about your neighbor, Lizzy Jones. Did you know her?"

"Yes?" She offered the word tentatively, as if afraid of answering wrong on a game show and losing out on the mega prize.

"Great!" Now I sounded like Bob Barker. And our next prize package is . . . "I've been hired to assist with some issues related to her baby's paternity, and I wondered if you could help me out." Not giving her a chance to refuse or hang up, I continued, "Were you friendly with her?"

"Uh . . . sorta. We did our laundry together sometimes, at the Laundromat. Once in a while we watched a little TV in the evenings. *Survivor.* It's not like we were friends, though. I mean, I've got a job and everything, and a boyfriend."

As if possessing a job and a boyfriend meant one couldn't have friends. Although I thought I knew what she meant: She and Lizzy were at different life stages and probably didn't have much in common. "I know what you mean," I said. "But when you got together, did she ever talk about the baby or the baby's father?"

Silence for a moment while Mina thought. "Well, she talked about the baby some. It was going to be a girl. I asked her if she had a name picked out, but she just kinda shrugged."

Because at that point she was still planning to hand the baby over to the Falstows.

"She mentioned moving to Virginia and going to college after the baby was born, but she never said anything about a boyfriend. I figured he'd knocked her up and hit the highway, you know?"

I felt a little let down, even though I hadn't really expected her to be able to name the baby's father. "Well, thanks anyway, Mina. Oh, did Lizzy ever have any friends over, any visitors that you noticed?"

"Just her mom."

What? Patricia Sprouse had told me she hadn't seen Elizabeth since the girl left home back in the spring. "Her mom? Are you sure?"

"Well, she didn't introduce me, if that's what you mean— but she was an older woman, and she always brought Lizzy stuff when she visited. You know, maternity clothes and groceries and stuff like a mom would bring. Come to think of it, though, she didn't look much like Lizzy. I mean, Lizzy's hair was dark, and she was on the short side. This woman had red hair, and she was really tall, taller than me."

A tall redhead. Jacqueline Falstow. Who had lied to me about not knowing where Elizabeth lived.

"Did you see her a lot?"

"A couple of times, both in the evening when I was headed out to start my shift."

"When did you last see her?"

Another pause. "Maybe two or three weeks before Lizzy . . . you know. She brought peanut butter cookies, and Lizzy offered me some the next day, but I'm allergic."

I started to make good-bye noises, but Mina stopped me. "Is the baby okay? I was worried . . ."

"She's doing great," I said, warmed by Mina's concern. I got her contact information, thanked her, and hung up.

"Trouble?" Albertine asked, plonking a glass of water in front of me.

Absently, I drank. "One of my witnesses has lied to me, not once but twice." Falstow had lied about not knowing where Elizabeth lived, and again about Elizabeth calling to say she wasn't going to give up the baby. Two strikes.

"Say it isn't so," Albertine said, feigning astonishment.

"Sad, isn't it?"

I dialed the Falstows' number but got an answering machine. I didn't leave a message. The element of surprise might serve me better, and I decided to make the Falstow house my first stop in the morning. It was time to meet Stefan, too. He was a strangely shadowy figure to me still, despite, I presumed, his equal partnership in the contract with Elizabeth. The Falstows and I were going to have a little come-to-Jesus meeting about the true nature of their dealings with Elizabeth Sprouse. Right now, though, I needed a date for the Wild West Casino Night.

I explained about the fund-raiser to Albertine and invited her to go along, but she shook her head. "Can't. I've got to close here tonight. My manager left early for his daughter's choir recital. How 'bout that cute policeman? I'll bet he's already got a six-shooter." Her lips curved in a wildly suggestive grin.

I rolled my eyes at her but dialed the phone. Detective Montgomery was out at a crime scene, a polite officer told me. I hung up and, after a moment's hesitation, dialed again.

15

The party was in full swing when Dan Allgood and I strolled through the doors of the Fine Arts Center. The huge Chihuly chandelier of topaz, orange, and gold glass squiggles glowed over an anachronistic crowd of saloon girls, cowboys, Indians, miners, and gamblers. Father Dan was the only priest in sight, fitting in with the Western atmosphere perfectly in an ankle-length black cassock and wire-rimmed spectacles, cowboy boots on his feet and a Bible tucked under one arm.

"Don't you think a priest with a saloon girl is a bit strange?" I'd asked when he came over to pick me up. I hitched up the fishnet hose I'd bought at Victoria's Secret on my way home and slipped on simple black pumps, not having any turn-of-the century footwear. I'd cinched the red satin skirt Gigi had lent me with a couple of safety pins at the waist and used Grandy's old cameo brooch to pin up a section of the skirt at midthigh to show the black netting underneath.

Dan applauded as I tried out a cancan step. "I'm trying to save you, of course," he said, thumping a hand on his Bible.

"Well, you have saved me, and I'm grateful," I said, tucking the tickets Gigi had given me into the low-scoop-necked black blouse I'd found at the back of a drawer. No way was Gigi's blouse going to fit me. "I'd've looked conspicuous on my own."

"Like you don't look conspicuous now?" His left brow flew up, and he grinned as his eyes ran from my modest cleavage to the not so modest length of fishnetted leg. My dark hair wisped around my forehead and neck despite my attempts to secure it atop my head and corral it with the feathered band Gigi had supplied. I'd layered on the mascara, used a bright red lipstick, and drawn a Cindy Crawfordesque beauty spot near the corner of my mouth with brown eyeliner. I felt like a cross between a saloon hooker and a flapper girl.

"You know what I mean." I punched him on the shoulder and opened the door. "C'mon. We're already late."

Getting into character, I sashayed across the floor toward the bar, craning my neck to spot Seth Johnson. Dan stuck by my side, his muscular good looks and slicked-back blond hair attracting a lot of sidelong looks from the women we strolled past. Shame on them . . . for all they knew he could be Catholic and celibate.

"What's your poison?" the bartender asked when we reached the front of the line. I opted for white wine, and Dan chose club soda and lime. He was driving.

"Will you be in trouble with your congregation if someone spots you at a gambling party?" I asked as we circled the room.

"Episcopalians are all about good causes," he said, "especially those that involve drinking and gambling. Care to try your luck?" He ushered me toward a blackjack table with only two people seated in front of the dealer. One was a black-hatted Western villain, complete with paunch, oiled mustachios, and spurs. The other man wore a gingham-checked shirt, modern jeans, and a watch with enough dials and gadgets to launch a space shuttle.

"Mind if we join you gentlemen?" I asked, trying to channel Jodie Foster in *Maverick*.

"Certainly, ma'am," the villain replied, scooting over one stool. "Take my seat, padre."

The dealer shuffled and slid cards toward us. I barely looked at my cards and placed a bet at random with the chips I'd bought at the door. I was too busy looking for Seth Johnson to pay attention to the cards.

"Take a hit." Dan nudged my elbow.

His body was warm and solid just inches from mine, and his breath held a pleasant hint of lime from his club soda. For a moment, I let myself be distracted by his smile; then I motioned for another card. Twenty-one. I flipped my cards, and the dealer paid up. The thrill of winning trickled through me, and I kissed Dan on the cheek.

"You must bring good luck," I said. Before he could reply, a familiar laugh caught my attention, and I swiveled to see Seth Johnson seated at a poker table situated near the entrance to one of the galleries. Four other men and a woman with dyed ostrich feathers tucked into a mass of ringlets were ranged around the table, concentrating on their cards.

"Don't leave now, little lady," the black-hatted man said as I slipped off the stool. "You're winning."

Dan started to get up, too, but I motioned him back.

"This'll probably go better if I can get him one-on-one," I said. "You stay here and make my fortune." I pushed my small pile of chips toward him.

"I guess he can't be much of a threat in this crowd," he said, after a narrow-eyed look in Johnson's direction. He subsided back on the stool, catching my wrist as I turned to go. "Be careful."

I nodded, squeezed his hand, and strolled across the room until I was within spitting distance of Seth Johnson. Dressed in white from the top of his ten-gallon hat to his snakeskin boots, Johnson looked every inch the nineteenth-century marshal, only without the chaw and bad teeth. A large gold star gleamed on his chest, and his belt sported a turquoise buckle the size of a salad plate. A pearl-handled revolver, either a genuine antique or a good fake, hung from a holster slung low on his hips. He nibbled on one edge of his gingery mustache as he studied his cards. I wondered if the woman beside him was his date, then decided she couldn't be because she was clearly over thirty—about ten years past her sell-by date as far as he was concerned. I watched the gamblers play a couple of hands, taking care to stay just outside Johnson's peripheral vision. A rocks glass with an inch of amber liquid sat to his left, and he sipped from it occasionally. The snick of the cards as the dealer dealt them and the occasional terse bid were all I overheard. Unlike most of the revelers laughing and groaning as the cards or the roulette ball dictated their fortunes, the players at Johnson's table looked grim and serious. Their expressions made me wonder what kind of stakes they were playing for.

When it became clear that they weren't going to take a

break anytime soon, I decided to take matters into my own hands. Swaying my hips to make the satin skirt swish against the net underskirt, I strolled up behind Johnson and slid my arms around his neck. "Seth, honey, I'm here to bring you good luck!"

He practically choked on his drink, jerking his head around to look at me. His brows snapped together. One of the other male gamblers, a Wilford Brimley look-alike, gave me a big grin, but two of the men frowned, obviously irritated at having their concentration broken.

"You can bring me some luck, sugar," Wilford said, patting his lap.

I sent him a saucy smile but remained draped over Johnson's shoulders. Leaning close, I whispered in his ear, "We need to chat about some fingerprints the police found in Elizabeth's apartment. A little birdie told me they might be yours." I smiled brightly at the other players.

He stiffened and then folded his cards together, tossing them on the table. "Gentlemen, Maggie, I'm going to sit out a round or two."

Wilford chuckled knowingly as Johnson rose, clamping an arm around my shoulders, and walked me back into the gallery behind the table. I waggled my fingers at the poker players as we turned a corner. We stood in a small square gallery, with huge abstract canvases, one per wall. Each was lit to show the play of colors and texture. For some reason, they struck me as angry.

"What the hell do you think you're playing at, Miss Swift?" Johnson said, swinging me around to face him, his hands on my shoulders.

"I could ask you the same question." I wrenched away from his grip. "I've learned a lot about you in the past couple of days. I have to admit I thought you might have fathered Elizabeth's baby—maybe raped her—but rumor says that's a virtual impossibility, so what took you to her apartment this summer?"

His face went white at my veiled reference to his impotence, and his eyes blazed with a fury that knocked me back a couple of steps.

"I believe I warned you when you came out to the ranch," he said from between clenched teeth. "You only get one warning."

Quick as a rattlesnake, his hand flashed out and grabbed my upper arm. He jerked hard, twisting me as he pulled so my back thudded against his chest, and clapped his hand over my mouth before I could do more than squeak.

I bit his finger hard and jabbed my elbow back into his gut. He let out a small "oof," and his grip loosened slightly. Ripping the unsecured gun from the holster at his side, I ducked under his arm and spun to face him, the gun leveled at his stomach. My hair flopped into my face, and my heart thudded in my chest.

Johnson raised one hand to shoulder height and held the other one up to inspect the damage I'd done to his finger. His posture was relaxed, and I sensed that the ungovernable fury that had seized him had faded. Pulling a hankie out of his pocket and dabbing at his finger, he said, "You don't really think I'd keep an antique like that loaded, do you?"

No, I didn't really. My reactions had been reflex. I popped the cylinder and inspected it. No bullets. Well, the revolver was heavy; I could use it as a club if he came at me again.

"What'd you think I was going to do, woman? Shoot you here in the museum and bury your body in a shallow grave at the ranch?" He laughed unpleasantly. "Not my style."

My thoughts had been running along those lines, but I didn't admit it. I stayed silent, letting the gun drop to my side but remaining alert.

"No, killing is messy. Besides, I don't fancy ending up in jail over a no-account nuisance like you. No, I've got other methods."

Although I tried to keep my face impassive, he must have caught the stiffening of my muscles, because he laughed again. "I understand your business isn't doing so well, and that your lease is coming up for renewal. You've also got a partner who's in desperate need of money, if my sources are accurate—and I'm sure they are. I'm sure she'd be amenable to a buyout offer. I could be your new partner."

Gigi, heretofore the bane of my professional existence, was suddenly looking like Abbott to my Costello, Ginger Rogers to my Fred Astaire, Cagney to my Lacey, the queen of partners. "You don't seem like the investigator type," I said calmly.

"Oh, I'm not. I'd sell off the assets, unless you could afford to buy me out?" When I stayed silent, he nodded. "Didn't think so. I'd say you'll be out of business in a couple of weeks. You'll have to leave the state to start up again because I'll make damn sure no one in this neck of the woods will hire your sorry ass. Say—don't you own a house you've been renovating? I sure hope you've been pulling all the correct permits, darlin', because every building inspector in the county is about to descend on you. And if I ever see so much as the tip of your snoopy little nose again, I might just have to find out who holds your mortgage and buy it up. If you're ten minutes late with a payment"—he snapped his fingers—"I foreclose."

I felt the ground slipping out from under me, like sand on an unstable dune. All I could think about was getting to Gigi, begging her not to sell out. I locked my eyes on his. "Money can accomplish a lot, but it can't stop rumors. And if I don't have a business to run, I won't have much else to do with my time besides investigate your business dealings and look into your wife's death a bit more closely. They may all be on the up-and-up—which I doubt—but you know how people are. 'If there's smoke, there's fire.' You may find the governor isn't quite so eager to be your buddy once word of your obsession with young girls gets out—and I'll make sure it gets out." I was proud of myself for keeping my voice hard and level. It didn't tremble with the fear threatening to overwhelm me. I had nothing without Swift Investigations, my house . . .

Johnson's eyes narrowed. We stood facing each other like two gunslingers at either end of a dusty cow-town Main Street. If we drew, we'd both end up dead.

"Charlie, I thought you'd ditched me." Dan stood just inside the doorway, his black-clad figure silhouetted against a canvas of swirling reds and purples and golds. He spoke easily, but his hands were balled into loose fists at his sides, and he moved like a lion ready to pounce. His eyes flashed to the gun in my hand. "Trying to steal her away, Sheriff?"

We made an uneasy triangle. Johnson's eyes jumped from Dan to me and back again. He and Dan were about the same height, but Dan outweighed him by a good twenty or thirty pounds, all of it muscle.

Johnson faked a laugh. "Hell, no, Father. Just having a little conversation about law and order on the frontier. I can't let the action at saloons and gambling parlors get out of hand, but I'm not against a little free enterprise, either. Keeps the cowhands happy, if you know what I mean." He winked.

I kept my eyes on him, wondering if he'd just agreed to a standoff. Dan put his arm around my shoulders, but I couldn't relax.

"My gun?" Johnson held out his hand.

After a moment's hesitation, I put the gun in it. My palm was damp with sweat where the butt had rested.

Ostentatiously wiping the gun off with his handkerchief, Johnson restored it to the holster. "If you'll excuse me, I've got a poker game waiting," he said. He spun on his booted heel and left.

I stayed still until I could no longer hear his footsteps clomping down the hallway. Then I collapsed against Dan, shivering. He held me against his chest, not saying anything until I regained some control.

"Want to tell me what that was all about?" He leaned back just far enough to study my face.

I blurted out the entire scene. I summed up with "So I learned nothing, and now he's out to destroy my business."

"This is what happens when you poke a rattlesnake with a stick," he said.

"Very helpful." I pulled away and glared at him.

"Do you think Gigi would sell to him?" he asked, ignoring my temper.

"Of course! She doesn't really want to be an investigator, and he can afford to make a tempting offer. And I've been a bitch to her," I added, almost as an afterthought. In reality, awareness of my less than welcoming treatment of her had been haunting me since Johnson first hinted at buying her out. It would serve me right if she sold her share of the business.

"Maybe she'll surprise you," Dan said, nudging me toward the doorway. "Look, unless you want to gamble the night away—"

"I've already gambled too much."

"Let's go home."

"What'd you do with my chips?" I asked.

"Turned them into a fortune, of course," he said, one corner of his mouth quirking up. "Isn't that what you told me to do?"

"Really, how much did you win?" If he'd turned my fifty dollars into a hundred, I'd be impressed.

"About five hundred."

"Dollars?" I stared at him.

"Uh-huh." He grinned at my astonishment. "I might have learned a thing or two about gambling in my misbegotten youth."

"And just where would this have been?"

He tapped his forefinger on my nose. "That's a story for another time."

On our way out the door, he dribbled the chips—all except my original stake of fifty dollars' worth—into the kettle set up to receive donations for the museum. Oh, what the heck . . . I tossed my chips in, too.

16

(Thursday)

I woke the following morning, heavy-eyed and worn-out, after a night of tossing and turning. I'd wanted to call Gigi as soon as I walked in the door, but it was after midnight. With the sun promising another hot day, I pulled on dark green twill slacks and topped them with a yellow silk-and-cotton-blend top in an effort to add some light to my tired skin. I tried phoning the office before I left the house, but Gigi wasn't in yet. I debated between heading straight to the office to wait for her and pursuing the case. Reluctantly, I opted for following up with Jacqueline Falstow.

A VW Beetle painted in the green and yellow of a local cleaning service blocked the Falstows' driveway when I arrived a little after eight. A fortyish Hispanic woman wearing green uniform slacks and top and a utility belt laden with feather duster, spray cleaner, paper towels, and other tools of the cleaning trade was lugging a vacuum from the car to the house.

"Mrs. Falstow is not here," she said when I asked. She set

the vacuum down and tweaked her short ponytail to tighten the elastic. "She volunteers at the Humane Society every Thursday morning, and Fridays, too, I think."

Good for her. Maybe abandoned animals were a baby substitute for her. "Is her husband here?"

She stared at me as if I'd asked if the sun rose in the west. "No. Of course not. I've never even seen Mr. Falstow. He is always at work."

Jacqueline it was, then. I returned to my car and pointed it in the direction of the Humane Society of the Pikes Peak Region, west of I-25 off the road to Manitou Springs. Made of a warm reddish wood and lots of glass, the Humane Society facility looked more like an upscale medical or dental building than a home for unwanted or abused pets. Glass doors gave way to neutral-colored tile and pale walls in the lobby. A bulletin board and a rack of flyers sat on the right, and an information desk dominated the left half of the reception area. Despite the antiseptic effect of the tiles and clean walls, an animal odor lingered, not completely obscured by a lemony air freshener. A slight young man with hair in a braid down his back looked up as I approached the desk.

"I'm supposed to meet Jacqueline Falstow here," I said with my winningest smile.

"In the kitty condos," he said, jerking his head toward a hallway. His eyes dropped back to the ledger he was studying.

"Thanks." I strode down the hall as if I knew where the hell I was going, enjoying the view of trees and grass through the huge plate glass windows that marched down one side of the hall. Pushing through a door, I found the cat area easily by following the mews. The ammonia scent of used kitty litter grew stronger as I opened another door into a room lined with what I guessed were the "kitty condos": wire cages stacked one atop the other with slide-out pans containing the litter. The room was well lit and cheerful, not depressing as I'd thought it might be. A glassed-in play area with carpeted steps and platforms held a variety of kittens busy pouncing on each other, leaping from level to level, or chasing their tails. A gray-striped kitten saw me and came to the glass, reaching up a paw as if to invite me in. Cute, even tempting, but I didn't need a pet.

"Can I help— Ms. Swift, what are you doing here?"

Jacqueline Falstow, clutching a long-haired white cat in her arms, stared at me, her eyes as green and unblinking as the cat's. They mirrored astonishment and maybe a little trepidation. Good.

I was in no mood for beating around the bush. "Looking for you. I talked to someone who overheard Lizzy's phone call to you after Olivia was born. She wasn't making arrangements to turn the baby over; she called to tell you she'd decided to keep her."

Jacqueline turned away to stow the cat in his condo, but not before I caught the leap of fear in her eyes. When she straightened from securing the cage door, her cheeks were flushed. "Is that the same 'someone' who thought Stefan and I hired Lizzy as a surrogate?"

Score one for her. I ignored the question. "Another witness has identified you as visiting Lizzy at her apartment on at least two separate occasions. You brought clothes and peanut butter cookies," I added to forestall the lie I saw coming. "Why did you lie to me and tell me you didn't know where she lived?"

"It was none of your business," she said heatedly. White fur clung to her camel-colored T-shirt and jeans beneath a canvas apron. She brushed at it with gloved hands. "It still isn't."

"Not if you don't know anything about who the baby's father is, or how Lizzy died," I agreed, "but your lies make me suspect you do."

"I don't!"

The agitation in her voice stirred up the cats, some of which shifted uneasily in their kennels. One lashed his tail as if egging her on.

"I think she called you that Sunday after Olivia was born and said you couldn't have her, that she was keeping her. You and your husband argued with her. Then, when you couldn't change her mind, you jumped in your car and drove to her apartment, maybe to try to convince her to give you the baby, maybe to take her by force. What went wrong? Did you push her, slap her? I've heard she could be irritating, and it must have pissed you off royally that she would lead you on about the baby and then decide to keep her. Did she fall and hit her head? I'm sure it was an accident, that you didn't mean to hurt her."

"She wasn't there," Jacqueline said wearily, moving a spray bottle of Windex off a step stool and sinking onto it. "Stefan and I—after she called—we argued about it. He didn't want to go see her; he preferred to take the legal route. He called Ziegler to get his advice about our 'options.' But taking her to court would take too long. I couldn't wait. I'd already been waiting for so long. So I snuck out while he was watching golf and went to Lizzy's apartment. You're right . . . I'd been there before, just a few times. She didn't really like it when I came,

241

but I couldn't help myself. I needed to know that she was still there, that the baby was doing well."

"She sent you e-mails."

"Yes, but that wasn't the same as feeling the baby kick against my hand." Her eyes glowed with remembered excitement, and she put a hand against her abdomen.

"How long after the call until you showed up at Lizzy's place?"

"About two and a half hours," Jacqueline said, her face tortured. "If only I'd gotten there sooner, maybe I could have saved her."

And gotten the baby, I thought, doubting she cared one iota about Elizabeth's fate. I still wasn't convinced she hadn't seen Elizabeth. "Was there anything different about her apartment? Did you see signs of a disturbance?"

"I couldn't see anything," she said, echoes of her frustration straining her voice. "I knocked and knocked and tried to peer in the window, but the blinds were down. I even knocked on her neighbor's door, thinking she might have seen Lizzy leave or something, but she wasn't home either. Finally, I just gave up and went home. Stefan never even knew I'd been gone."

The white cat meowed, a raspy, demanding sound, and she stuck a finger through the two-inch-square mesh to stroke his head. After submitting to the caress for a moment, he laid his ears against his skull and slashed at her finger with bared claws. She jerked her hand back.

"Not nice, Mo," she admonished him. "That's why we wear gloves," she said, turning to me and waggling her fingers. "Not all the kitties appreciate the care we give them."

"My witness says you were there again on Tuesday," I lied, hoping to squeeze a few more drops of honesty out of her.

She sighed and closed her eyes for a moment. They held nothing but deep weariness when she reopened them. "I went back every day, sometimes twice a day, until I read that Lizzy was dead. Then I gave up."

No, then she went to the funeral and tried to pry information out of Patricia Sprouse. This was one very determined and resourceful woman. As I thought about what else to ask her, the door opened, and a woman stood on the threshold, holding a young boy by the hand and cradling an infant swaddled in several yards of white blanket in her other arm.

"Come pick out the kitty you want, Robbie," she said to the boy. He dashed forward and pressed his face against the glass behind which the kittens tumbled. I smiled at his eagerness as he left little handprints on the glass I was pretty sure Jacqueline had just shined. I turned to her, expecting to see rueful amusement in her face, only to see her gaze clamped to the baby, the hunger in them approximating the look a vampire might give a pint of A-Pos.

Never underestimate the power of obsession. I slipped out of the room without saying good-bye, and she didn't even notice my departure.

Getting back on I-25, I made a quick call to Falstow Construction and learned that Stefan Falstow was on a job site, a high-rise office building going up on the south end of Castle Rock, a town midway between Colorado Springs and Denver.

"Do you mostly do commercial building?" I asked the help-ful receptionist.

"About half commercial and half residential," she said. "We've got a lovely new community of single-family homes and townhomes, Prairie View, going up east of Black Forest. I'd be happy to send you a brochure if you're in the market for a new home. The models are just stunning and are open from nine to five thirty weekdays and Saturdays and noon to five on Sundays." She reeled off the hours in a singsong voice brim-ming with good cheer. She probably moonlighted at Christ-mas as one of the elves coaxing nervous kiddies onto Santa's lap at the mall.

I gave her the agency address and sped up I-25, hoping the state troopers were busy elsewhere. Apparently they were, be-cause I reached my exit without getting a ticket. I could see the high-rise from the interstate and wound my way to it. A large maroon, navy, and white sign announcing FALSTOW CON-STRUCTION told me I'd arrived. Construction sites have always reminded me of anthills, and this one was no exception. Work-ers in overalls and hard hats scurried around the base of the building and swarmed over its steel superstructure. If I nar-rowed my eyes and peered through my lashes, all I could see was yellow hard hats bobbing like the bits of food or grit ants carried. Shouts, clangs of metal on metal, and the chugging engines of large machinery made the site a lot noisier than an anthill. Locating the office in a trailer, I climbed the two por-table steps.

A wave of damp-smelling air-conditioning from a window unit washed over me as I entered. Rubbing my suddenly goose-pimpled arms, I asked the man sitting at a desk where I could find Stefan Falstow. He pointed, and I turned to see the tall man with his neatly trimmed beard and a hard hat emerge from an office. The hard hat read STEF in precisely applied electrical tape. He wore a white button-down shirt tucked into gray slacks, but no tie or jacket. His face was tanned and lined by the sun; drooping lower lids below brown eyes gave him the aspect of a bassett hound.

His voice was brusque as he looked at me and said, "You were at the Sprouse woman's house. Make it quick. I'm due to take a look at some plumbing."

"I'll walk with you," I said, eager to extend our talk beyond the five seconds he was going to allocate if we stayed in the office.

He grunted something I took for assent and pointed to a row of hard hats slung on pegs beside the door. Interpreting the gesture as a command to put one on, I seized one and slapped it on my head as I followed him out the door. He was a couple of inches over six feet and moved rapidly over the rutted ground of the site. I trotted to keep up, trying to fasten the helmet as I moved.

"I'm Charlotte Swift," I said, not bothering to try to shake hands since he was half a step ahead of me. "I've talked to your wife a couple of times about the baby you were hoping to adopt."

"You're the PI that's trying to find her father," he said, shooting a look over his shoulder. "Any luck? If you find him, I'll pay him a healthy sum to allow us to continue with the adoption. Enough to send him to college. He's probably just some teenager who wouldn't know what the hell to do with a baby, anyway."

"Maybe." I didn't contradict him, although I thought it was unlikely. "Mrs. Falstow told me you're the one who handled all the legal details, the insurance and so on. Can you tell me how you got together with Elizabeth—Lizzy—in the first place?"

He lifted a hand in response to a "Hey, Stef" greeting from a man trundling a wheelbarrow into the building before answering me. "What did Jacqueline tell you?"

"She didn't seem sure where you met," I hedged, alerted by his too casual tone.

"I—we—met her through my lawyer," Falstow said.

"Ziegler."

"Right." He ducked through a framed doorway, and I followed. Inside the building it was darker, colder, despite the lack of walls and the August sunshine turning the I-beams to shadow stripes on the ground. "Watch your step."

He was always a step or two in front of me, keeping me from reading his face. Yet I got the sense he was evading my questions. "So, refresh my memory, did you suggest Lizzy to Ziegler, or is he the one that knew her first?"

"I don't know many teenagers." He ducked the question again. "Hey, Austadt, what the hell do you think you're doing there?" He marched toward a worker doing something with metal pipes.

I cycled his evasions through my brain, virtually certain his reluctance to outright deny having known Elizabeth meant he'd run into her somewhere. I wondered again where he might know her from. I knew now it wasn't from the high school, since Falstow was childless. Where did people meet? School, church, work, social events . . . I couldn't see Jacqueline or Falstow fitting in with the believers at the Church of

Jesus Christ the Righteous on Earth. Work—Lizzy wasn't a welder or mason on a construction site; she sewed pillows and slipcovers and curtains for model homes. Bingo! The tumblers in my mind clicked into place. I'd've bet my last dollar that Designer Touches had the contract to decorate the Prairie View model homes.

Falstow tromped toward me, his face fixed in a scowl. I didn't know if he was angry with me or the plumber he'd just chewed out. "Look, Ms. Smith—"

"Swift."

"Sure. Sorry. I've got some things to deal with here today, and I don't have time—"

"I understand. Just tell me: Are you happy with the work Lizzy did on your Prairie View model homes? I've heard they're lovely."

He was silent for a moment, one hand plucking at his beard.

"It wouldn't take me two seconds to confirm that Designer Touches decorated those models and find out when they completed the job," I prompted him.

A nailgun thudded above us as if counting the seconds. Ka-chunk . . . ka-chunk . . . ka-chunk . . .

Finally, Falstow gave in. "Okay, okay, I knew the girl and suggested her to Ziegler when he brought up the idea of a private adoption. I didn't want Jacqueline to know because she's insanely jealous and would've jumped to all sorts of hurtful conclusions."

Probably the same ones running through my mind. "Was Lizzy pregnant when you met her?"

"Hell, yes! See, that's what I mean!" He gave a disgusted shake of his head. "I was on the site one day last January when she came running out of the model we'd almost finished and puked in the yard—the toilets weren't working yet. I thought she had food poisoning or something and wanted to call a doc. She said no, she was pregnant."

"What made you think to ask her if she wanted to put her baby up for adoption?" I asked, skeptical that his encounter with Elizabeth had been as simple and brief as he portrayed it.

"Hell, she wasn't much more than a baby herself. Despite the"—he cupped his hands in front of his chest to approximate breasts—"she couldn't have been more than sixteen or so. I thought it was worth talking to her when Zieg explained how private adoptions work. She was *happy* to let us have the baby, seemed relieved to have someone to cover the medical expenses. I didn't get the feeling she could rely on her folks."

"Apparently she wasn't as happy as you thought," I said, "since she decided not to give up the baby."

"Yeah, she turned out to be a real bitch."

I raised my eyebrows, and his scowl deepened. "She broke my wife's heart. And if you or she thinks I'm going to stand still for that . . ."

He talked as if Elizabeth were still alive. "So you raced over to her apartment after she called and—"

"The hell I did! I called my lawyer."

I believed him on that. He seemed like the type who would have his lawyer on speed dial and would summon him if a worker got a paper cut (to forestall a workmen's comp claim), if he was involved in a fender bender (to sue the pants off the guilty party), or had trouble collecting on a rebate promise from a big-box store (to send the message that no one cheats Stef Falstow).

"Okay. So the last time you saw Lizzy Jones was . . . ?"

He glanced at his watch and headed back toward the building entrance. I was glad to get out into the sun's glare again, although I blinked several times in the brightness. "When we signed the contract in mid-March."

"Your wife told me Lizzy came for dinner a couple of times and that she visited her at the apartment."

"The baby was—is—Jacquie's thing," he said, waving a dismissive hand. "If Lizzy was at the house for dinner, it was when I was away on business or out for the evening. I know Jacquie went to her apartment a couple of times, but I certainly didn't."

"You don't sound too enthused about the baby," I observed as we arrived back at the trailer. I pulled the hard hat from my head, running my fingers through my flattened hair to fluff it.

"There aren't many guys my age who get excited about infants and the birthing process and all that," he said defensively, "but once she's out of diapers, I'll teach her the right way to hammer a nail into a board, take her to Rockies games, and hope to God she likes tools more than she likes boys. So whoever has that baby ought to be on notice: I paid for her, and she's mine." With that, he stomped up the stairs and banged open the office door. It slammed shut on the rebound, so I left my hard hat on the edge of one step and headed for my car. I made notes about the interview with Falstow before starting the engine and driving back toward Colorado Springs.

―――

Once on I-25, I called the office to check in. Gigi answered with a cheery "Swift Investigations!"

"Any messages?"

"Oh, hi, Charlie. Yes, Melissa Lloyd called and wants you to meet her at Designer Touches as soon as possible. I was just going to buzz you."

"Did she say what she wants?" I looked at my watch. I'd pass Monument on my way back from Castle Rock, so the detour wouldn't be a big pain.

"No. Oh, and we got a call from a law firm downtown, one of the ones I called, and they have some process-serving work for us. I'm going down there in just a few minutes to pick up the paperwork. It goes to some guy in Fountain."

"Great." I made a mental note to keep an eye on the six o'clock news to see what Gigi had in her repertoire besides burning down fast food joints, busting meth labs, and scuttling golf carts. "Um, Gigi, will you be back at the office later?"

"Probably. Why?"

"Something came up last night I'd like to talk about."

We agreed to meet late that afternoon and hung up.

I arrived at Designer Touches half an hour later to find Melissa engaged in conversation with a young couple looking at fabrics. She caught my eye and signaled she'd be with me soon. I drifted around the showroom, wishing I had enough spare change to buy a pair of pebbled glass and slate table lamps. With ecru shades, they gave off a homey glow that would be perfect in the living room when I finished renovating it. The price tag practically singed my fingers, however, and I decided I could make do with something from Target or Lowe's.

"Ms. Swift. Charlie."

Melissa Lloyd appeared at my elbow, looking ill at ease.

Wearing a cream jersey dress and medium-heeled sandals, her hair scraped back in the usual French braid, she looked cool and professional. She waved good-bye to the young couple as they left, then turned back to me. "I asked you to come here because . . . well . . ."

"Is something wrong?" I asked as she trailed off. "Is Olivia okay?"

"She's fine," Melissa said. "What I wanted to say is that I don't need you to keep looking for her father."

My eyebrows arced toward my hairline. "You found him?"

"No. I just don't—"

She turned away and click-clacked across the parquet floor to her desk. I followed. Plucking a piece of paper from her desk, she handed it to me.

I studied the check. She'd made it out for more than she owed. "This is too much," I said. The check would go a long way toward keeping Swift Investigations in the black for the month, but I felt let down. Once I took on a case, I liked to see it through to the end. I felt like I'd been benched late in the fourth quarter.

"I wanted to thank you for all the effort you put in. I—"

"Did you turn the baby over to CPS, is that it?"

"No!"

Her eyes slid away from mine to study the odds and ends on her desk. For the first time, I noticed a photo of Olivia in an elaborate wood frame. The penny dropped.

"You want to keep her."

"Yes," Melissa admitted. "I never planned . . . I never thought . . ." She laid her palms flat against her flushed cheeks. "I guess I owe you an explanation."

She didn't really, but I didn't disagree.

"C'mon." She flipped the sign on the store's door to CLOSED and led me to a small break room apparently shared with the store that abutted hers. It featured a table with four chairs, a sink, a microwave, a refrigerator, and a vending machine. "Pepsi, right?" She plunked quarters into the machine and handed me a cold soda, getting a 7-Up for herself.

"Thanks." I took a long swallow and seated myself in one of the orange plastic chairs.

Melissa joined me. "I was abused as a child," she said baldly. "My father beat me. You don't need all the gory details. Suffice it to say I was put into the system when I was ten and bounced from foster home to foster home for a few years. Elizabeth's father was one of my foster 'dads.'"

Her emotionless statement rocked me back in my chair. "I had no idea—"

"Why would you?" She smiled, a wry twist of her lips. "I never thought I'd be a good parent. All the literature says kids who are abused are more likely to become abusers. Plus, I had no good role models, no one to teach me how a good parent does it." She rolled the soda can between her palms. "So I was afraid to have children."

I could relate to that. Being serially abandoned with various relatives while my parents traveled the world had left me wary of having children, too. "Then Olivia arrived on your doorstep."

"Exactly. You have no idea how petrified I was. Scared and angry. Scared I would do something wrong, angry that I'd been put in this position. Ian's reaction didn't help much, either," she said. "He's always liked it being just the two of us, has never pushed for children. But caring for Olivia has changed me. Yes, I'm tired. Yes, I make mistakes . . . Did you know you're supposed to put babies to sleep on their back? I was putting Olivia on her tummy until I saw something about it on one of those morning shows. But I haven't hurt her. I haven't felt the slightest urge to hurt her, not even when she cries for hours and I can't get to sleep and I don't know what's wrong. All I want to do is make her feel better."

"You love her."

"Yes." She nodded, her face shining with wonder. "And I want to keep her. So, can you just stop looking for her father? I don't care who he is anymore."

"You're the client. But I have to warn you that I think you're going to have a legal battle on your hands." I told her about Jacqueline Falstow's obsession with the baby and her husband's readiness for war with lawyers as the weapon of choice. "Patricia Sprouse might get in on the action, too, if her husband will let her."

"I've already talked to a lawyer," she said fiercely, "and he thinks I've got a good chance. Regardless, I've got to try."

"Okay, good luck." I rose and shook her hand. "What about Elizabeth's death? Aren't you curious about what happened?"

"The police can deal with that," she said dismissively. "It doesn't have anything to do with me and Olivia."

I thought otherwise but kept my mouth shut. I was almost positive Elizabeth's death was tied up with the baby in some way, but it would serve no purpose to make an issue of it with Melissa. Besides, as she'd pointed out (and Montgomery would heartily agree), the murder was a police matter.

Feeling strangely let down, with no place in particular to go now that I was off the case, I drifted back to my car, sitting for a moment before keying the ignition and pulling out of the parking lot.

Gigi was waiting for me when I entered the office. I stopped on the threshold, taken aback by the pink and black tiger-striped jacket and slacks she wore over a pink T-shirt stretched to its limits. The cast now sported black stripes markered on over the pink and a rudimentary cat's face with exaggerated whiskers.

"Dexter drew it. Isn't it cute?" she asked, noting the direction of my gaze and waving her arm in the air.

"He's quite the artist." Not sure how to broach the subject of Johnson and his buyout threat, I procrastinated by getting a Pepsi and then pulling my chair over toward Gigi's desk. She looked at me, her blue eyes curious.

"You wanted to talk about something?"

"Yes. I . . . I wanted to talk about the business." I wished I'd rehearsed this, or at least planned what I wanted to say. The Falstow interviews had kept me busy most of the day, though, and Melissa's bombshell had occupied my thoughts on the drive back from Monument. I struggled on, feeling my way slowly.

"When I left the Air Force, investigating and police work were all I knew. I didn't want to be a cop, because that would've been trading one uniform and male-dominated bureaucracy for another. I wanted to own my own business, to answer to no one. So I set up shop as a PI. I had virtually no cash on hand—

I'd used my separation pay to buy my house—and an attorney friend suggested your husband might like to invest, strictly as a silent partner."

I studied Gigi's face to see how the mention of Les affected her, but she merely nodded for me to go on.

"Business was slow for the first few years, but a couple of years ago I found my niche, began concentrating on missing persons cases, and began to turn a profit, a small one. I've been paying myself a salary barely enough to live on and was hoping to buy Les out within a couple of years."

"You told me," Gigi said, beginning to look wary.

I forced myself to continue. "So, when you showed up, wanting to be an active partner, drawing a salary, I . . . I didn't react well. I thought you'd be a drain on the agency, and I was used to making all the decisions without considering anyone else, so I wasn't very fair to you. I shoved you into all sorts of situations you weren't ready to handle, hoping you'd give up and go back to hairdressing. You surprised me by coping better than I expected. How did the process serving go today?" I asked, putting off the rest of what I needed to say.

"Great!" she said happily. "I got his address off the paperwork, knocked on the door, and handed the envelope over. He even said thank you."

"You've got a knack for it," I said. "You're so . . . sympathetic looking that people don't run when they see you coming."

"You mean I'm a dumpy, middle-aged woman who doesn't look like a threat," she said drily but with a hint of a smile.

"Not looking like a threat is helpful in this line of work," I temporized, "and nobody wearing pink tiger stripes is dumpy. Look, Gigi, what I'm trying to say—"

"Does this have anything to do with that lawyer who came by this morning offering to buy out my share of the business?" she asked. Her foot tapped nervously beneath the desk, and I wondered what kind of shoes went with pink tiger stripes. I resisted the urge to look.

"Yes," I said bluntly.

Her lower lip trembled, and her eyes darkened with hurt. "You want me to sell—"

"No! God, no! I want you to stay."

"You do?"

"Honestly, in the best of all possible worlds, I'd own this business free and clear all by myself," I said, "but if I have to have a partner, I'd rather have you than anyone else."

The truth surprised me. Gigi had grown on me in the couple of weeks we'd been together. Yes, she irritated me, and I doubted I'd ever come to appreciate her decorating style or fashion sense, but she did relate better than I did to some of the people we interviewed—okay, a lot of them—and her society contacts had already paid off. Maybe, if we put some thought and effort into it, we could make more money together than I'd been making on my own or than she'd make as a hairstylist.

"Oh, I'm so glad to hear you say that. Because you know what? I like being a PI!" Her face glowed. "When Les left and I realized I'd have to go back to work, I'd've just as soon shot myself, if it wasn't for the kids. I didn't know anything except hairdressing and nails, and the thought of massaging Tina Brandenburg's scalp or pumicing Jemima Danforth's feet made me want to curl up and die. It took years to get that crowd to accept me when I married Les—they copied my accent, and I can't tell you how many redneck jokes I had to pretend to laugh at—so just the thought of working in a salon made me throw up. Literally."

I hadn't thought of it like that. Going from being one of the in crowd to little better than a servant would be more than a saint could bear.

"So when I found the partner paperwork for Swift Investigations, I felt like my guardian angel had swooped down to save me. I know I kind of thrust myself on you," she added more tentatively, "but I didn't have any PI training or useful skills, so I thought the only thing I could do was pretend to be confident and try to learn, learn, learn as fast as I could. Instead, I just kept screwing up. I'm sorry."

Resisting the urge to turn this into an apology fest, I said briskly, "There are several places we can send you to get some useful training in surveillance techniques and skip tracing and the like. The budget's tight, but we can probably finagle it somehow, especially if we continue to get process-serving work. And I promise I'll make more of an effort to include you in what I'm working on, to help with some on-the-job training."

"That'd be great!" Gigi breathed. "Now, about my gun—"

"We'll go to the range tomorrow," I promised, "and see about some lessons." It was probably my civic duty to call the range owner and warn him, but I was sure he, as a small business owner, carried insurance against the possibility of one customer accidentally winging another. I'd look in my storage room tonight, see if I could dig out the Kevlar vest I hadn't worn since leaving the OSI.

I stood, hesitating for a moment, wondering if the musty smell making my nose wrinkle was coming from Bernie.

"Thanks for not selling out," I said. "I know Johnson must have offered you a lot of money, and, well, I appreciate it."

"Some things are more important than money," she said. "At the opening of the new art museum building last year, Seth Johnson was making up to Kendall, running his hand up and down her arm, eyeing her like she was a mouse and he was a rat snake. Rat is right—she's only fourteen! I wouldn't sell that man a bite of roadkill stew if he was starving." She nodded her head emphatically. "What did you do to make him so angry?"

I told her about the encounter at the Wild West Casino Night. Her eyes got bigger and bigger, and she caught her breath when I reached the part about Johnson grabbing me. Her only comment when I finished, though, was "You bit his finger? Gross me out, as Kendall would say. Did you get a rabies shot?"

We both dissolved into laughter. Our giggles were drowned by the phone. Still chuckling, Gigi picked it up. "Swift Investigations. For you," she said, handing the receiver across her desk.

"Swift."

"Charlie, she's gone!" Melissa's frantic voice clawed at me. "Olivia's been kidnapped!"

17

~m~

"I only went in for a minute, and when I came back, she was gone," Melissa cried.

"Slow down," I said calmly. "Take a deep breath and tell me what happened. Inside from where?"

She drew a ragged breath. "After you left, I decided to shut up shop for the day and go home. I was doing some gardening in the front yard, pulling weeds. Olivia was in her bouncy seat. The phone rang, and I went in to answer it. I was back in under a minute, a minute and a half at most, I swear! And she was gone."

"Have you called the police?"

"No! No, I can't do that. They'll take her away." Sobs echoed down the phone line.

I let the stupidity of that statement hang in the air between us for a moment. "Olivia's safety is the most important thing, right? Trust me when I say the police are best equipped to deal with this."

"This is your fault! No one knew I had the baby except

you. Who did you tell about Olivia?" Melissa said, accusation and fear and anger tangled in her voice.

My conscience pricked. Jacqueline Falstow. I hadn't told her where Olivia was—I had all but led her to the Lloyds' door. I could just see her cruising the neighborhood streets in the area where we'd had our run-in, looking for a baby the right age. Had she seen Melissa with Olivia? A worse thought crept into my head. Maybe she'd followed me this morning from the Humane Society to her husband's job site, then to Designer Touches. I didn't think I'd been followed, but I couldn't be sure. The phone book would have yielded Melissa's address. Jacqueline was definitely smart enough to put two and two together and come up with Olivia. A shiver ran down my spine. Was she really desperate enough for a baby to risk a kidnapping charge?

Gigi was waggling her brows and mouthing "What?" at me. I grabbed a pencil and wrote *Olivia kidnapped* on a slip of paper. She cocked her head to read as I wrote and gasped when she caught on. I turned my back to her to concentrate on Melissa.

"Who was on the phone?" I asked.

"What?"

"The phone. When you went inside to pick it up, when you left Olivia alone, who was on the phone?"

"It was a wrong number. Some guy looking for Wanda Something. What's it matter?" She sounded impatient, on the edge of relapsing into hysteria.

A ploy, maybe, to separate her from the baby? If so, the kidnapper had to have been nearby. "While you were gardening, did you see any vehicles? Were there any pedestrians?"

"I don't know!"

"Think, Melissa!" My voice was a verbal slap, telling her to pull herself together. "Every minute we waste lets the kidnapper get another mile down the road. Was there anyone at all on the street, especially anyone you didn't know?"

Silence, broken only by her ragged breathing, was the only response for thirty seconds. Finally, she said, "There was a man walking a Rottweiler, but I'm pretty sure he just moved into the house on the corner. A couple of cars went past, and a pickup truck, I think. I wasn't really watching the road . . . my back was mostly to it."

"You're doing well," I told her. "Was one of the cars a Lexus, by any chance?"

"I don't know! Why? Do you know who it was?" She seized on my hesitation like a baseball fan grabbing at the last World Series ticket.

"Maybe," I finally admitted. "I'll check it out. But you need to call the police, Melissa. If I'm wrong about who's got the baby, the police are the only ones with the resources to find her, put out a multistate alert, get the word out to the airlines and bus companies."

"Okay, okay," she said, crying again. "All I want is for Olivia to be safe."

"I'll call," I said. "You stay home, by the phone. The police will be out there to talk to you ASAP, and maybe there'll be a ransom call. I've got my cell if you need to reach me."

Hanging up before she could protest, I dialed Montgomery's number. "Thank God," I said when he answered.

"What is it, Charlie?" he asked, my voice telling him this wasn't the time for banter.

I filled him in as quickly as I could.

"We'll get detectives over there pronto," he said, "and we'll probably have to call in the FBI. What's the address?"

I gave it to him and listened as he relayed it to someone. When he came back on the line, I said, "I know who took the baby, Montgomery. Jacqueline Falstow. It had to be her." I explained.

"Slow down," Montgomery commanded. "You have zero evidence that this Falstow woman took the baby. You're not even sure she knew where the baby was."

"Who else could it be? Surely you're not going to suggest it was a random thing? Coincidences like that just don't happen."

"Sure they do." He talked louder to be heard over my sputtering. "I'm not saying this is a coincidence, but I can't get a warrant for the Falstows' house on what you've got. There's not a judge in the county that would sign it."

"Then I'll find another way in," I said. "I feel like it's my fault. I've got to do something."

"Don't do anything stu—" he started to say, but I hung up. Whirling, I crossed to the small safe, worked the combination, and withdrew my H&K 9 mm, ejecting the cartridge and slamming it back in with the heel of my hand.

"I'm coming with you."

I had forgotten Gigi. She stood between me and the door, purse slung over one shoulder, a look of determination on her face. I didn't have time to argue with her. "We'll take your car," I said. "Jacqueline Falstow might recognize mine."

"Let's roll." Gigi charged out the door ahead of me, purse braced under her arm like a battering ram. With her pink tiger stripes, all she needed was kitty ears on her head to look like a refugee from *Josie and the Pussycats: The Golden Years.*

Riding in the Hummer conferred a feeling of power. We were above most of the other traffic and could look down on weary commuters tuning their radios, sipping their Big Gulps, picking their noses, and dozing at stoplights. The mass of steel enclosing us would ward off artillery shells, I was pretty sure, and be unfazed by a head-on collision with a foreign aluminumobile. I understood for the first time why Les had bought this car.

"Kinda cool, isn't it?" Gigi said.

"Yep," I admitted, gripping the dash as Gigi cut in front of a station wagon and accelerated. "What kind of gas mileage does it get?"

"About a half mile to the gallon."

I gave Gigi directions to the Falstows' and fell silent, plotting my strategy for when we arrived. Unfortunately, I came up with nothing more radical than ringing the doorbell and asking to see Olivia. I was plotting contingency courses of action when Gigi swung the car into the circular driveway and skidded to a stop. I braced myself against the door and shot her a look.

"Sorry," she said sheepishly. "Les says—said—I drive like a NASCAR reject with Parkinson's."

Ouch. Nice guy, that Les. Not that he was wrong in this case. I got down from the Hummer and waited for Gigi to come around from the driver's side before ascending the steps to the front door and ringing the bell.

"Are you going to use your gun?" Gigi whispered from a step below me.

"No." My gun would stay tucked into my purse. I wasn't even sure why I'd brought it. I focused my ears on sounds coming from within the house but heard nothing. Certainly not approaching footsteps.

"No one's home," Gigi said after several long moments. "What do we do now? Break in?"

"That would be illegal," I said crushingly, cupping my hand against the glass panels beside the door, straining to see inside. Nothing.

"I've got lock picks," Gigi said helpfully, jangling a key ring loaded with slim metal instruments.

I stared at them, then raised my eyes to hers. "Where did you get those?"

"eBay."

"Do you know how to use them?" Not that I planned to let her; I was just curious.

She shook her head, her forehead wrinkling. "No. They didn't come with directions. The guy I bought them from said he was sure I could find someone around here to teach me how."

"Yeah, if you drove over to Cañon City." Site of the high-security prison. "Put those back in your purse." Morbid curiosity made me wonder what else she had in there—grenades?—but an instinct for self-preservation kept me from asking. "Let's check the back."

As on my earlier visit, the back gate was open. No one lounged at the pool when we got there, though. The clear aquamarine water was as smooth as an untouched cup of Jell-O, and the CD player sat silently on the table.

"Where do you suppose she is?" Gigi asked, looking around

as if expecting to spot Jacqueline crouched under the chaise lounge or hiding behind the barberry shrubs growing near the house.

That was the sixty-four-thousand-dollar question. I ground my teeth in frustration. Maybe Jacqueline and Olivia were seated in the first class cabin of a jet heading for Costa Rica or Tanzania. I didn't know if you needed a passport for an infant. If so, maybe they were driving through Kansas or on a plane headed to Seattle or Sacramento or San Antonio. I had no way of finding out. Montgomery could do it with a few phone calls—check airline manifests and suchlike—but I knew he wasn't going to.

Just as I opened my phone to call Stefan Falstow's office, see if I could get a lead on Jacqueline there, I heard tires crunch on asphalt at the front of the house. Someone had pulled into the driveway. I trotted toward the gate in time to meet Jacqueline Falstow as she came through it, a bag of groceries in her arms, a puzzled look on her face. When she saw me, her brows drew together and she backed up a step.

"What are you doing in my yard?"

Was that fear in her voice, or only the natural irritation of a homeowner who finds unwanted guests in her backyard? I kept walking. "Where's the baby, Mrs. Falstow?"

"What are you talking about?" Confusion mixed with the annoyance in her face.

"Olivia. Roberta. Whatever. Lizzy Jones's baby. Where is she?"

One hand flew to her half-opened mouth, and the bag of groceries dropped unheeded to the ground. A carton of eggs oozed yolk onto the grass, and a bottle of olive oil shattered when it hit the flagstone walk, splattering Jacqueline's legs with oily splotches. She didn't seem to notice. "Roberta! What's happened to her?"

"She was kid—taken from the house where she was staying," I said carefully. It dawned on me that I might have been wrong about Jacqueline stealing the baby. Unless she was the best actress since Meryl Streep, she couldn't fake the emotions chasing across her face.

"You let someone take her? What if they hurt her? What if she's scared and crying? What will happen to my baby?" With each question, her pitch rose until she was virtually shrieking, and she rushed at me, mashing runaway blueberries underfoot, her hands curled into claws.

She was blocking access to the gate, so I retreated toward the pool. Despite the fact she was taller, I didn't have much doubt I could take her down if I had to. I was uncomfortably aware, however, that I was standing on legal ground about as solid as quicksand. I was trespassing in her yard; if I hit her and she made a complaint, I was screwed. My backward progress had landed me on the decking around the pool. I held up my hands placatingly and cast a swift glance behind me, not wanting to end up wet.

Gigi, so far silent, piped up. "Look, Mrs. Falstow, we're all worried about the little baby, but Charlie can't get on with finding her if you don't calm down. If you don't have the baby, you need to let us get back to looking for her."

"Who are you?" Jacqueline asked, slowing in her pursuit of me. Her head swiveled from me to Gigi, trying to keep an eye on both of us.

"Gigi Goldman, my assoc— my partner," I said.

Gigi shot me a gratified look and beamed, and I realized it was the first time I'd used the P-word. It hurt, but not as much as I would've thought.

"I don't have Roberta," Jacqueline said, tears streaking mascara down her face. "I've never even seen her." Her hands dropped to her sides, and Gigi approached her, throwing a comforting arm around her shoulders.

"There, there," Gigi said. "It'll all work out."

I marveled at the way her presence seemed to calm Jacqueline, even though I thought it doubtful that it would all work out the way Jacqueline hoped. With relatives wanting the baby, and the father still unaccounted for, I held out little hope she'd be cuddling the baby in her expensive nursery anytime soon . . . if ever.

As Gigi led the sobbing Jacqueline to the back door, I headed out the gate, knowing Gigi would have better luck calming Falstow if I stayed out of sight. Determined to cover all the bases, I checked Falstow's car. She'd left the doors open, and the scent of sun-warmed bananas drifted out. Nothing but groceries in the backseat—no sign of a safety seat or baby paraphernalia. Climbing into the Hummer, I waited for Gigi to appear.

She did, five minutes later, her cheerful face drawn down with empathy. "That poor woman," she said, starting the car.

"Any sign of the baby in there?" I asked.

She shook her head. "None. She took me up to show me the baby's room—"

"Of course she did."

"—and it's clear there's never been a baby in there. I feel sorry for her."

"Me, too, but there's nothing we can do to help her." I was pissed at myself for wasting so much time. We were that much farther behind the kidnapper now, all because I'd been sure I knew who had taken the baby, and I was wrong. My phone rang as I was mentally flagellating myself. Montgomery.

"Did you get anything?"

His voice singed the line. "Not even the admission that a kidnapping took place."

"What!"

"Your Melissa Lloyd denies that a baby is missing. If you'd told me she had the baby in the first place, we might have been able to force her to produce it, but the way it is . . ."

"I don't frigging believe this!" I hit the dashboard with frustration. The Hummer wasn't fazed by my fury. "I did not make this up! She called me not an hour ago, panicked. She told me—"

"Chill, Charlie." Montgomery's voice was calm. "She's lying to us. I've never met anyone who lies so badly. She's nervous as a cat in a room full of rocking chairs, but we can't budge her on her story. She kicked us off the property. Maybe if you came out here and had a go at her . . ."

"On my way." I hung up and told Gigi where we were headed. I occupied the drive imagining the various tortures I'd use on Melissa to get her to admit the truth. Not only was she slowing down our hunt for Olivia, she was making me look like a fool in front of Montgomery.

As Gigi wove in and out of the traffic on I-25, my brain finally kicked into gear. Unless this was a totally random kidnapping—a coincidence I just couldn't buy—Olivia was taken by someone who knew she was at the Lloyds' house. Who *knew* that Melissa had the baby? Not the Falstows. Not the Sprouses. Not Linnea or Jack or Seth Johnson. I did. Melissa did. Her husband did. I punched in Melissa's number. "Where's your husband?" I asked when she picked up the phone.

"Ian?"

Did she have more than one? "Yes, Ian," I said.

"Arizona. I told you. Why do you . . . ?" Her voice petered out, then came back at a higher pitch. "Oh, no! He wouldn't! When I told him I want to keep Olivia, he . . . Even though he's never wanted kids, I'm sure I can talk him into . . . He'll be a great father."

He wasn't winning any prizes so far. "Look, when he and Elizabeth met, what did—"

"They didn't know each other," Melissa cut in, confused. "Ian doesn't hang at the store very often."

No, they had met when Elizabeth hung the drapes at the Lloyd house. I remembered Ian's unease when I stopped by, the dropped paintbrush. I wondered at what point he'd realized he was sleeping with his wife's daughter. Surely he hadn't known when he seduced her. Or had she seduced him? I mulled it over, barely conscious of Melissa sputtering in the phone and Gigi casting me anxious looks. On the whole, I was inclined to think Elizabeth had initiated the affair. Everyone from Linnea to Aurora Newcastle to Frieda Vasher suspected Elizabeth's motives for trying to locate her birth mother. No one thought she was looking for a lovey-dovey reunion. What, then? I thought I knew: revenge.

I didn't have time to figure it all out or explain my thinking to Melissa. Every minute we wasted gave Ian more time to . . . I stopped myself from imagining what Ian might want to do with the baby whose DNA could tie him to a murder victim. "Melissa! Try to get hold of Ian. Try his cell phone, his office, his hotel. If you get him, say—" What could she say?

"His truck has one of those theft-tracking GPS systems."

It took me a moment to process the words Melissa had whispered. "It does? Great. Call the company and tell them the truck's been stolen. Then you can tell Lieutenant Montgomery, and he'll—"

"No police."

"Melissa, you have to tell the police. This is kidnapping. Olivia's in danger. Ian might—"

"He'd never hurt a baby."

Right, and he'd never have an affair with a teenager, or kill said teenager. What did she think—he was taking Olivia to the park to feed the ducks? "You've got to—"

"No." Her voice was implacable. "He's my husband. I'll find out where the truck is, and *you* get Olivia back."

"Call me right back, as soon as they get a position on the truck," I said without explicitly agreeing not to tell the police. She might be crazy, but I wasn't. As I dialed Montgomery's number again, I filled Gigi in on my thoughts and told her, "At the next exit, get off and head south." My instincts told me Ian would be headed back to Arizona. He'd need to establish an alibi for himself there, regardless of what he did with Olivia.

"I can do better than that," Gigi said.

Before I could guess what she planned, she wrenched the Hummer's wheel to the left, and the heavy vehicle wallowed onto the median. The tires spun on the grass, and I jounced forward, stopping myself with a hand on the dash. "Gigi!" The word was torn from my lips as she engaged a lower gear and the Hummer lurched into a depression, careened over a boulder at an angle that almost tipped me onto Gigi, and slammed into the southbound lane of traffic, broadside to the oncoming cars.

"Oops!"

I shut my eyes, waiting for the crash, the grinding of metal ripping into metal, hoping the Hummer had side-impact airbags. Gigi stepped on the accelerator, and the vehicle shot across all three lanes of traffic and onto the verge as two cars and a semi flashed by, all the drivers leaning hard on their horns. Before I could recover my breath, Gigi spun the wheel again and merged into the southbound flow of traffic.

"That was close." She gave me a sunny smile.

I looked at her with something approaching awe. Before I could say anything, Montgomery's voice squawked, and I bent to recover my cell phone from the floor. I filled him in, and he cursed. "Damn the woman. I need to contact the FBI. Call me back when you get the coordinates for Lloyd's vehicle. I'm going to *persuade* the Lloyd woman to tell me the truth so we can get in on this properly."

The way he ground out "persuade" had me envisioning an iron maiden or a waterboard. My phone emitted a low-battery beep. Uh-oh. "Gotta go," I told Montgomery.

"Where are we going?" Gigi asked.

"Hell if I know."

We lapsed into silence, barreling south down I-25 for two long minutes until my phone rang again. The caller ID told me it was Melissa. "Where is he?" I said in lieu of "hello."

Catching my sense of urgency, she read out a set of coordinates without any small talk or tears. I scribbled them on the back of a Jiffy Lube receipt tucked in the sun visor. "The truck's been there for ten minutes, the technician told me," Melissa finished.

"Tell Detective Montgomery—" My phone died. "Shit!"

Taking three deep breaths, I turned to Gigi. "Does this thing have a GPS?"

She chuckled, sounding very southern. "Honey, this thing has every kind of navigating device short of sonar. Les is really into gadgets. We even have a weather station—"

"How do I use it?" I cut her off, examining the box she gestured at.

She shrugged her soft shoulders and overcorrected as the Hummer drifted into another lane. Horns blared. I held on to the dash and poked the coordinates into the GPS device. It lit up, and a velvety female voice began issuing instructions. We were just fourteen miles from our destination. Hallelujah!

"It's just like geocaching," Gigi said, steering around a Hyundai that was only doing twenty miles an hour over the speed limit.

"Geo what?"

"Geocaching. It's a game. You get coordinates from some site on the Internet and use them to find a treasure, only usually the treasure's not anything to write home about. Anyway, Dexter's really into it, and we went—Les and Dex and Kendall and me—one time last fall, and, well . . . never mind. Anyway, it's just like this"—she nodded at the small display—"following the map to a treasure."

Only in this case the treasure was a baby.

18

As we drew closer to the blip representing Lloyd's truck, I began to wonder if he'd dumped it. He could have switched cars, caught a taxi to the airport, hopped a bus. I was willing to rule out Jet Skis and gondolas, but any other form of transportation was still in play. I clenched and unclenched my hands as Gigi, following the directions of the sultry GPS voice, swung off I-25 and trundled along a service road. "There." She pointed.

A couple of acres of cars, trucks, and vans of all descriptions surrounded the twenty-first-century shopping mecca: Walmart. Sun glinted off chrome, mirrors, and highly polished paint jobs, bumping the temperature at least five degrees. The heat rose off the asphalt and vehicles in a visible, shimmering wave. Maybe it was all a mirage? I groaned at the prospect of locating Lloyd's truck in the huge lot. I felt like Horton trying to find the thistle with the Whos on it in the thistle field. My hope dwindled because I was sure Ian had abandoned the car, assuming no one would notice it. I just couldn't imagine a kidnapper stopping off to pick up groceries at discount prices.

As I worried, and tried to gin up another plan for finding Lloyd and Olivia, Gigi cruised down the aisles, keeping one eye on the GPS display. "It should be in the next row," she said, her voice breathless with excitement. "What kind of car are we looking for, anyway?"

"A maroon F-150 with a camper top," I said, pulling up an image of the truck from my visit to the Lloyd home. "Maybe there'll be a clue in it to tell us where he's headed," I said with faint hope. "It's—"

"Look!"

My eyes followed Gigi's outstretched arm. I couldn't believe it. The maroon truck, its door ajar, squatted between a yellow Mini Cooper and a rusted-out El Camino that was once red. A man who might have been Lloyd had his head and torso inside the passenger compartment, apparently trying to load something into the seat.

"Park him in," I ordered Gigi, grasping the dashboard.

She bounced on her seat, tore down the aisle like a drag racer, and stopped with a lurch directly behind the F-150. Due to the size of the Hummer, she was also blocking the Mini Cooper's exit, but that couldn't be helped.

"Perfect," I said, unbuckling and jumping to the ground. I hesitated for a moment; if Lloyd was armed, I might be putting the baby in danger by confronting him. Maybe now that we had him cornered, I should wait for the police to show up. I was sure Montgomery had talked Melissa into cooperating by now. A baby's wail jolted me forward. Relief tingled through me at the auditory evidence that Olivia was alive. I felt Gigi's bulk crowding me from behind.

"Hey, you can't put that baby in the front seat," she said indignantly before I could motion her to silence. "It isn't safe!"

With a muffled "Damn," Ian Lloyd pulled his head out of the front seat, banging it on the roof. His cursing escalated; a passing shopper hauled her toddler into her arms and cupped her hands over his ears.

Rubbing the bleeding gash on his forehead, Lloyd looked from me to Gigi, wild-eyed, as Olivia continued to screech.

"Let me have that baby," Gigi said, elbowing past Lloyd to reach into the truck. "There, there, honey, it'll be okay," she soothed, working mother magic on the car seat straps and gentling the squalling infant against her bosom. "Phew, you're a stinky, aren't you? No wonder you're so unhappy." She shot an accusatory look at Ian. "Diapers?"

"In the bag." He nodded toward a Walmart bag on the pavement at his feet. A scowl twisted his face. "That's why we stopped. Well, for that and the car seat. She couldn't sit up so I couldn't use the seat belt on her and she was rolling around on the seat so I had to drive with one hand holding her so she wouldn't fall. Then she pooped and I don't know what Mel's been feeding the kid, but it stank like a herd of pigs had crowded into the cab, I kid you not, and then—"

"You mean you drove that poor baby all the way from Monument to here without a safety seat?" Gigi's horrified voice brought stares from interested shoppers.

"That's illegal!" piped up a skinny woman holding a snotty-nosed toddler of indeterminate gender by one hand.

"Enough." I made shooing motions, and the bystanders who seemed inclined to linger proceeded reluctantly toward the store. "Take the baby to the Hummer, Gigi," I suggested. The unrelenting caterwauling was driving me insane. Even Lloyd looked like he thought it was a good idea. Gigi scooped up the bag with the Huggies peeking out the top and stalked to the car muttering, "The stupid man's got the car seat in backwards, and I'll bet he didn't even get wipes or powder for your sweet little bottom."

I put a hand on Lloyd's arm as he started to inch away. "Uh-uh. You and I can sit here and have a nice conversation while we wait for the police."

"The police!" He looked around as if searching for SWAT personnel behind lampposts or under the plastic swimming pools displayed by the store entrance.

"Kidnapping's a crime, in case you didn't know, and so is murder."

"It was an accident."

"Which? The kidnapping or the murder?"

"Both. Well, Beth's death." His brown eyes beseeched me.

I let out a long breath compounded of sadness and relief. At least he wasn't going to deny it. "She's your baby, isn't she?"

"Olivia? Yeah." His gaze drifted toward the Hummer, where Gigi had the baby laid flat on the seat—my seat—and was efficiently changing her diaper. The smell drifted to me. I was not riding back in the Hummer. "I wasn't going to hurt her, you know." He seemed anxious that I believe him. "I was going to take her to New Mexico or Arizona and leave her at a fire station or hospital. I just needed to get her away from here."

"Because she linked you to Elizabeth."

He nodded. "But I wouldn't harm a baby. I couldn't."

"I think interrupting the kidnapping to buy a car seat will count in your favor," I said, unable to totally despise the man. I believed him when he said he wouldn't have hurt Olivia. On the other hand . . . "How did you hook up with Elizabeth?"

He sighed heavily and wiped a hand down his face. "I met Beth soon after she started working for Melissa, and she was . . . well, no one would've guessed she was only sixteen. I bought her story about her husband being deployed and everything. You won't believe this, but—"

"She came on to you, didn't she?"

He arched his eyebrows into the shock of sandy hair dropping across his brow. "Yeah. How did you know?"

I shrugged, leaning back against the warmth of the truck's hood. Lloyd followed suit. "Lots of the folks I talked to knew she was trying to find her birth mom—your wife—and a few of them seemed concerned about her motives. It seemed to me that maybe she was looking for revenge?" I turned my head to watch his reaction.

He looked at me as if I were a psychic. Just call me Madame Carlotta and cross my palm with silver.

"That's what she said! When she called me after the baby was born—I was in Arizona—and told me she needed money. She threatened to tell my wife about our affair and called it 'delicious revenge.' When I asked her why the hell she wanted revenge on Melissa, who'd never been anything but kind to her—giving her sewing work and all—she told me about Mel being her mom. I was floored. I had no idea. Mel never said—"

The look of betrayal on his face made me almost feel sorry for him. Almost.

"She spit out all this stuff about Mel abandoning her and

her father getting killed on 9/11 and her stepfather being abusive. She blamed it all on Mel. When I tried to make her see reason, she slapped me." He put a hand to his cheek as if still feeling the blow. Pale tan freckles sprinkled the back of his hand. "When she hit me, I lost it. I hit her back." His hands shook, and he clenched them together in his lap. "She fell and—" He pointed down to a dent in the metal bumper directly beneath where we were leaning. I scootched away.

"Would you please move that tank? I need to get out."

The owner of the Mini Cooper, a woman in a turquoise jog bra and nylon shorts that showed the tanned, corded legs of a marathoner, stood impatiently behind Gigi. Her tapping Pearl Izumi–shod foot and tight jaw told me she needed to try a little meditation or yoga to relieve her stress. Or maybe a Valium.

"It's a Humvee, not a tank," Gigi said instructively, her attention still on the baby kicking her legs on the front seat. "Tanks are tracked vehicles, not wheeled, like—"

"I don't care what you call this mountain of steel that only an irresponsible, ecologically careless criminal would drive. Just move it! My lima beans are defrosting." She flung a hand toward her Mini, piled high with bags of groceries.

I stepped toward the woman, poised to grab her by the shoulders if it looked like she was going to turn violent. I couldn't altogether blame her; shopping at Walmart had that effect on me, too.

"Don't get your panties in a wad," Gigi said, bringing Olivia to her shoulder and patting her. "As soon as I put the baby in her car seat"—she nodded toward us and the truck— "I'll—Charlie!"

The warning in her voice made me turn in time to see Ian Lloyd sidling between parked cars two aisles over. Shit! Cursing for letting myself be lulled by his penitent manner, I took off after him. His legs were longer, but I was more maneuverable, threading my way through parked cars and startled shoppers like an agility dog on uppers. Lloyd reached the edge of the parking lot before I did, cast a glance behind to check on my progress, and broke into a sprint that took him around the side of the Walmart. By the time I rounded the corner, breathing heavily, he was climbing into the cab of a Fluffy-Wip truck that had been off-loading crates at the dock stretching the length of the Walmart. Several other trucks cozied up to the dock like piglets to a sow, and a forklift shifted pallets from one with a Del Monte logo. The Fluffy-Wip truck's driver, sprawled on his butt where Lloyd had apparently yanked him out of the cab, was scrambling to his feet.

I pounded toward the truck, determined not to let Lloyd escape. The truck driver in his red and white uniform jumped for the door handle and missed as Lloyd engaged the gears and pulled away from the loading dock. A scraping, tearing sound was drowned by a metallic clatter as the truck's ramp fell from the dock and began to drag across the asphalt, sparks flying as Lloyd picked up speed. I debated standing in the truck's way but decided I couldn't count on Lloyd to stop. His face, through the windshield, was set in grim lines, his brows drawn down and his lips thinned. I was suddenly not so sure Elizabeth's death had been an accident.

I was contemplating running up the ramp—but how could I get to Lloyd once inside the refrigerated truck?—when the Hummer squealed around the corner, Gigi gripping the wheel in white-knuckled hands. What had she done with Olivia? The thought barely had time to whip through my head before I saw her steer the Hummer onto a collision course with the truck.

"Gigi, don't!" I yelled. I watched helplessly as the two vehicles growled toward each other. The space between them shrank rapidly. When it seemed like they must collide, both drivers chickened out. The Hummer skidded to the right, leaving thirty-foot-long rubber marks on the pavement, but the trailer of the delivery truck, a victim of its own momentum and the sudden turn, came gradually up onto two wheels and then, as if in slow motion, listed toward the ground with a wrenching sound of wounded metal. With the popping of caps and a pressurized hissing, whipped cream oozed out of the trailer. The air filled with a sugary smell.

I dashed toward the cab, still upright, and pulled a dazed Lloyd to the ground. He came unresisting, all fight drained out of him. "Olivia?" he asked, his eyes tracking toward the Hummer.

"I hope not," I said, steering him toward the Hummer with his arm twisted up, none too gently, between his shoulder blades.

"I couldn't risk hurting her," he said. "I had to stop."

The man had some semblance of a conscience if he was willing to give up his break for freedom to avoid injuring the baby that might have been in the Hummer; maybe Elizabeth's death was an accident. I'd let the courts figure it out.

The pink-tiger-striped Gigi emerged from the Hummer, hands patting her hair into place, as we drew within ten feet.

I peered around her into the front seat. "The baby?"

"With Melissa," she said.

"Melissa?"

"She drove up with Detective Montgomery just as you took off after the baby-napper here. I came after you because I thought you might need some help."

"I did. Thanks."

We smiled at each other as three police cars swarmed around the corner, light bars pulsing and sirens screeching.

"Thank goodness," Gigi said, and then, "Oh, my."

I looked over my shoulder to see a horde of happy Walmart shoppers snatching containers of Fluffy-Wip from the wreck, some spraying the froth into their mouths, others using it to coat their friends, and one enterprising young tagger drawing swirly whipped cream letters on the side of the trailer. He'd gotten a ten-foot high F-U-C spelled out by the time I handed Lloyd over to a uniformed policeman who cuffed him, Mirandized him, and led him away.

"I love whipped cream," Gigi said, watching the revelers wistfully.

"Me, too." The baby was safe. Lloyd was on his way to prison. What better way to celebrate than by spraying strangers with whipped cream substitute? "Let's do it."

We hurried to the ankle-deep pool of whipped cream surrounding the trailer and fished for unopened cans. A Golden retriever, flocked with whipped cream, shook itself vigorously, coating us with a mist of sticky dairy product. Gigi lost her footing trying to get out of the line of spray and plopped onto her bottom, trying to hold her cast up to avoid the goo. She was giggling, so I figured she wasn't hurt. Reaching down to help her up, I slipped, too. If you can't beat 'em, join 'em: I aimed my can at Gigi and depressed the nozzle. That's where we were when Montgomery found us—and the news cameras. Swift Investigations made the *Live at Five* broadcast for the third time in a week.

19

~~~

(Saturday)

The following Saturday, nine days after the whipped cream frolic at the Walmart and the rescue of baby Olivia, I was in the office early, planning to put in a couple of hours on paperwork before spending the afternoon basking poolside in the bikini I hadn't gotten to wear yet this summer. An apartment complex just a mile from Swift Investigations had a resort-style pool and lax security measures: No one would know I didn't live there if I showed up with my towel and Pepsi, acting like I belonged. It was ninety-five degrees, and I was rushing through my billing, anxious to slide into the cool water, when the door opened and a soft voice said, "Miss Swift?"

"Charlie," I said automatically, looking up to see Wes Emmerling standing awkwardly on the threshold.

"C'mon in," I said. "Want a Pepsi?"

"Uh, sure."

Wearing khaki cargo shorts and another Emmerling T-shirt—no mud accessories this time—he accepted the can as he sat in the chair in front of my desk. He placed a manila envelope on the desk to free his hands for opening the Pepsi. His bangs flopped into his eyes.

"What's up?" I asked, suspecting I knew. I eyed the envelope but didn't reach for it.

"I got the results."

I knew what results he meant without his having to say. He'd come in the day we rescued Olivia to tell me he was going to have the DNA test. I'd given him Olivia's DNA profile Melissa had provided the day we met for his lab to use as a comparison. It probably wasn't quite in keeping with the spirit of client confidentiality, but the courts would have ordered Melissa to produce the baby for a test if Wes went that route, and I wanted to spare Olivia any extra needle sticks.

"And?"

"She's mine." He barely breathed the words.

Yowza. If I had a hundred bucks for every time I'd heard those words in connection with this baby, I could retire. My mind flashed briefly to Ian Lloyd and the desperate actions he'd taken, all because he believed Elizabeth when she told him Olivia was his. How different things would be for so many people if Elizabeth hadn't lied. Or, I thought, maybe she truly didn't know whose baby it was and chose to believe it was Ian's because he was the one in a position to bankroll her new life. Would she really have gone to Virginia? I wondered. Would she have contacted Wes? I pushed back in my chair and took a long breath. "What are you going to do?"

"What should I do?" He didn't look like a father; he looked like what he was—a nice, naive kid on the verge of adulthood, a little more together than some, but an unlikely prospect for single fatherhood.

"I can't tell you that. Have you told your folks?"

He shook his head. "No. My dad—"

How come this guy couldn't seem to finish any sentence that started with "my dad"? "Don't you think they're the best ones to advise you? Would they want to raise the baby, or help you raise her?"

He shrugged again, looking frustrated.

"Look, Wes." I leaned forward, putting my forearms on the desk. "There's going to be a battle over this baby. Right now, she's with Elizabeth's killer and his wife, Elizabeth's biological mother, because everyone thinks he's the father. Elizabeth signed a contract with a nice couple who are desperate for a baby, though, and they're going to fight for custody in court. Even if you don't want to raise Olivia, as her father, you could have some say in who gets her. I know it's a lot of responsibility, but with knowledge comes responsibility." I nodded at the envelope on the desk. "If you weren't ready to take it on, you wouldn't have had the test."

He rose and pocketed the envelope, looking resolute. And scared. He left his Pepsi untouched on the edge of the desk. "Thanks, Miss Swift."

"Charlie," I called after him. I watched the door for several moments after it closed behind him, not sure what course of action I was hoping he'd take. Sometimes it's easy to know what the right thing is but hard to make yourself do it. Other times, choosing the right course is a challenge in itself. As Elizabeth no doubt realized too late.

(Sunday)

The next night, Gigi and I sat at Albertine's bar with its owner, drinking piña coladas, Pepsi, and martinis (the James Bond classics, not the frou-frou kind), respectively. The bar was closed, but Albertine had offered drinks on the house in return for the story of our capture of Ian Lloyd. Tonight, she shimmered in silver and aqua lounging pajamas and made quite a contrast with Gigi, who was in the outfit I thought of as her canary suit. She sported a yellow cast to match and was hopeful the doctor would take it off completely in another ten days.

"So where's the baby now?" Albertine asked when Gigi finished telling her how many showers she'd needed to get the whipped cream stickiness out of her hair.

"With Melissa, for the moment. Since Ian's apparently the biological father and is out on bail awaiting trial, the court ruled in their favor." I threw in the "apparently" because I knew Ian wasn't Olivia's dad but I didn't want to out Wes Emmerling. "The Falstows are fighting it, however, and who knows what'll happen if Ian gets convicted." Or if Wes comes forward.

"If?" Gigi said. She looked at me wide-eyed over the rim of her glass. "What do you mean 'if'? He killed Elizabeth. He kidnapped little Olivia."

I shrugged, inured to the capriciousness of the legal machine. "Oh, the DA will push it, but with no witnesses to Ian's encounter with Elizabeth, he might well be able to convince a jury her death was accidental, and since the baby seemingly was—is—his, the kidnapping charges sort of evaporated. Melissa swore it was all a misunderstanding."

Albertine rolled her eyes as Gigi said, "That's just not right."

I agreed with her, but what could you do? Melissa had felt guilty enough, though, or grateful enough, to let me borrow Olivia for the morning. I'd driven the baby—asleep in her car seat, thankfully—to Denver and introduced her to Aurora Newcastle. She was at Purple Feet, working, but an oxygen tank trailed her now, a clear hose snaking from her nostrils. Her skin was like parchment, despite the rosy glow reflected by her pink dress, but her eyes were still bright and clear and focused on Olivia as I handed over the awakening baby. Olivia stared up at Aurora, unblinking, her eyes unbelievably blue and wondering.

"Let me tell you about your mom," Aurora said, cradling the baby in her arms and walking down the nearest aisle, the oxygen cart trundling behind. "I met her when she was just a little older than you . . ."

She kissed Olivia's forehead an hour later when I told her we had to go, and a new sense of peacefulness wafted from her. I suspected she'd be dead within the month and felt sad.

Albertine recalled my drifting thoughts.

"What about that Johnson fellow?" she asked, sliding another Pepsi down the bar to me. "What was he doing at Elizabeth's apartment? Didn't you say some kid saw his car there?" She looked from me to Gigi, who was bobbing her head enthusiastically, remembering her role in finding Mikey the Spy.

I popped the can open and took a long swallow before answering. "Well, since Johnson's not talking to me and Montgomery tells me the police see no need to interview him, given how things turned out, the best we can do is speculate. I'd guess he was having one last go at trying to convince Elizabeth to marry him. She was proven fertile, after all."

"You sound like she was a brood mare," Albertine objected.

"I think that's basically how he saw his wives."

"He's getting married again, you know," Gigi put in.

I blinked at her.

She nodded and bit into the slice of pineapple decorating her glass. "To Hannah Wittinger. Her mom told me yesterday. They're having a small private ceremony." She grinned at our astonishment.

"How old is this Hannah? Fifteen?" Albertine asked scathingly.

"Twelve?" I guessed.

"Seventeen," Gigi said. "Dexter went out with her a couple of times."

We were silent a moment, pondering the stupidity of people confronted with money and power. Or at least I was. The Wittingers were letting Seth Johnson buy their daughter as breeding stock. I gave the marriage two years, tops.

"Eighteen months," Albertine said, apparently reading my mind. "Are they tying the knot at the Church of the Hypocritical Pastor and Domestic Abuse Perpetrator on Earth?"

Gigi and I laughed at her renaming of Sprouse's church.

"Uh-uh." Gigi shook her head. "The Wittingers are Catholic. Seth's converting to marry Hannah."

I wondered cynically if Seth was that much in love with Hannah or if the Catholic stance on in vitro fertilization was more to his liking. Either way, it sounded like Pastor Zach was going to be up a creek without a sponsor. So much for his dreams of TV evangelist fame. I couldn't say I was sorry for him, although I did pity his wife, who, as far as I knew, had still not even been able to see her grandchild.

"Let's get some dinner," Gigi suggested. "I'm hungry. I've been doing that South Beach Diet and I could eat a whole loaf of bread with a giant helping of fettucine alfredo." She patted her plump thighs ruefully.

"Zio's sounds good," Albertine agreed.

"Can't," I said airily, sliding off the bar stool. I bent to fuss with the strap of my high-heeled sandal, letting that account for my heightened color when I straightened up. "I have plans."

"Plans?" Gigi echoed.

"A *date*?" Albertine asked, the corners of her eyes crinkling.

"Maybe."

"Ooh, is it that hunky priest who took you to the fundraiser?" Gigi asked.

Was Dan Allgood hunky? I tabled that thought for another time.

"I'll bet you made up with that fine man you pissed off in here last week," Albertine guessed.

"Let's just call him Bachelor Number Three." I waved to them over my shoulder as I strolled toward the door. I didn't need Montgomery tracking me down here and fueling their speculations. Especially since it was just a payback dinner he said he owed me for helping him file the Sprouse case under CLOSED. It wasn't a real date. I'd've dressed in my black silk pants and the clingy green peasant top even if I'd been going to Zio's with the girls. Really.

"See you tomorrow, bright and early," Gigi called. "Remember, we've got five appointments with new clients."

Nothing like a little free TV advertising. "See you tomorrow, partner."

I didn't even wince when I said it.